THE PENGUIN CLASSICS

EDITED BY E. V. RIEU

L64

THE
THOUSAND AND ONE
NIGHTS

*The Hunchback · Sindbad
and Other Tales*

TRANSLATED
WITH AN INTRODUCTION BY
N. J. DAWOOD

PENGUIN BOOKS

Penguin Books Ltd, Harmondsworth, Middlesex
U.S.A.: Penguin Books Inc., 3300 Clipper Mill Road, Baltimore 11, Md
AUSTRALIA: Penguin Books Pty Ltd, 762 Whitehorse Road,
Mitcham, Victoria

—

This selection first published as Penguin 1001 in 1954
Reissued as a Penguin Classic 1955
Reprinted 1961

Made and printed in Great Britain
by R. & R. Clark Ltd
Edinburgh

CONTENTS

INTRODUCTION

THE folk-tales which have collectively survived in what is known as *The Thousand and One Nights* owe their origin to three distinct cultures: Indian, Persian, and Arab. They can be regarded as the expression of the lay and secular imagination of the East in revolt against the austere erudition and religious zeal of Oriental literature generally.

Written in a simple, almost colloquial style, and depicting a unique world of all-powerful sorcerers and ubiquitous jinn, of fabulous wealth and candid bawdry, these tales have little in common with the refined didacticism of Classical Arabic literature and have therefore never been regarded by the Arabs as a legitimate part of it. Yet it is a remarkable paradox that to the non-Arab world, and particularly to the West, the *Nights* is to-day the best known and most widely read book of Arabic authorship, while the more serious works of Classical Arabic literature, for the most part untranslatable verse, remain quite unfamiliar. In fact, in the course of the past two centuries the *Nights* has attained, mainly through the medium of translation, the status of a universal classic and has come to be recognized as such.

This is not surprising. The tales themselves are masterpieces of the art of story-telling. In inventiveness and sheer entertainment value they stand supreme among the short stories of all time. And in their minute accuracy of detail and the vast range and variety of their subject-matter they constitute the most comprehensive and intimate record of medieval Islam.

The original nucleus of the *Nights* was derived from a lost Persian book of fairy-tales called *Hazar Afsanah* (A Thousand Legends), which was translated into Arabic about A.D. 850. The Arab encyclopaedist Al-Mas'oodi (d. A.D. 956) makes a casual reference to this book in his *Murooj al-Dhahab* (The Golden Meadows). He tells us that 'the people call it "A Thousand and One Nights"' and goes on to give a brief account of the Prologue which resembles that of our *Nights* in outline. Modern scholarship has traced this Prologue, which contains the framework story, back to Indian folk-lore. But there is no evidence that this 'Thousand and One Nights' of Mas'oodi contained the same stories that have come down to us in the manuscripts of the *Nights*, except the framework story. Several of the tales were undoubtedly taken, in some shape or form, from *Hazar Afsanah*; for they have unmistakable parallels in Indian and Persian folk-lore. The Arab *rawis*, or professional story-tellers, knew how to add local colouring to the foreign tale and how to adapt it to native surroundings. In the course of centuries other stories, mainly of Baghdad and Cairo origin, gathered round this nucleus, and, to make up the number of a thousand and one nights, more local folk-tales, generally of poor composition, were unscrupulously added by the various scribes and redactors.

The final recension of this heterogeneous material was made in Egypt, probably in Cairo, by an unknown redactor towards the end of the 18th century. Written in a language which constantly borders on the vulgar dialect, and in which the original marked differences of style and idiom are still apparent, this version has come to be regarded as the 'standard' text of the *Nights*. The present translation follows Macnaghten's Calcutta edition (1839–42) of this text, but the generally parallel first Bulaq edition (1835) has also been consulted wherever the Macnaghten text seemed faulty.

The Thousand and One Nights was first introduced to the Western world by Antoine Galland (1646–1715), a French orientalist and gifted story-teller who had travelled widely in the Middle East. His *Mille et une Nuits*, published in twelve volumes between 1704 and 1717, had a great popular success and was itself almost at once rendered into several European languages. Galland was by no means a faithful translator. He selected his materials and skilfully adapted them to contemporary European tastes, emphasizing the fantastic and the miraculous and carefully avoiding the candid references to sex. Nevertheless the Galland version possesses a vigorous narrative style and can still be read with enjoyment.

It was during 1706–8 that the first English rendering of the *Nights* made its appearance. Known as the 'Grub Street version', it was translated from Galland's French by an unknown hack-writer. This version, stilted and dull as it may well appear to the modern reader, established the popularity of the *Nights* with successive generations of Englishmen and was read with delight by the English Romantics in their childhood. For it was a very long time before an attempt to render a direct translation from the Arabic was made. In 1838 Henry Torrens published a literal translation of the first fifty Nights in which he tried to give the feeling of the original. But to-day his version makes tedious reading. It was followed by E. W. Lane's translation (3 vols., 1839–41), a bowdlerized selection intended for the drawing-room. His notes are very valuable and show his deep knowledge of Egyptian life in the early 19th century. The first complete translation was made by John Payne (9 vols., 1882–4) and published in a limited edition of 500 copies. The rendering of this version is in sophisticated archaic English and its style is even more ponderous than that of any of its predecessors. In 1885–6 the last, and most celebrated, of the direct translations was published. This was Sir Richard Burton's (10 vols., with five supplemental vols.).

In translating *The Thousand and One Nights* Burton wrote, as he himself puts it, 'as the Arab would have written in English.' He 'carefully sought out the English equivalent of every Arabic word ... and never hesitated to coin a word when wanted.' The result was a curious brand of English, a language which no Englishman has spoken or written at any time:

But she rejoined by saying, 'Allah upon you both that ye come down forthright, and if you come not, I will rouse upon you my husband, this Ifrit, and he shall do you to die by the illest of deaths'; and she continued making signals to them.

Thus I did for a long time, but at last I awoke from my heedlessness and, returning to my senses, I found my wealth had become unwealth and my condition ill-conditioned and all I once hent had left my hands.

'This, then, is the rede that is right: and while we both abide alive and well, I will not cease to send thee letters and monies. Arise ere the day wax bright and thou be in perplexed plight and perdition upon thy head alight!' Quoth he, 'O my lady, I beseech thee of thy favour to bid me farewell with thine embracement'; and quoth she, 'No harm in that.' So he embraced her and knew her carnally; after which he made the Ghusl-ablution; then, donning the dress of a white slave, he bade the syces saddle him a thorough-bred steed. Accordingly they saddled him a courser and he mounted and, farewelling his wife, rode forth the city at the last of the night, whilst all who saw him deemed him one of the Mamelukes of the Sultan going abroad on some business.

What Burton gained in accuracy he lost in style. His excessive weakness for the archaic, his habit of coining words and phrases, and the unnatural idiom he affected, detract from the literary quality of his translation without in any way enhancing its fidelity to the original. The notes are far more entertaining than the text.

In spite of Torrens, Lane, and Burton, however, the average English reader's acquaintance with the *Nights* begins and ends with the nursery adaptations. And it is this fact, as well as the absence of a readable version, which constitutes, in my opinion, the best justification for a fresh translation.

It has been my aim in this selection to present the modern reader with an unexpurgated rendering of some of the well-known tales in contemporary English. I have sought to reconcile faithfulness to the text and to the spirit of the original with fidelity to modern English usage. I have sometimes felt obliged to alter the order of phrases and sentences where English prose logic differs from Arabic. As the Macnaghten text, on which this translation is based, has never been properly edited, I have often found it necessary to make my own emendations. In the tale of *The Hunchback*, for instance, I have substituted Al-Muntasir Billah (who reigned in the year of the Flight 247, A.D. 861) for Al-Mustansir Billah (whose reign was more than three centuries and a half later) to avoid an obvious anachronism. I have generally tried to do without footnotes by bringing their substance up into the text itself whenever it reads obscurely. The only Arabic words used in this translation are those which have been assimilated into the English language, such as Caliph, Vizier, Cadi, etc.

Here I must also mention that the verses have been left out. Apart from the fact that they tend to obstruct the natural flow of the narrative, they are completely devoid of literary merit. Internal evidence consistently shows that most of the verses were injected at random into the text by the various redactors. I have also ignored the division of the tales into nights.

And now a few words on the tales themselves. *Sindbad the Sailor* dates back to the time when Baghdad and Basrah had reached the zenith of their commercial prosperity. Originally the cycle seems to have been an independent work. It has many touches which remind one strongly of the *Odyssey*. Like Homer's epic, its background is the sea. The tale of the *Third Voyage* has much in common with Book IX; the Black Giant is Polyphemus the Cyclops seen through Arab eyes. Yet it is almost certain that the author or authors of these tales did not know Homer. What they did know was the Odysseus legend, which, in the course of centuries, had reached the Arabs in the form of a romantic tale of sea adventures.

The Hunchback is an excellent example of the framework system of the *Nights*: the interlacing of several stories into an organic whole. It is full of social criticism and presents the reader with an admirable picture of life in medieval Baghdad, particularly in its underworld. Above all it has, in the humorous figure of the barber, one of the most skilfully drawn characters in Oriental fiction.

The Fisherman and the Jinnee combines Moslem superstition with Persian and Indian folk-lore. It is one of the oldest and simplest tales in the entire collection.

Khalifah the Fisherman is a humorous fantasy. It belongs to that group of Baghdad folk-tales which have Haroun Al-Rashid as their hero.

Ma'aruf the Cobbler is a sophisticated social satire. It is one of the stories which were added to the *Nights* at a comparatively late period in Egypt.

The Young Woman and her Five Lovers and *The Tale of Kafur the Black Eunuch* are short farcical skits, the first satirizing bureaucratic corruption, the second the extravagances of mourning in Islamic countries.

Finally, I would like to express here my gratitude to Dr E. V. Rieu, C.B.E., the Editor of the Penguin Classics, for all that I have learnt from him about the art of translation and for the keen interest he has taken in this book.

N. J. D.

Warlingham, *November 1953*

IN THE NAME OF ALLAH
THE COMPASSIONATE
THE MERCIFUL

PRAISE be to Allah Lord of the Creation, and blessing and peace eternal upon the Prince of Apostles, our master Mohammed.

¶ The annals of former generations are lessons to the living: a man may look back upon the fortunes of his predecessors and be admonished; and contemplate the history of past ages and be purged of folly. Glory to Him who has made the heritage of antiquity a guide for our own time!

¶ From this heritage are derived the Tales of the Thousand and One Nights, together with all that is in them of fable and adventure.

THE PROLOGUE

❧

The Tale of King Shahriyar and his Brother Shahzaman

IT is related – but Allah alone is wise and all-knowing – that long ago there lived in the lands of India and China a Sassanid king who commanded great armies and had numerous courtiers, followers, and servants. He left two sons, both renowned for their horsemanship – especially the elder, who inherited the kingdom of his father and governed it with such justice that all his subjects loved him. He was called King Shahriyar. His younger brother was named Shahzaman and was king of Samarkand.

The two brothers continued to reign happily in their kingdoms, and after a period of twenty years King Shahriyar felt a great longing to see his younger brother. He ordered his Vizier to go to Samarkand and invite him to his court.

The Vizier set out promptly on his mission and journeyed many days and nights through deserts and wildernesses until he arrived at Shahzaman's city and was admitted to his presence. He gave him King Shahriyar's greetings and informed him of his master's desire to see him. King Shahzaman was overjoyed at the prospect of visiting his brother. He made ready to leave his kingdom, and sent out his tents, camels, mules, servants, and retainers. Then he appointed his Vizier as his deputy and set out for his brother's dominions.

It so happened, however, that at midnight he remembered a present which he had left at his palace. He returned for it unheralded, and entering his private chambers found his wife lying on a couch in the arms of a black slave. At this the world darkened before his eyes; and he thought: 'If this can happen when I am scarcely out of my city, how will this foul woman act when I am far away?' He then drew his sword and killed them both as they lay on the couch. Returning at once, he gave orders for departure, and journeyed until he reached his brother's capital.

Shahriyar rejoiced at the news of his approach and went out to meet him. He embraced his guest and welcomed him to his festive city. But while Shahriyar sat entertaining his brother, Shahzaman, haunted by the thought of his wife's perfidy, was pale and sick at heart. Shahriyar perceived his distress, but said nothing, thinking that he might be troubled over the affairs of his kingdom. After a few days, however, Shahriyar said to him: 'I see that you are pale and care-worn.' Shahzaman answered: 'I am afflicted with a painful sore.' And he kept from him the story of his wife's treachery. Then Shahriyar invited his brother to go hunting with him, hoping that the sport might dispel his gloom. But Shahzaman declined, and Shahriyar went alone to the hunt.

While Shahzaman sat at one of the windows overlooking the King's garden, he saw a door open in the palace, through which came twenty slave-girls and twenty Negroes. In their midst was his brother's queen, a woman of surpassing beauty. They made their way to the fountain, where they all undressed and sat on the grass. The King's wife then called out: 'Come, Mass'ood!' and there promptly came to her a black slave, who mounted her after smothering her with embraces and kisses. So also did the Negroes with the slave-girls, revelling together till the approach of night.

When Shahzaman beheld this spectacle, he thought: 'By Allah, my misfortune is lighter than this!' He was dejected no longer, and ate and drank after his long abstinence.

When he returned from the hunt Shahriyar was surprised to see his brother restored to good spirits and full health. 'How is it, my brother,' asked Shahriyar, 'that when I last saw you, you were pale and melancholy, and now you look well and contented?'

'As for my melancholy,' replied Shahzaman, 'I shall now tell you the reason: but I cannot reveal the cause of my altered condition. Know then, that after I had received your invitation, I made preparations for the journey and left my city; but having forgotten the pearl which I was to present to you, I returned for it to the palace. There, on my couch, I found my wife lying in the embrace of a black slave. I killed them both and came to your kingdom, my mind oppressed with bitter thoughts.

When he heard these words, Shahriyar urged him to tell the rest of his story. And so Shahzaman related to him all that he had seen in the King's garden that day.

Alarmed, but half in doubt, Shahriyar exclaimed: 'I will not believe that till I have seen it with my own eyes.'

'Then let it be given out,' suggested his brother, 'that you intend to go to the hunt again. Conceal yourself here with me, and you shall witness what I have seen.'

Upon this Shahriyar announced his intention to set out on another expedition. The troops went out of the city with the tents, and King Shahriyar followed them. And after he had stayed a while in the camp, he gave orders to his slaves that no one was to be admitted to the King's tent. He then disguised himself and returned unnoticed to the palace, where his brother was waiting for him. They both sat at one of the windows overlooking the garden; and when they had been there a short time, the Queen and her women appeared with the black slaves, and did as Shahzaman had described.

Half demented at the sight, Shahriyar said to his brother: 'Let us renounce our royal state and roam the world until we find out if any other king has ever met with such disgrace.'

Shahzaman agreed to his proposal, and they went out in secret and travelled for many days and nights until they came to a meadow by the seashore. They refreshed themselves at a spring of water and sat down to rest under a tree.

Suddenly the waves of the sea surged and foamed before them, and there arose from the deep a black pillar which almost touched the sky. Struck with terror at the sight, they climbed into the tree. When they reached the top they were able to see that it was a jinnee of gigantic stature, carrying a chest on his head. The jinnee waded to the shore and walked towards the tree which sheltered the two brothers. Then, having seated himself beneath it, he opened the chest, and took from it a box, which he also opened; and there rose from the box a beautiful young girl, radiant as the sun.

'Chaste and honourable lady, whom I carried away on your wedding-night,' said the jinnee, 'I would sleep a little.' Then, laying his head upon her knees, the jinnee fell fast asleep.

Suddenly the girl lifted her head and saw the two

Kings high in the tree. She laid the jinnee's head on the ground, and made signs to them which seemed to say: 'Come down, and have no fear of the jinnee.'

The two Kings pleaded with her to let them hide in safety, but the girl replied: 'If you do not come down, I will wake the jinnee, and he shall put you to a cruel death.'

They climbed down in fear, and at once she said: 'Come, pierce me with your rapiers.'

Shahriyar and Shahzaman faltered. But the girl repeated angrily: 'If you do not do my bidding, I will wake the jinnee.'

Afraid of the consequences, they proceeded to mount her in turn.

When they had remained with her as long as she desired, she took from her pocket a large purse, from which she drew ninety-eight rings threaded on a string. 'The owners of these,' she laughed triumphantly, 'have all enjoyed me under the very horn of this foolish jinnee. Therefore, give me your rings also.'

The two men gave her their rings.

'This jinnee,' she added, 'carried me away on my bridal night and imprisoned me in a box which he placed inside a chest. He fastened the chest with seven locks and deposited it at the bottom of the roaring sea. But he little knew how cunning we women are.'

The two Kings marvelled at her story, and said to each other: 'If such a thing could happen to a mighty jinnee, then our own misfortune is light indeed.' And they returned at once to the city.

As soon as they entered the palace, King Shahriyar put his wife to death, together with her women and the black slaves. Thenceforth he made it his custom to take a virgin in marriage to his bed each night, and kill her the next morning. This he continued to do for three years, until a clamour rose among the people, some of whom fled the country with their daughters.

At last came the day when the Vizier roamed the city in search of a virgin for the King, and could find none. Dreading the King's anger, he returned to his house with a heavy heart.

Now the Vizier had two daughters. The elder was called Shahrazad, and the younger Dunyazad. Shahrazad possessed many accomplishments and was versed in the wisdom of the poets and the legends of ancient kings.

That day Shahrazad noticed her father's anxiety and asked him what it was that troubled him. When the Vizier told her of his predicament, she said: 'Give me in marriage to this King: either I shall die and be a ransom for the daughters of Moslems, or live and be the cause of their deliverance.'

He earnestly pleaded with her against such a hazard; but Shahrazad was resolved, and would not yield to her father's entreaties.

'Beware,' said the Vizier, 'of the fate of the donkey in the fable:

The Fable of the Donkey, the Ox, and the Farmer

'THERE was once a wealthy farmer who owned many herds of cattle. He knew the languages of beasts and birds. In one of his stalls he kept an ox and a donkey. At the end of each day, the ox came to the place where the donkey was tied and found it well swept and watered; the manger filled with sifted straw and well-winnowed barley; and the donkey lying at his ease (for his master seldom rode him).

'It chanced that one day the farmer heard the ox say to the donkey: "How fortunate you are! I am worn out with toil, while you rest here in comfort. You eat well-sifted barley and lack nothing. It is only occasionally that our master rides you. As for me, my life is perpetual drudgery at the plough and the millstone."

'The donkey answered: "When you go out into the field and the yoke is placed upon your neck, pretend to be ill and drop down on your belly. Do not rise even if they beat you; or if you do rise, lie down again. When they take you back and place the fodder before you, do not eat it. Abstain for a day or two; and thus shall you find a rest from toil."

'Remember that the farmer was there and heard what passed between them.

'And so when the ploughman came to the ox with his fodder, he ate scarcely any of it. And when the ploughman came the following morning to take him out into the field, the ox appeared to be far from well. Then the farmer said to the ploughman: "Take the donkey and use him at the plough all day!"

'The man returned, took the donkey in place of the ox, and drove him at the plough all day.

'When the day's work was done and the donkey returned to the stall, the ox thanked him for his good counsel. But the donkey made no reply and bitterly repented his rashness.

'Next day the ploughman came and took the donkey again and made him labour till the evening; so that when the donkey returned with his neck flayed by the yoke, and in a pitiful state of exhaustion, the ox again expressed his gratitude to him, and praised his sagacity.

'"If only I had kept my wisdom to myself!" thought the donkey. Then, turning to the ox, he said: "I have just heard my master say to his servant: 'If the ox does not recover soon, take him to the slaughterhouse and dispose of him.' My anxiety for your safety prompts me, my friend, to let you know of this before it is too late. And peace be with you!"

'When he heard the donkey's words, the ox thanked him and said: "To-morrow I will go to work freely and willingly." He ate all his fodder and even licked the manger clean.

'Early next morning the farmer, accompanied by his wife, went to visit the ox in his stall. The ploughman came and led out the ox, who, at the sight of his master, broke wind and frisked about in all directions. And the farmer laughed so, he fell over on his back.'

When she heard her father's story, Shahrazad said: 'Nothing will shake my faith in the mission I am destined to fulfil.'

So the Vizier arrayed his daughter in bridal garments and decked her with jewels and made ready to announce Shahrazad's wedding to the King.

Before saying farewell to her sister, Shahrazad gave her these instructions: 'When I am received by the King, I shall send for you. Then, when the King has finished his act with me, you must say: "Tell me, my sister, some tale of marvel to beguile the night." Then I will tell you a tale which, if Allah wills, shall be the means of our deliverance.'

The Vizier went with his daughter to the King. And when the King had taken the maiden Shahrazad to his chamber and had lain with her, she wept and said: 'I have a young sister to whom I wish to bid farewell.'

The King sent for Dunyazad. When she arrived, she threw her arms round her sister's neck, and seated herself by her side.

Then Dunyazad said to Shahrazad: 'Tell us, my sister, a tale of marvel, so that the night may pass pleasantly.'

'Gladly,' she answered, 'if the King permits.'

And the King, who was troubled with sleeplessness, eagerly listened to the tale of Shahrazad:

THE TALE OF THE
HUNCHBACK

ONCE upon a time, in the city of Basrah, there lived
a prosperous tailor who was fond of sport and merriment. It was his custom to go out with his wife from
time to time in quest of pleasure and amusement. It
chanced that one evening, when they were returning
home from a long jaunt, they met a sprightly little
hunchback whose comic aspect banished grief and sorrow from his presence and drove away all care. Elated
with drink, he was clashing a tambourine and singing
gleefully. The tailor and his wife were so amused at the
hunchback's drollery that they invited him to spend the
evening with them as their guest. The hunchback accepted, and when they had returned to the house, the
tailor hurried out to the market-place, where he bought
some fried fish, bread, and lemons, and honey for dessert.

The three sat down to a hilarious meal. Being fond of
practical jokes, the tailor's wife crammed a large piece
of fish into the hunchback's mouth and forced him to
swallow it. But, as fate would have it, the fish concealed a big, sharp bone which stuck in his throat and
choked him; so that when they examined him, they
found, to their horror, that the hunchback was dead.

The tailor lifted up his hands and exclaimed: 'There
is no strength nor power save in Allah! Alas that this

man should have met his fate at our hands, and in this fashion!'

'Your cries are of no avail,' said his wife. 'We must do something!'

'What *can* we do?' whimpered the tailor.

'Rise,' she said, 'and take the body in your arms; we will cover it with a shawl and carry it out of the house this very night. I will walk in front, crying: "My child is ill, my poor child is ill! Who will direct us to a doctor's house?"'

Encouraged by her plan, the tailor wrapped up the hunchback in a large silken shawl and carried him out into the street; his wife lamenting: 'My child! My child! Who will save him from the foul smallpox?'

So all who saw them whispered together: 'They are carrying a child stricken with the smallpox.'

Thus they proceeded through the streets, inquiring for the doctor's house as they went, until at last they were directed by the passers-by to the house of a Jewish doctor. They knocked, and the door was opened by a black slave-girl.

'Give your master this piece of silver,' said the tailor's wife, 'and beg him to come down and see my child; for he is very ill.'

When the girl went in to call the doctor, the tailor's wife slipped into the vestibule and said to her husband:

'Leave the hunchback here and let us run for our lives!'

The tailor propped up the body at the bottom of the staircase, and the pair made off as fast as their legs could carry them.

The Jew rejoiced on receiving the piece of silver. He rose in haste, and hurrying down the stairs in the dark, stumbled against the corpse and toppled it over. Terrified at the sight of the lifeless hunchback, and thinking that he himself had just killed him, the Jew called on Moses and Aaron and Ezra and Joshua son of Nun, and bethought himself of the Ten Commandments, and wrung his hands, crying: 'How shall I get rid of the body?' Then he took up the hunchback and carried him to his wife and told her what had happened.

'Why, then, do you stand there doing nothing?' exclaimed the terrified woman. 'If the corpse is still here by day-break, we are lost! Come, we will carry the body up to the terrace and throw it into the house of our neighbour the Moslem.'

Now the Moslem was the steward of the royal kitchens, from which he seldom departed with his pockets empty. His house was always infested by cats and mice, which ate the butter, the cheese, and the corn; and on fine nights the dogs of the neighbourhood came down and feasted on the contents of his kitchen. So the Jew and his wife, carrying the hunchback, climbed down from their terrace into their neighbour's house, and propped him up against the wall of the kitchen.

It was not long before the steward, who had been out all day, returned to his house. He opened the door and lighted a candle – then started at the sight of a man leaning against the wall of his kitchen. 'So our thief is a man after all!' he thought; and taking up a mallet, he cried: 'By Allah, to think that it was you, and not the cats and the dogs, who stole all that meat and butter! I have killed almost all the cats and dogs in the district and never thought of you and your like, who come prowling down the terraces.'

So saying, he knocked down the hunchback with the mallet and dealt him another blow upon the chest as he lay on the ground. But the angry steward soon found that the hunchback was dead. He was seized with fear, and exclaimed:

'There is no strength nor power save in Allah! A curse upon the meat and the butter, and upon this night which has witnessed your death at my hands, you wretch!' Then, perceiving his deformity, he added: 'Is it not enough that you are a hunchback: must you also be a kitchen thief? O Allah, protect me in your mercy!'

The steward took up the hunchback, and, carrying him on his shoulders, left the house. The night was already approaching its end. He walked with his burden through the deserted streets until he entered a lane leading to the market-place, and came to a shop that stood on a corner. There he leaned the hunchback up against the wall, and hurried away.

Soon after, a Christian, who was the King's broker, passed through the lane on his way to the public baths. Fuddled with drink, he reeled along muttering to himself, 'Doomsday has come! The Last Judgement has come!' and staggering from one side of the lane to the other. When he came close to the hunchback he stopped, and without noticing him, turned round to make water.

Now it so chanced that earlier in the evening the Christian had been robbed of his turban and was forced to buy another. Therefore, when he suddenly saw the figure of the hunchback against the wall, the drunken broker, imagining that he was about to snatch off his new turban, took him by the throat and knocked him down with a resounding blow. Then he raised a great outcry, screaming and cursing and calling out to the watchman of the market-place.

The watchman arrived to find a Christian beating a Moslem. 'Rise up and let go of him!' he shouted; and when he found that the hunchback was dead, he exclaimed: 'A pretty state of things when a Christian dares to kill a Believer!'

Confounded at the swift dispatch of his victim, the Christian began to call on Jesus and Mary: thus, as the proverb has it, intoxication departed and meditation came in its place. And the watchman took hold of the Christian broker, and manacled him, and dragged him away to the Governor's house.

In the morning the Governor gave orders for the hanging of the Christian. The town-crier proclaimed his crime in the streets, and a gallows was set up in the heart of the city. Then came the executioner, and, in the presence of the Governor, he placed the Christian beneath the gallows and threw the rope round his neck.

At this moment the King's steward pushed his way through the crowd, crying: 'Do not hang him! It was I who killed the hunchback!'

'Why did you kill him?' asked the Governor.

'It all happened,' replied the steward, 'when I returned home last night and found him in my house, about to break into the kitchen. I struck him with a mallet and he fell down dead upon the instant. In despair, I carried him to a lane adjoining the market-place. Is it not enough to have killed a Moslem?' added the steward passionately. 'Must a Christian also die on my account? Therefore, hang no man but me!'

When he heard this the Governor set the Christian free and said to the executioner: 'Hang this man instead, on the grounds of his own confession.'

The executioner led the steward to the scaffold and had just placed the rope round his neck, when the Jewish doctor forced his way through the crowd, crying out: 'Do not hang him! I am the man who killed the hunchback!' And the Jew related to the Governor his own version of the hunchback's death. 'Is my sin not great enough that I have killed a man unwittingly?' he added. 'Must another be killed through my crime, and with my knowledge?'

On hearing this the Governor gave orders that the Jew be hanged in place of the steward. But when the rope was placed round his neck, the tailor came forward and cried out: 'Do not hang him! None killed the hunchback but myself!' And he related to the astonished assembly the circumstances of the hunchback's death.

The Governor marvelled at the story of the hunchback, and said: 'This episode ought to be recorded in books.' And he ordered the executioner to set the Jew at liberty and to hang the tailor.

'Would to heaven they would make up their minds,' muttered the executioner, who was becoming impatient at the delay. 'The day will end before we hang any of them.' And he resolutely placed the rope round the tailor's neck.

Now the hunchback, who was the cause of all this commotion, was the King's jester and favourite companion. When the King found that the hunchback had been absent from the royal palace all night and the next morning, he ordered some of his attendants to seek him. They soon returned to inform him of the hunchback's death and his self-confessed murderers.

'Go to the Governor,' said the King to his Chamberlain, 'and bring them all before me.'

The Chamberlain hurried at once to the city square, where the executioner was about to hang the tailor. 'Stop! Stop! Do not hang him!' shouted the Chamberlain, rushing through the crowd. And before the executioner could complete his work, the Chamberlain informed the Governor of the King's orders, and took him to the royal palace, together with the tailor, the Christian, the Jew, the steward, and the hunchback's body.

When they had all been admitted to the King's presence, the Governor kissed the ground before him, and related to him all that had happened. The King marvelled greatly, and gave orders that the story be inscribed on parchment in letters of gold. Then the King asked those who were present: 'Have you ever heard a story more marvellous than that of the hunchback?'

The tailor came forward, and said:

The Tailor's Tale

OF all the tales of marvel that I have heard, your majesty, none surpasses in wonder the incident which I witnessed yesterday. Early in the morning, before I met the hunchback, I was at a breakfast party given by a friend to some twenty tradesmen and craftsmen of the city, among them tailors and drapers and carpenters and others. As soon as the sun rose and the food was set before us, our host ushered into the room a handsome, but noticeably lame, young man, richly dressed in the Baghdad fashion. The young man greeted the company, and we all rose to receive him. But when he was about to be seated, he caught sight of an old man in our midst who was a barber; whereupon he refused to sit down and made for the door again. We all hastened to prevent him, and the host, swearing that he should not leave the house, held him by the arm and earnestly pleaded with him to explain his abrupt departure.

'Sir,' he answered, 'do not try to detain me. If you must know, it is the presence of this sinister barber that compels me to leave at once.'

Our host was greatly astonished at these words, and we all wondered why the young man, a stranger in this city, should have taken such offence at the barber's presence. We begged him to tell us the reason.

'Gentlemen,' he answered, 'this barber was the cause of a grave disaster which befell me in Baghdad, my native city; thanks to him my leg was broken and I am now lame. I have sworn never to sit in the same room with him, nor live in any town where he resides. This is why I left Baghdad, yet here I find him again. Not another night will I spend in this city.'

'By Allah,' we said, 'let us hear your story.'

The barber hung his head, as the young man proceeded to tell of his adventure.

The Tale of the Lame Young Man and the Barber of Baghdad

You must know that my father was one of the chief merchants of Baghdad and I was his only son. When I attained manhood my father died, leaving me great wealth and a numerous retinue of slaves and servants. From that time I began to live sumptuously, wearing the richest clothes and eating the choicest dishes. But I always shunned the company of women, for Allah had made me strangely indifferent to their allurements.

It so chanced, however, that one day, as I was walking along a narrow lane in Baghdad, a crowd of women barred my way. To avoid them I slipped into a quiet alley, and sat down upon a bench. I had not been there long, when a window in the house opposite was flung open, and there appeared a young girl who was like the full moon in her beauty. She was watering the flower-pots on her window-sill, when she happened to glance around and caught sight of me; whereupon she shut the window and disappeared. Love suddenly burned like a flame in my heart, and my soul was enthralled with the vision of her loveliness. I sat lost in my new-born passion, till sunset, when the Cadi of Baghdad came riding by, with slaves before him and servants behind him. Imagine my feelings, gentlemen, when I saw him dismount and enter the very house where the young girl lived; for at that moment I realized that she was the Cadi's daughter.

I returned home downcast and melancholy, and threw myself upon my bed. My slave-girls came in and anxiously sat around me, afraid to inquire the cause of my dejection. Presently, however, there entered an old woman of the house who at once understood the truth of my condition. She sat at my bedside and comforted me, saying: 'Tell me everything, my son, and let me be your messenger.'

When she had heard my story, she said: 'You must know that this girl lives with her father the Cadi in the strictest seclusion. I myself am a frequent visitor at their house, and will undertake to be the means of your union. Take heart, and do not despair.'

I was greatly consoled by her words, and the next day my people rejoiced to see me restored to good spirits. The old woman departed on her mission, but soon returned crestfallen. 'My son,' she said, 'do not inquire the outcome of my visit. Scarcely had I begun to speak of you, when the girl cried: "Hold your tongue, old woman, or you shall receive the treatment you deserve."'

Seeing that this news had dashed my spirits, the old woman added: 'But do not fear, I shall shortly approach her again.'

My anguish was renewed. After a few days, however, she came to me and said: 'Rejoice, I bring you good news! Yesterday I again visited the girl. When she saw me in tears, she asked me the cause of my grief. Weeping bitterly, I replied: "I have come from a youth who is languishing with love for you." Her heart was moved, and she asked: "Who is the youth of whom you speak?" "He is the flower of my life," I answered, "and as dear to me as my own son. Some days ago he saw you at your window, watering your flowers. He loved you from that moment. But when I told him of your harsh response he began to pine away, and took to his bed, where he now lies dying." "And all this on my account?" asked the girl, moved with pity. "Yes, by Allah," I replied. "Go back to him," she said, "give him my greetings and say my love is even greater than his. Ask him to come to me on Friday next, before the midday prayers. I shall let him in myself and bring him up to my chamber. But he must leave me before my father returns from the mosque."'

On hearing this, I was transported with joy and handsomely rewarded the old woman for her labours. My sickness left me, and my household rejoiced at my recovery.

When Friday came, I made ready for the great occasion, putting on my finest robes and sweetest perfumes, and then sat waiting for the hour of midday prayers. But the old woman hinted that a visit from the barber might do much to improve my appearance. I called my slave and said to him: 'Go to the market-place and

B

bring me a barber. See that he is a man of sense who will attend to his business and will not split my head with idle chatter.' The slave went away and brought back with him a barber who was none other than the odious old man you see before you.

As soon as he entered, the barber remarked upon my pallor; and when I explained that I had but recently recovered from an illness, he congratulated me, saying: 'May Allah preserve you, sir, from all misfortune, all distress, all grief, and all sorrow!'

'Allah grant your prayer!' I replied.

'Now tell me, sir,' he said, 'do you wish to be shaved or to be bled? You doubtless know that the famous Ibn Abbas (may Allah rest his soul in peace!) has said: "He who has his hair cut on a Friday shall ward off seventy calamities." And to the same authority is also attributed the maxim: "To let blood on a Friday averts weakness of sight and a host of other diseases."'

'Enough of this talk, old man!' I cried. 'Come now, begin shaving my head at once.'

He rose, and produced from his pocket a large bundle. Imagine my astonishment when I saw him take from it, not a razor or a pair of scissors as one might have expected, but an astrolabe consisting of seven plates of polished silver. He carried it to the middle of the court-yard, and, raising the instrument towards the sun, gazed intently at the reflection for a long time. Then he came back to me and said solemnly: 'Know, that of this day, Friday the tenth of Safar in the year two hundred and fifty-three after the Flight of the Prophet (upon whom be Allah's blessing and peace), and twelve hundred and thirty-one in the year of Alexander the Great, there have elapsed eight degrees and six minutes; and that, according to the strictest rules of computation, the planet

Mars, in conjunction with Mercury, is this day in the ascendant: all this denoting an auspicious moment for hair-cutting. Furthermore, my instrument manifestly informs me that it is your intention to pay a visit to a certain person, and that of this nothing shall come but evil. There is also another sign in connexion with a certain matter, of which I would rather not speak.'

'By Allah!' I cried, 'this is intolerable! You weary me with your tedious chatter, and what is more, your forebodings are far from encouraging. I sent for you to shave my head. Do so at once and cease your babbling!'

'If only you knew the gravity of the impending disaster,' he said, 'you would listen to my counsel and heed the portent of the stars!'

'Doubtless,' I cried, 'you are the only astrologer among the barbers of Baghdad: but, allow me to tell you, old man, you are also an impudent mischief-maker and a frivolous chatter-box.'

'What more would you have?' cried he, shrugging his shoulders. 'Allah has sent you one who is not only a barber of great repute, but also a master of the arts and sciences: one who is not only deeply versed in alchemy, astrology, mathematics, and architecture, but also (to mention only a few of my accomplishments) well schooled in the arts of logic, rhetoric, and elocution, the theory of grammar, and the commentaries on the Koran. Add to all this the maturity of judgement that can only be acquired through long experience of the world. Your late father, young man, loved me for my discretion; and it is the memory of his goodness and kind favours that prompts me to render you an honest service. Far from being a meddlesome gossip, as you seem to suggest, I am, in fact, renowned for my gravity

and reserve; on account of which qualities people call
me the "Silent One". Instead of crossing and thwarting
me, young man, it would be much more befitting to
thank Allah for my sound advice and my concern for
your well-being. Would that I were a whole year in your
service, that you might learn to do me justice!'

Here I exclaimed: 'You will surely be my death this
day!' But when the old man was about to resume his
soliloquy, I felt as though my gall-bladder would burst,
and I said to my slave: 'In Allah's name, give this man
a quarter of a dinar and show him out; for I do not wish
to have my head shaved after all.'

'What kind of talk is this?' cried the barber. 'By
Allah, I will accept nothing before I have shaved you.
You must know that I would regard it as a pleasant
duty and a great honour to serve you even without payment. For although you do not seem to appreciate my
merits, I appreciate yours. I remember one Friday when
I was sent for by your late father (may Allah have mercy
upon him: he was a man of rare munificence). I found
him entertaining a company of visitors. He welcomed
me as he might have welcomed an old friend, and said:
"I beg you to let me a little blood." At once I took out
my astrolabe, computed the height of the sun, and soon
ascertained that the hour was clearly unpropitious for
blood-letting. I did not hesitate to tell him the truth.
He accepted my judgement, and readily agreed to wait
for a favourable moment. Incidentally, it might interest
you to know that, while we waited, I composed half a
dozen verses in his praise and recited them before the
company. Your father was so pleased with them that
he ordered his slave to give me a hundred and three
dinars and a robe of honour. When the auspicious hour
had come and the operation was completed, I asked him

in a whisper: "Why did you pay me a hundred and *three* dinars?" "One dinar is for your wisdom," he replied, "one for the blood-letting, and one for the pleasure of your company; as for the remainder and the robe of honour, pray accept them as a slight reward for your excellent poem."'

'Then may Allah have no mercy on my father,' I burst out, 'if he ever had dealings with a barber like you!'

'There is no god but Allah, and Mohammed is his Prophet!' exclaimed the barber, laughing and shaking his head. 'Glory to him who changes others and remains himself unchanged! I always took you for a sensible and intelligent young man: now I see that your illness has slightly affected your head. You would do well to remember that Allah in his sacred book mentioned with especial praise those who curb their anger and forgive their fellow-men. However, I will forgive you. As I was saying, neither your father, nor your grandfather before him, ever did anything without first seeking my advice. You have doubtless heard the proverb: "He who takes good counsel is crowned with success." Now you will find no one better versed in the ways of the world than myself: and here I stand, waiting to serve you. What I cannot understand, however, is that you seem to be a little tired of me, when I am not in the least tired of you. But the high esteem in which I hold your father's memory will always make me mindful of my duty to his son.'

'By Allah,' I yelled, 'this has gone too far!' I was about to order my slaves to throw him out of the house, when he suddenly began to damp my hair, and before I knew what was happening, my head was covered with lather.

'I shall take no offence, sir,' continued the wretched old man, quite unruffled, 'if you are a little short-tempered. Apart from the strain of your recent illness, you are, of course, very young. It seems but yesterday that I used to carry you to school on my shoulders.'

Unable to contain myself any longer, I said solemnly: 'My friend, I must beg you to proceed with your work.' Then, I rent my clothes and began to shriek like a maniac.

When he saw me do this, the barber calmly produced a razor and began to strop it, passing it up and down the piece of leather with deadly deliberation. At length, he held my head with one hand and shaved off a few hairs. Then he raised his hand and said: 'I do not suppose that you are aware of my standing in society. These hands of mine have dressed the heads of kings and princes, viziers and noblemen. Have you not heard the poet's eulogy in my praise? —'

At this point I interrupted him, crying: 'You have stifled me with your nonsense!'

'It has just occurred to me that you might be in a hurry,' said the barber.

'I am indeed!' I shouted, 'I am indeed!'

'Well, well,' he went on, 'haste is a precept of the Devil, and leads only to ruin and repentance. The Prophet has said: "The best enterprises are those that are carried out with caution." I wish you would tell me the purpose of your hurry, as it is yet nearly three hours to midday prayers.' Here the barber paused, and then added: 'But the fallacies of mere conjecture are not to be relied upon by a man of my learning.'

So saying, he flung away the razor, took up the astrolabe, and went out into the courtyard. There he observed the sun for a long time, and at last came back, saying:

'It is now three hours to midday prayers, neither one minute more nor one minute less.'

'For Allah's sake,' I cried, 'hold your tongue: you have goaded me beyond endurance!'

Again he took up the razor and proceeded to strop it as he had done before. Scarcely had he removed a few hairs, when he said: 'I am somewhat anxious about you. It would be in your own interest to tell me the cause of your haste. For, as you know, your father and grand-father never did anything without consulting me.'

I realized that I should never be able to elude his persistent questioning. To cut the matter short, I said that I had been invited to a banquet at the house of a friend, and begged him to cease his impertinence.

At the mention of a banquet the barber exclaimed: 'This reminds me that I myself am expecting a few friends at my house to-day. But I have forgotten to provide anything for them to eat. Think of the disgrace!'

'Do not be troubled over this matter,' I replied. 'All the food and drink in my house is yours if you will only finish shaving my head.'

'Sir,' he cried, 'may Allah reward you for your generosity! Pray let me hear what you have for my guests.'

'Five different meat dishes,' I answered, 'ten stuffed chickens finely broiled, and a roasted lamb.'

'Be so good,' he said, 'as to let me look at them.'

I ordered the food to be brought before him, together with a cask of wine.

'How generous you are!' he exclaimed. 'But the incense and the perfume are wanting.'

I then ordered my slave to set before him a box containing aloe-wood, musk, and ambergris, the whole worth not less than fifty dinars. Time was running short, so I said: 'All this is yours; only, for the sake of

Mohammed, on whom be Allah's blessing and peace, finish shaving my head!'

'Pray allow me to see the contents,' he replied.

My slave opened the box, and the barber put aside his razor, and sat down on the floor examining the incense. He then rose and, taking up his razor again, held my head and shaved off a few hairs.

'My son,' he said, with great satisfaction, 'I do not know how to thank you. The party I am giving to-day will owe a great deal to your bounty. Although none of my guests might be considered worthy of such magnificence, they are all quite respectable. First, there is Zantoot, the bath-keeper; then Salee'a, the corn merchant; Akrasha, the fruiterer; Hamid, the dustman; Silat, the grocer; Abu Makarish, the milkman; Kaseem, the watchman; and last, but by no means least, Sa'eed, the camel-driver. Each one of them is a delightful companion, and has a song and a dance of his own invention; and, like your humble servant, neither inquisitive nor given to idle talk. In truth, no description of my friends can do them justice. If, therefore, you would care to honour us with your company, you will have a more pleasant time, and we will all be the happier. One reason, in my opinion, why you would do well not to visit those friends of yours, is the possibility of meeting some busybody who will split your head with incessant chatter.'

Choking with rage, I burst into a fit of hysterical laughter, and said: 'I should be delighted to come some other time. Shave my head now, and let me go my way. Besides, your friends must be waiting for you.'

'But how I long to introduce you to these excellent fellows!' he continued. 'Once you meet them, you will give up all your friends for ever.'

'May Allah give you joy in them,' I said. 'I shall doubtless have the pleasure of meeting them one day.'

'Well, well,' said he, shrugging his shoulders, 'if you needs must go to your friends, I will now carry to my guests the presents with which you have favoured me. As I do not stand upon ceremony with them, I will return without delay to accompany you to your banquet.'

Here I lost all control of myself and cried: 'There is no strength nor help save in Allah! Pray go to your friends and delight your heart with them, and let me go to mine; for they are waiting for me.'

But the barber cried: 'I will not let you go alone.'

'The truth is,' I said, 'that no one may be admitted to the house where I am going except myself.'

'Aha!' he exclaimed. 'It must be a woman, then, or else you would allow me to accompany you. Yet I am the right man for that kind of adventure, and could do much in an emergency; especially if, as I suspect, the woman proves to be a deceitful whore. Why, you would probably be murdered! Furthermore, you know how ruthless the Governor is about such irregular dealings, particularly on a Friday.'

'Vile old man,' I cried, 'how can you speak so to my face?'

'Did you imagine,' retorted the barber, 'that you could conceal such a design from me? My sole concern, young man, is to serve you.'

Afraid that my servants might hear the barber's remarks, I made no answer.

The hour of prayer had come and the imams had already begun their sermons, when at long last the barber finished shaving my head.

'Take away this food to your house,' I said, 'and

when you return we will go together to the banquet.'

But he would not believe my words. 'You want to get rid of me and go alone,' he replied. 'Think of the trap that may have been set for you! By Allah, you shall not leave the house until I come back to accompany you and watch over your safety.'

'Very well,' I said, 'but you must not be late.'

The barber took all the meat and drink I had given him and left me in peace. But the damnable dog hired a porter to carry the things to his house, and hid himself in one of the neighbouring alleys.

The muezzins had now intoned their blessings on the Prophet from the minarets of the city. I rose in haste and flung on my cloak and ran as fast as I could to the girl's house. Finding the door open, I hurried up the stairs to her apartment. But I had scarcely reached the first story when the Cadi arrived. Seized by a great fear, I rushed to one of the windows overlooking the alley, and was confounded to see the barber (Allah's curse be upon him!) sitting at the doorstep.

Now it so happened that immediately on his return from the mosque, the Cadi took it into his head to beat a maid-servant. She raised an uproar, shrieking and screaming. A black slave interceded for her, but the furious Cadi fell upon him also, and the slave joined in the shrill tumult, yelling for help.

Imagining that it was I who was the victim, the incorrigible barber set up a great outcry in the street, tearing his clothes and scattering dust upon his head. 'Help! Help!' he cried. 'My master is being murdered by the Cadi!'

Then, running frantically to my house with a great crowd following him, he roused my people and my servants; and before I knew what was happening, they all came, men and women, to the Cadi's house, with torn clothes and loosed tresses, lamenting: 'Alas! Our master is dead!'

When he heard the loud clamour in the street, the Cadi ordered a slave to find out what had happened. The slave quickly returned and said: 'At the door there is a great multitude of men and women. They are all shaking their fists and crying: "Our master has been murdered!"'

The Cadi rose in anger, and opening the door, was amazed to find an infuriated mob shouting threats at him.

'What is the meaning of this?' he asked indignantly.

'Dog! Pig! Murderer!' shouted my servants. 'Where is our master?'

'What has your master done to me,' asked the Cadi, 'that I should kill him?'

'You have just been flogging him,' replied the barber. 'I myself heard his cries.'

'But what has your master done that I should flog him?' repeated the Cadi. 'Who brought him to my house?'

'Wicked old liar,' answered the barber, 'do not pretend to be so innocent; for I know the whole truth and every detail of the matter. Your daughter is in love with him and he with her. When you caught him in the house you ordered your slaves to flog him. By Allah,' added the barber vehemently, 'the Caliph himself shall judge this outrage! Give us back our master, or else I shall have to enter by force and rescue him myself.'

Embarrassed and perplexed, the Cadi said: 'If you are not lying, come and bring him out.'

When I saw the barber push his way through the door, I desperately looked about for a means of escape, but could find none. At length I saw in one of the rooms a great wooden chest which was empty. I jumped into it and pulled down the lid, holding my breath. Immediately after, the barber ran into the room. He looked right and left, and, instantly divining where I was, lifted the chest upon his shoulder and scrambled with it down the stairs. But as he rushed through the door, the barber tripped over the threshold, hurling me out of the chest into the crowded street. My leg was broken; but my single thought at that moment was to fly for my life. I took from my pockets handfuls of gold and threw them to the crowd. Whilst they were busy scrambling for the coins, I made off, hobbling through the back streets as fast as I could go.

The barber pursued me from one lane to another, crying: 'The blackguards would have killed my master! Praise be to Allah who aided me against them and saved my master from their hands!'

Then, calling out to me as he ran, the barber continued: 'Now you see the fruits of your rashness and impatience! Had not Allah sent me to your rescue, you would not have escaped alive to-day. I have risked my life in your service; but you would not even hear of taking me with you. However, I will not be angry, for you are very young and exceedingly rash and foolish.'

Writhing with the pain in my leg and the anguish in my heart, I turned on my heel and solemnly said to the jabbering monster at my back: 'Is it not enough that you have brought me to this pass? Must you also hound me to my death in the midst of the market-place?' Then, entering a weaver's shop near by, I begged asylum of him and implored him to drive the barber away.

As I sat in the back room, I thought: 'If I return home, I will never be able to rid myself of this fiend.

He will pursue me like a shadow, and I cannot endure the sight of him!'

I sent out for witnesses and wrote my will, dividing my property among my people. I appointed a guardian over them, and committed to him the charge of the young and the aged, and also the sale of my house and other estates. I then left Baghdad and came to live in your city, imagining that I had for ever freed myself from this monster. Yet no sooner had I stepped into this house than I found him sitting amongst you as an honoured guest. How, then, can my heart be at ease or my stay be pleasant, when I am under the same roof as the man who did all this to me and was the cause of my lameness?

The young man (continued the tailor) refused to sit down, and went away. When we had heard his story, we turned to the barber and asked: 'Is it true what this young man has said of you?'

'By Allah, gentlemen,' replied the barber, 'I must assure you that had it not been for my sagacity, resourcefulness, and personal courage this youth would have surely died. He should, indeed, be thankful that his folly cost him merely his leg, and not his life. This young man has accused me of being talkative and meddlesome – two vices from which, unlike my six brothers, I am entirely free. To prove to you the falseness of this charge, however, I shall now tell you the following story, and you shall judge for yourselves that I am a man not only of few words but also of great generosity and chivalry.'

The Barber's Tale

THE little adventure I am about to relate occurred to me some years ago during the reign of Al-Muntasir Billah (may Allah have mercy upon him: he was a truly munificent Caliph and a righteous man).

One day the Caliph was incensed against ten men, and he ordered his lieutenant to bring them before him. It so chanced that just as they were being embarked on a boat to cross the Tigris, I was taking the air along the river-bank. Drawing close to them, I thought to myself: 'This must be a pleasure party. They will probably spend the day in this boat eating and drinking. By Allah, I will be their guest and make merry with them.'

I jumped into the boat and sat in their midst. But as soon as we set foot on the opposite bank, the Governor's guards took hold of us and put chains round the necks of the men, and round my neck also. Yet I never breathed a syllable (which, I submit, is but a proof of my courage and discretion). Then they dragged us away to Al-Muntasir's court, and led us before the Prince of the Faithful.

When he saw us, the Caliph called the executioner and said to him: 'Strike off the heads of these ten wretches!'

The executioner made us kneel down in a row before the Caliph; then he unsheathed his sword and beheaded the unfortunate men.

Seeing me kneeling still at the end of the row, the Caliph cried, 'Why did you not kill the tenth man?'

The executioner counted aloud the ten heads and the ten bodies that lay on the ground; and the Caliph turned to me and said: 'Who are you, and how did you come to be among these criminals?'

Then, and only then, did I decide to break my silence.

'Prince of the Faithful,' I replied, 'I am called the "Silent One" and my wisdom is proverbial. I am a barber by trade and one of the seven sons of my father.' I then explained how I was mistaken for one of the prisoners, and briefly outlined my life's history.

When he was satisfied that I was a man of rare qualities, the Caliph smiled, saying: 'Tell me, noble sheikh, are your six brothers like you, distinguished for their deep learning and the brevity of their speeches?'

'Gracious heavens!' I replied. 'Each of them is such a disreputable good-for-nothing, that you almost dispraise me by comparing me with them. Because of their recklessness, stupidity, and unusual cowardice, they have brought upon themselves all kinds of misfortunes and bodily deformities: the first is lame, the second loose-limbed and disfigured, the third blind, the fourth one-eyed, the fifth ear-cropped, and the sixth had both his lips cut off. Were it not for the fear that you might take me for an idle gossip I would gladly tell you their stories.'

Thereupon the Prince of the Faithful gave me leave to relate to him the story of my first brother.

The Tale of Bakbook
The Barber's First Brother

Know, Prince of the Faithful, that the eldest of my brothers, he who is lame, was in his youth a tailor and lived in Baghdad.

He used to ply his trade in a little shop which he rented from a wealthy man, who himself lived in the upper storey of the building. In the spacious basement below a miller worked at his mill and kept his ox.

One day, as he sat sewing, my brother chanced to raise his eyes and caught sight of a young woman looking out at the passers-by from an oriel window above his shop. She was the landlord's wife, and was as beautiful as the rising moon. Bakbook fell in love with her at first sight. He could sew no more and passed the whole day in gazing at her. Next morning he opened his shop at an early hour and sat sewing; but each time he sewed a stitch, his eyes wandered towards the window, and with every minute that passed, his longing for her grew more passionate.

On the third day, however, the woman, perceiving his love-sick gaze, cast at him a sidelong glance and smiled seductively. She then disappeared from the window, and shortly afterwards her slave-girl came to him with a parcel containing a length of red flowered silk.

'My mistress sends you her greetings,' said the girl, 'and desires you to make her, with your own good hands, a shirt from this material.'

'I hear and obey,' replied my brother.

Bakbook set to work at once, so that the shirt was ready before the evening. Early next morning the slave-girl came to him again, and said: 'My mistress greets you and inquires if you slept well last night, for she herself, she says, could scarcely sleep a wink, thinking of you.'

Then the girl placed before him a piece of yellow satin, adding: 'From this my mistress wishes you to make her two pairs of drawers, and to have them ready by the evening.'

'I hear and obey,' replied my brother. 'Give her my most tender greetings, and say to her: "Your slave prostrates himself at your feet and waits your will and pleasure."'

He worked assiduously till the evening, when the woman looked out from her window, now smiling, now winking at him; so that Bakbook persuaded himself that he would soon enjoy her. Presently the slave-girl came to the shop and took the two pairs of drawers.

That night my brother lay on a sleepless bed, thinking of all the delights that were in store for him, and next morning the slave came again and said: 'My master wishes to speak to you and desires you to come into the house.'

Thinking that this was but a device to further the woman's intrigue with him, Bakbook gladly followed the slave-girl, and when he entered, he greeted his landlord, kissing the ground before him. The young woman's husband threw him a great roll of silk, and said: 'Make me a few shirts from this, good tailor.'

My brother went back to his shop and worked so diligently, not allowing himself a moment for food or rest, that twenty shirts were ready by the evening. At supper-time he carried them to his landlord.

'How much do I owe you?' asked the landlord.

But as Bakbook was about to say: 'Twenty dirhams', the young woman made a sign to him that he should accept no payment. And the shallow-pated Bakbook, who did not for a moment suspect that the fair woman of his dreams was in league with her husband to make an ass of him, refused payment despite his woeful penury.

Early next morning the slave again came to him and said: 'My master wishes to speak with you.'

As soon as Bakbook entered, the landlord handed

him a roll of stuff, saying: 'Make me five pairs of trousers.' He took the rascal's measurements and went back to his shop.

After three days of painful drudgery, my brother finished the trousers; and when he proudly carried them to their owner, the landlord complimented him on his needlework and loaded him with praises. But just as he put his hand into his pocket to take out his purse, the young woman again signed to Bakbook to accept no payment. So he feebly murmured a refusal and went back to his shop in exceedingly low spirits. For he was now not only afflicted with a love-sick heart and an empty stomach, but was also reduced to beggary.

However, to repay Bakbook for the services he had rendered them, the young woman and her husband decided to marry him to their slave-girl. My brother accepted without hesitation, and looked forward to becoming, in a sense, a member of the family. On the evening of the wedding they called him to their house and counselled him to spend the bridal night at the mill in the basement. Nothing, they assured my brother, was more conducive to connubial bliss than such a beginning.

After the marriage ceremony, the credulous Bakbook waited in the basement for his bride. But when she failed to come down he was obliged to sleep in that dreary place alone. At midnight he was awakened by the whip of the miller, who, at the instigation of the landlord, had tied my brother to the grinding-stone. He heard the miller's voice, saying: 'A plague on this lazy ox! The corn is waiting to be ground, and the customers are demanding their flour.'

Then the miller lashed Bakbook with his whip, crying, 'Rise up, and turn the mill!'

Yelling and screaming, my brother began to go round and round the mill-stone, and continued to do so for the rest of the night.

Early in the morning, the slave-girl to whom he had been married the night before, came down to the base-ment. Seeing him still tied to the mill-stone, she un-fastened him and said with affected concern: 'We have just heard of this unfortunate mistake. My mistress lacks words to express her grief.'

Bakbook was so overcome with exhaustion that he could make no answer.

Soon after, the clerk who had drawn up the marriage-contract appeared. He greeted my brother, saying: 'Allah give you a long and happy life, my friend!' Then, perceiving the haggard look on Bakbook's face, he added: 'If I am not mistaken, what a night of sport you must have passed, with billing and cooing and coupling from dark till day!'

'Allah confound all liars, you thousandfold scoun-drel!' retorted my brother. 'Your contract and blessings have caused me to turn a mill all night.'

When the clerk heard the story of the unhappy bride-groom, he said: 'I think I know the reason. Your star is at variance with that of your bride. I can, for a small fee, draw you up a more auspicious contract.'

But my brother refused to listen to him and told him to go and play his tricks elsewhere.

He resumed his work with renewed determination, hoping to make a little money with which to buy some-thing to eat. But while he was sitting at his needlework, the young woman appeared at the window. With tears running down her cheeks, she swore to him that she knew nothing of what had happened at the mill that night. At first Bakbook would not listen to her pleading;

but before long her sweet words won his heart again, and all his troubles were forgotten.

For many days afterwards my brother sat sewing contentedly. One day the slave came to him and said: 'My mistress greets you and wishes to inform you that her husband is to spend the night at the house of a friend. She invites you to come to her at the fall of evening.'

Now you must know that the young woman and her husband had conspired to ruin my brother. The land-lord had said to his wife: 'How shall we entice him into the house, so that I may seize him and drag him before the Governor?' And the wicked woman had answered: 'Let me play another of my little tricks on him, and he shall be paraded through the city as an example to others.'

In the evening my brother (who, alas, knew nothing of women and their cunning) was led by the slave to the landlord's house. The young woman welcomed him, saying: 'We are alone at last, thank heavens!'

'Waste no time,' urged my brother. 'First kiss me, and then ...'

But before he could finish his sentence, the husband burst into the room. He gripped my brother, crying: 'By Allah, the Governor himself shall judge this out-rage!'

Turning a deaf ear to Bakbook's pitiful entreaties, he dragged him away to the Governor, who whipped him, and mounted him upon a camel, and drove him through the streets of the city. Great crowds watched the spec-tacle, shouting: 'Thus shall adulterers be punished!'

During the procession Bakbook was thrown off the camel's back and broke his leg. Furthermore, the Gov ernor banished him from Baghdad. But I took pity on him and carried him back in secret to my house, where I have fed and clothed him ever since.

The Caliph was much amused by my story. He ordered a gift to be bestowed upon me, saying: 'You have spoken well, my silent sheikh.'

'Prince of the Faithful,' I replied, 'I will not accept this honour until I have told you the stories of my other brothers; although, indeed, I fear that you may think me a little talkative.'

And thereupon I began to relate the tale of my second brother.

The Tale of Al-Haddar
The Barber's Second Brother

My second brother, Prince of the Faithful, is called Al-Haddar, and was in his younger days as skinny and loose-limbed as a scarecrow.

One day, as he was slouching along the streets of Baghdad, an old woman stopped him, saying: 'I have an offer to make you, my good man, which you can accept or refuse as you think fit.'

'Tell me what it is,' said my brother.

'First,' continued the old woman, 'you must promise that you will talk but little and ask no questions.'

'Speak, then,' replied Al-Haddar.

'What would you say,' whispered the old woman, 'to a handsome house set about with beautiful gardens, where you may drink to your heart's content and embrace a pretty girl from night till day?'

'How is it, good mother,' said Al-Haddar, 'that you have chosen me from all others to enjoy this marvel?'

And what quality of mine has pleased you?'

'Did I not tell you,' replied the old woman, 'to ask no questions? Be silent, then, and follow me.'

My brother followed the old woman, his mouth watering at the delights which she had promised him, until they came to a magnificent palace, at the doors of which stood numerous slaves and attendants. As he entered, my brother was stopped by one of the servants, who demanded: 'What is your business here?' But his guide promptly intervened, saying: 'He is a workman whom we have hired for a certain task.'

The old woman led him up to the second storey, and then ushered him into a great pavilion hung round with rich ornaments. He had not waited long before a young woman of shining beauty came in, surrounded by her slave-girls. Al-Haddar rose and bowed to the ground before her, and she welcomed him in a most amiable fashion. When they had all sat down, the slaves placed delicate sweetmeats before their mistress and her guest, and as she ate, the young woman jested with my brother and made a great show of affection to him. Although she was laughing at him all the while, my imbecile of a brother perceived nothing and fancied, in the excess of his passion, that the young woman was enamoured of him and would soon grant him his desire.

When the wine had been laid before them, there entered the pavilion ten beautiful girls singing to the accompaniment of lutes. The young woman plied Al-Haddar with wine, and while he drank she began to stroke his cheeks, more with violence than with affection, and ended by slapping him hard on the nape of his neck. My brother rose angrily, and would have left the house had not the old woman reminded him, with a wink, of his promise. Determined to control himself, he went back in silence; but no sooner had he resumed his seat than the young woman and her servants fell upon him, slapping and cuffing him until he almost fainted. Upon this Al-Haddar made up his mind that he was not to be trifled with any longer, and resolutely made for the door. But the old woman hastened to prevent him, whispering: 'Be patient a little, and you shall win her.'

'How long, pray,' retorted Al-Haddar, 'have I to wait? Never in all the days of my life have I been so vilely treated.'

'Once she is heated with wine,' replied the old woman, 'she will be yours.'

Al-Haddar was prevailed upon to stay in the pavilion. Presently, however, the young woman ordered her slaves to perfume my brother and besprinkle his face with rose-water. When they had done so, she called one of her slave-girls and said: 'Take your master and do to him what is required. Then bring him back.'

Not knowing what lay in store for him, my brother allowed himself to be conducted into a neighbouring room. The old woman soon joined him and said: 'Be patient. Only little remains to be done and you shall enjoy her.'

'Tell me,' said Al-Haddar, his face brightening, 'what would she have the slave do with me?'

'Nothing but good,' replied the old woman. 'She will only dye your eyebrows and shave off your moustaches.'

'As for the dyeing of my eyebrows,' said Al-Haddar, 'that will come off with washing: it is the shaving of my moustaches that I cannot endure.'

'Beware of crossing her,' replied the old woman, 'for her heart is set on you.'

My brother patiently suffered the slave-girl to dye his eyebrows and remove his moustaches. But when the girl returned to her mistress to inform her that the task had been accomplished, the young woman said: 'There remains only one other thing to be done: his beard must be shaved off.' So the slave went back to him and told him of his hostess's orders.

'How can I,' said the blockhead, deeply perplexed, 'permit that which will disgrace me in the eyes of my fellow-men?'

But the old woman answered: 'She cannot love you otherwise: your face must first be as smooth as that of a beardless youth. Be a little more patient, and you shall attain your desire.'

My brother hopefully submitted to the slave-girl, who shaved off his beard and made up his face with red and white. When he was brought back to the young women, they were so amused by his grotesque appearance that they fell over on their backs and rolled laughing on the floor. The young woman complimented him on his looks and pressed him to dance before them. This he did, and while he hopped and capered about, they pelted him with citrons, lemons, and oranges, and flung at his head every cushion that came to hand. When he was about to drop down unconscious, the old woman whispered in his ears: 'Now you have nearly attained your desire: there are no more blows, and one thing only remains to be done. It is her custom when overcome with wine to let no one approach her until she has put off all her clothes. When this is done, she will order you to do the same yourself and to run after her. You must obey her in every particular and run after her from one room to another until you catch her.'

Presently the young woman began to unrobe herself,

and ordered the half-conscious Al-Haddar to put off his clothes. When they were both stark naked, she said to my brother: 'If you want anything, run after me until you catch me.'

With this she tripped out of the pavilion and rushed in and out of many rooms and galleries, Al-Haddar chasing her in a frenzy of desire. At length, she slipped into a darkened chamber, and as he was scampering after her, the floor suddenly gave way beneath him. In a twinkling he found himself in the market of the leather-merchants.

When the merchants saw Al-Haddar drop down in their midst – naked, shaven, with his eyebrows dyed, his face painted, and his manhood manifest, they booed him, and clapped their hands at him, and thrashed his bare body with their hides, until he fell down senseless. Finally they threw him on a donkey's back and took him to the Governor, who asked: 'Who can this man be?'

'He fell down upon us,' they answered, 'through a hole in the Vizier's house.'

The Governor sentenced him to a hundred lashes and banished him from the city. As soon as this news reached me, I set out to search for him, and when I found him, brought him back in secret to Baghdad and made him a daily allowance of food and drink. But for my courage and generosity, I would not have taken such pains to succour such a fool.

I now beg you, Prince of the Faithful, to listen to the story of my third brother.

The Tale of Bakbak
The Barber's Third Brother

M Y third brother, he who is blind, Prince of the Faithful, is called Bakbak.

One day, as he was begging in the streets of Baghdad, Destiny directed his steps to a certain house. He knocked at the door, hoping that he might be given a coin or something to eat. The master of the house called out from within: 'Who is there?' But my brother, who was well versed in the tricks of his profession, would not answer before the door was opened. Again he heard the master of the house call out at the top of his voice: 'Who is knocking?' and still he made no reply. Bakbak then heard the sound of approaching footsteps, and the door was opened.

'What do you want?' asked the master of the house.

'Some little thing for a poor, blind man, in the name of Allah,' replied my brother.

'Give me your hand,' said the man, 'and follow me.'

Bakbak stretched out his hand, and the man took him within and led him up from one flight of stairs to another until they reached the roof of the house: my brother thinking at every step that he was about to be given some food or money. There the man stopped and asked Bakbak a second time: 'Now, what do you want?'

'Some little thing,' repeated my brother, 'in the name of Allah.'

'Then may Allah have pity on you,' replied the man, 'and open a door for you elsewhere.'

'Could you not have given me that answer when we

were below?' cried my brother indignantly.

'Vile wretch,' retorted the master of the house, 'why did you not say you were a beggar when you first heard my voice?'

'What are you doing with me?' asked my brother helplessly.

'I have nothing to give you,' the man answered.

'Then guide me down the stairs,' said Bakbak.

But the master of the house coolly replied: 'The way lies open before you.'

Unaided, my brother groped his way back to the stairs. But when he was some twenty steps from the bottom, his foot slipped, and he rolled down, nearly breaking his skull.

As he left the house, two of his blind fellow-beggars heard his groans and went to ask him what had happened. He dolefully described to them the treatment he had received, adding: 'Now, my brothers, there is no way left for me but to go to our house and take something from our common savings; or else I shall be hungry for the rest of this ill-omened day.'

Now all this time, the man from whose house my brother had just been so amiably dimissed was following Bakbak and his blind companions, and heard all that they said to each other. He continued to walk quietly behind them until they reached their dwelling. When the three had entered, he slipped into the house without a sound. Then said my brother to his friends: 'Shut the door quickly and search the house lest any strangers should have followed us.'

When he heard my brother's words the man, who was an accomplished thief, noiselessly caught a rope that was hanging from the ceiling, and, climbing it, held fast until the blind men had inspected every corner. They then sat down beside my brother and brought out their money and began counting it. It was more than twelve thousand dirhams. When they had finished, one of them took a coin and hurried out of the house to buy something to eat, while the other two put back the silver in its hiding-place beneath the tiles.

When their companion returned, they all sat down to eat. During the course of their meal, however, my brother gradually became aware of a fourth pair of jaws chewing by his side. 'There is a stranger in our midst!' shouted Bakbak, and as he stretched out his hand and groped around him, it struck against the thief.

The three men closed upon the stranger, punching and kicking him, and crying out: 'A thief! Help, good Moslems! A thief, help!'

But as soon as the neighbours and the passers-by came to their rescue, the thief shut his eyes, pretending to be blind like the three beggars. 'Take me to the Governor, good Moslems,' he cried out passionately, 'for, by Allah, I have important information to give him.'

At once the crowd seized the four and led them to the Governor's house.

'Who are these men?' asked the Governor, when they were brought before him.

'Noble Governor,' cried the thief, 'nothing but the whip can make us confess the truth. Begin by flogging me, and then these others!'

'Throw this man down and thrash him soundly,' said the Governor.

The guards threw down the pretended blind man and fell upon him with their whips. When his buttocks had received the first few lashes, he yelled and opened one of his eyes; and after a few more he opened the other.

'Wicked impostor,' cried the Governor, 'so you are not blind after all!'

'Grant me your pardon,' replied the thief, 'and I will tell you the whole truth.'

The Governor nodded assent, and the man continued: 'For a long time we four have pretended to be blind beggars, entering the houses of honest Moslems and gaining admittance to their harems and corrupting their women. We amassed a large fortune, amounting to twelve thousand dirhams in silver. But when I demanded my share to-day, they rose against me and beat me. I beg protection of Allah and of you; and if, noble Governor, you doubt the truth of my confession, put them to the whip and they will open their eyes.'

'Scoundrels!' roared the Governor. 'Dare you deny Allah's most gracious gift and pretend to be blind?'

The first to suffer was my brother. In vain he swore, by Allah and by all that is holy, that none of them was blessed with sight. They continued to whip him until he fainted.

'Leave him till he comes to,' cried the Governor, 'and then whip him again!'

The others received a similar treatment; nor did they open their eyes in spite of the impostor's repeated exhortations. Then the Governor sent his guards to fetch the money from my brother's house. A quarter of it he gave the thief, and kept the remainder for himself. Furthermore, he banished Bakbak and his friends from the city.

When I heard of my brother's misfortunes I set out to search for him and brought him back in secret to my house, where he has lived ever since.

The Caliph laughed heartily at my story, and said to

his attendants: 'Give him a reward and show him out of the palace.'

'By Allah,' I replied, 'I will accept nothing until you have heard the stories of my other brothers.'

The Tale of Al-Kuz The Barber's Fourth Brother

MY fourth brother, one-eyed Al-Kuz, Prince of the Faithful, was at one time a butcher and sheep-breeder in Baghdad. He catered for the rich and the high-born, so that he amassed great wealth and became in time an owner of many herds of cattle and large estates.

He continued to prosper until a certain day when, as he was attending to his customers, an old man with a long white beard entered the shop and asked Al-Kuz to weigh him some mutton. My brother did so, and when he examined the money which he had received from the stranger, he was so struck by the unusual brilliance of the coins that he kept them in a separate coffer. For five months the old man bought meat regularly from my brother, and each time he paid him Al-Kuz put the bright, new coins aside.

One day, wishing to buy some sheep, my brother opened the coffer and found, to his astonishment and dismay, that it was filled only with little rounds of white paper. He set up a great clamour, beating himself about the face and calling out to the passers-by, until a huge crowd gathered round him. Whilst he was telling them his story, the old man himself came forward with the glittering coins ready in his hand as was his custom. My brother sprang upon him and, taking him by the throat, cried: 'Help, good people! Here is the scoundrel who has robbed me!'

But this did not seem to perturb the old man, who calmly whispered to my brother: 'Hold your tongue, or I will put you to public shame!'

'How will you do that, pray?' shouted Al-Kuz.

'By charging you here and now,' replied the old man, 'with selling human flesh for mutton!'

'You lie, accursed reprobate!' yelled my brother.

'None is more accursed,' rejoined the old man, 'than he who at this moment has a human corpse hung up in his shop instead of a sheep!'

'If you can prove this crime against me,' said Al-Kuz, 'my life and all my property are yours!'

Accepting the challenge, the old man turned to the by-standers and cried out: 'Good Moslems, for months this butcher has been slaughtering his fellow-men and selling us their flesh as mutton. If any one doubts this, let him enter the shop and see for himself!'

The crowd rushed in, and what should they see hanging from one of the hooks but the corpse of a man! Struck with horror, the infuriated mob gripped Al-Kuz, crying: 'Blasphemy! Sacrilege!' And those who were his oldest clients and dearest friends turned against him and beat him. In the hubbub, the sorcerer (for such was the wicked old man) struck my brother in the face, knocking out his left eye.

Then the crowd carried Al-Kuz and the supposed corpse to the chief of the city's magistrates. 'Your honour,' said the sorcerer, 'we bring before you a criminal who for months has been murdering human beings and selling their flesh as mutton. We call upon you to perform Allah's justice; and here are all the witnesses.'

My brother tried to defend himself, but the judge

would not listen to him, and sentenced him to five hundred lashes. He confiscated all his goods and banished him from the city; and, indeed, had Al-Kuz been poor, he would have put him to a cruel death.

Penniless and broken, my brother left Baghdad and journeyed many days and nights until he arrived in the chief city of a foreign land. There he set up as a cobbler, making a precarious living in a little shop.

One day, as he was walking along the street, he heard the neighing of horses and the beating of hoofs. Upon inquiry he was informed that the King was going out hunting, and Al-Kuz stopped to watch the procession pass by. Chancing to glance over his shoulder, the King caught sight of my brother's face, and with a start turned away his head, crying: 'Allah preserve us from the evil eye and from the portent of this day!' At once he turned his horse about and rode back to his palace, followed by the troops. As for my brother, he was set upon by the King's slaves and beaten, and then left for dead by the roadside.

Al-Kuz was so perplexed at this stroke of ill-fortune that he betook himself to one of the King's attendants and related to him what had happened. The courtier burst into a fit of laughter, and said: 'The King cannot bear the sight of a one-eyed man, especially if it is the left eye which is missing. Indeed, in this land death is the usual penalty for such a disfigurement.'

When Al-Kuz heard this he decided to fly the country, and set out at once for a far-off town where no one knew him. Many months afterwards, as he was taking a walk one day, he suddenly heard in the distance the neighing of horses and the beating of hoofs. He took to his heels in great panic, searching in vain for a hiding-place. At length he found himself on the threshold of a great door, and, pushing it open without a moment's thought, entered a long passage. Scarcely had he advanced one step, when two men sprang upon him, crying: 'Allah be praised that we have caught you at last! We have passed three sleepless nights in fear of your malice.'

'But, good people,' said my brother, 'what offence have I committed?'

'You are plotting to kill the master of this house and to ruin us all!' they replied. 'Was it not enough to reduce him to poverty, you and your friends? Where is the dagger with which you threatened us yesterday?'

So saying, they searched Al-Kuz and found his soling knife in his belt.

'Good people,' whimpered my brother, 'have fear of Allah and let me tell you the whole of my story!'

But they refused to listen to him. They beat him and tore his clothes to tatters. His body being thus uncovered, they saw the marks of whipping on his back. 'Black-souled reprobate,' they cried, 'these scars bear testimony to your other crimes!' Then they dragged him away to the Governor.

My brother tried to defend himself, but the Governor gave a deaf ear to his entreaties. 'Wretched criminal!' he cried indignantly. 'One need only look upon your back to see that you have practised every kind of crime!' And he ordered Al-Kuz to be given a hundred lashes.

Then the Governor's men hoisted Al-Kuz on the back of a camel, and drove him through the streets, crying: 'Thus shall house-breaking ruffians be punished!'

When I heard of my brother's misfortunes, I set out for his city, and searched for him until I found him. I then brought him back in secret to Baghdad, where he

C

has lived under my care and protection ever since.

That is the story of Al-Kuz. But do not think, Prince of the Faithful, that it is in any way more extraordinary than the tale of my fifth brother.

The Tale of Al-Ashar The Barber's Fifth Brother

MY fifth brother, he who is cropped of both his ears, Prince of the Faithful, is called Al-Ashar. In his youth he was very poor, and used to beg alms by night and spend the proceeds by day. When our father died, we each inherited a hundred pieces of silver. For many weeks Al-Ashar did not know what to do with his share, and at length he decided to be a glass-merchant. He bought some glass-ware with his hundred dirhams, and, placing the articles in a large basket before him, sat at a corner in a busy thoroughfare.

On a certain Friday, as he squatted in his accustomed place, he sank into a reverie, and thought to himself:

'I have invested the whole of my capital in this glass-ware. It cost me a hundred dirhams and I shall no doubt sell it for two hundred. With the two hundred I shall buy more glass, which I shall sell for four hundred. I shall go on buying and selling till I make a large fortune. With this I shall buy all kinds of essences and jewellery, and make a vast profit. Then I shall be able to afford a splendid house, with slaves, and horses, and gilded saddles. I will eat the choicest dishes, drink the rarest wines, and be entertained in my own house by the sweetest singers of the city.

'When I have made a hundred thousand dirhams, I shall send for the subtlest marriage-brokers and instruct them to find me a wife among the daughters of kings and viziers. I shall perhaps ask for the hand of the Grand Vizier's daughter, for I hear she is a girl of incomparable beauty. I shall offer her a marriage-portion of a thousand pieces of gold; and should her father withhold his consent I will carry her away by force. I will buy ten young eunuchs to attend upon me, and dress myself in regal robes. My saddle shall be adorned with priceless jewels, and as I ride through the city to the Vizier's house, with slaves before me and servants behind me, men will bow reverently as I pass by them, greeting and blessing me.

'When I enter the Vizier's house, he will stand up to receive me. He will give me his own place and will himself sit down at my feet. Two of my eunuchs shall carry purses with a thousand dinars in each; one I shall lay before the Vizier as his daughter's marriage-portion; the other I shall present him as a gift, in proof of my worthiness and munificence. I shall be solemn and reserved, and for every ten words he addresses to me I shall answer with two. Then I shall return to my house. And when one of my future wife's relations returns my visit, I will give him gold and a robe of honour; but if he brings me a present, I will return it to him, so that he will know how proud my spirit is.

'I will myself appoint the wedding-day, and then make preparations for the bridal festivities. On the wedding-night I will put on my most splendid robes, and, surrounded by my guests, will recline upon a mattress of gold brocade. I will turn my head neither to the right nor to the left, but will look straight in front of me with an air of authority and contemptuous unconcern. When

my bride is brought before me, decked with jewels and
radiant like the full moon, I will not even look at her.
Her women will plead with me, saying: "Our lord and
master, here stands your wife, your slave, waiting for
you to honour her with a gracious look." They will kiss
the ground before me. I will cast one glance at her and
resume my disdainful air. They will then conduct her
to the bridal chamber, and I will rise and change into a
finer robe. I shall order one of my slaves to bring me
five hundred pieces of gold, which I shall scatter among
my wife's attendants. Then I will go to my bride; and
when I am left alone with her, I will neither speak to
her nor even look at her. Presently the bride's mother
will come in, kissing my head and hand, and saying:
"My lord, look upon your slave-girl, who yearns for
your favour; speak to her and heal her broken spirit."
I will make no answer. She will throw herself down
at my feet, kissing them again and again, and saying:
"Your slave is a beautiful virgin and she has seen no
man but you. On my knees I beg you to cease humbling
her, or her heart will break!" Then the bride's mother
will rise, and, filling a cup with wine, will give it to her
daughter, who will offer it to me with all submission.
But I, leaning idly upon my elbow among the gold-
embroidered cushions, will take no notice of her. With
a trembling voice she will say: "I beg you, my lord, to
take this cup from the hand of your slave and servant."
But I will maintain my dignified silence. She will raise
the cup to my mouth, pressing me to drink from it.
Then I will wave it away with my hand, and spurn her
with my foot, thus –'

So saying, Al-Ashar kicked against the basket of glass-
ware, knocking over the contents and crashing them in
fragments to the ground.

My brother began to beat himself about the face, tearing his clothes and wailing, as the people went by to the midday prayers. Some stopped to say a kind word to him, and some passed by, taking no notice of his lamentation. Whilst he sat bitterly mourning the loss of all his worldly possessions, a woman rode by on her way to the mosque. She was very beautiful, and as she passed, surrounded by her servants, a sweet odour of the rarest musk hung about her. Moved with pity for my brother, she sent to inquire the cause of his distress. When she heard his story she called one of her servants and said: 'Give this unfortunate man the purse you are carrying.'

The servant took from his belt a heavy purse and gave it to Al-Ashar, who, on opening it, found that it contained five hundred pieces of gold. He almost died for joy, and fervently called down Allah's blessing on his benefactress.

Carrying the great purse, my brother returned to his house a rich man. He sat thinking of the happy turn of his fortune, and was on the point of spinning another vision, when he was roused by a knocking at the door. He went to open it, and found on the threshold an old woman whom he had never seen before.

'My son,' said the old woman, 'the hour of Friday prayers is almost past, and I have not yet made the necessary ablutions. I beg you to let me come into your house, so that I may prepare myself.'

Al-Ashar politely invited her to enter. He brought her a ewer and a basin, and retired to delight his eyes with his treasure.

A few minutes afterwards the old woman appeared in the room where my brother was sitting. She knelt and bowed twice in prayer and called down blessings on my brother. He thanked her, took two dinars from the purse, and offered them to her. But the old woman refused the gold with dignity, saying: 'Put this money back into your purse. If you have no need for it, return it to her who gave it to you.'

'Do you know her?' asked Al-Ashar in a transport of joy. 'I beg you to tell me how I can see her again.'

'My son,' she replied, 'I have served that lady for many years. I assure you that she has a great liking for you. But she is married to a rich, old man. Rise, my son, take with you all your money lest a thief should steal it, and follow me to the lady's house. When you are alone with her, let your words be loving and your deeds lusty. Thus shall her beauty and all her wealth be yours.'

Bursting with happiness, Al-Ashar rose, took all his gold, and followed the old woman until she stopped at a great house and knocked. The door was opened by a Greek slave-girl, and the old woman went in, followed by my brother. Al-Ashar soon found himself in a spacious hall, hung with rich tapestry and spread with rare carpets. He sat down on a cushion, holding his turban on his knees, and had not waited long before a young woman, attired in splendid silks and blessed with more loveliness than the eyes of men had ever seen, appeared before him.

Al-Ashar rose to his feet as she entered, and when she saw him she welcomed him with a seductive smile. She took him by the hand and led him to a richly carpeted room, where they sat dallying together for an hour. Then the young woman rose from his side, saying: 'Stay here till I return.'

Whilst my brother was waiting, the door was flung

wide open and there entered a tall black slave, holding an unsheathed sword in his hand.

'Vilest of men,' cried the Negro, 'who brought you to this house, and what are you doing here?'

My brother's tongue stuck in his throat and he did not know what to answer. The slave took hold of him and, stripping him of his clothes, beat him savagely with the flat of his sword until he fell down unconscious. Taking him for dead, the Negro called out in a terrible voice, and immediately a slave-girl ran in with a tray of salt. He filled my brother's wounds with salt, but Al-Ashar, who soon recovered his senses, neither moved nor uttered a sound lest he should kill him. Then the black slave gave another terrible cry, and the old woman appeared.

She gripped Al-Ashar by the feet and, dragging him into a dark cellar, threw him upon a heap of corpses.

For two days Al-Ashar remained among the dead, and would himself have surely perished had not Allah made the salt with which his wounds had been treated the means of preserving his life; for it prevented his flesh from festering and checked the flow of blood. At night-time, when his strength had returned a little, Al-Ashar crawled on all fours groping for the door. Having at length found it, he made his way, with Allah's help, out of the cellar to the vestibule, and concealed himself there. Next morning the old woman left the house in search of another victim; and before she had time to shut the door behind her, my brother slipped out without a sound, and made off as fast as his legs could carry him to his own house.

When his wounds had healed, Al-Ashar began to plan a punishment for the old woman and her accomplices.

He kept a watchful eye on her movements and acquainted himself with her daily haunts. As soon as he was restored to his normal vigour, he disguised himself as a traveller from a foreign land. He tied to his waist a large bag filled with glass fragments, which seemed as though it were bursting with coins, hid a sword under his robe, and went out to seek the old woman.

When he saw her, Al-Ashar said with an uncouth foreign accent: 'Good mother, have you a pair of scales in which I can weigh nine hundred pieces of gold? I am a stranger here and do not know anyone in this city.'

The old woman answered: 'One of my sons is a money-changer, and has all kinds of scales. I will take you to him before he leaves his house, and he will gladly weigh your gold for you.'

My brother followed her until she stopped at the door of the sinister house. The young woman herself opened for them, and her old servant whispered to her: 'I have brought you some fat meat to-day.' Then the young woman took my brother by the hand and led him to her room, where she did with him as she had done on the first occasion. Then she retired as before, and presently the black slave appeared with his naked sword.

'Rise up,' roared the Negro, 'and follow me!'

My brother rose, and as the slave turned his back, Al-Ashar drew his sword and sprang upon him, striking his head off with one blow. He then dragged him by the feet to the cellar and called out to the slave-girl, who promptly appeared with her tray of salt. Seeing Al-Ashar with a sword in his hand, she ran in terror out of the room. But he overtook her and killed her. He next called out to the old woman, and when she appeared, he cried: 'Black-souled hag, do you recognize me?'

'I do not, indeed,' replied the old woman.

'Know, then,' shouted my brother, 'I am the man to whose house you came to do your washings, and whom you betrayed so wickedly!'

The old woman implored him on her knees to pardon her, but with one stroke of his sword Al-Ashar cut her in two pieces. He then set out to look for her mistress. When he found her, the terrified young woman entreated him to spare her life. His heart was softened, and he pardoned her.

'How did you fall into the power of this black slave?' he asked.

'Three years ago,' she replied, 'before I was imprisoned in this house, I was a slave in the service of a merchant of this city. The old woman was a frequent visitor at our house. One day she invited me to accompany her to an entertainment. I accepted gladly, and, putting on my best clothes and taking with me a purse of one hundred dinars, went out with her. She led me to this house, where the Negro has kept me and made me the instrument of his crimes ever since.'

Al-Ashar ordered her to conduct him to the place where the stolen gold was hidden. He stood dumbfounded as she opened one coffer after another, all filled with glittering coins.

'You will never be able to carry all this gold alone,' she said. 'Go and bring some porters to take it out of the house.'

Al-Ashar went out at once and soon came back with ten strong men. But, on his return, he found the doors wide open and the girl and most of the money gone. He realized that the young woman had deceived him. Nevertheless, he contented himself with what she had left behind. He emptied the closets of their valuables and took everything to his house.

Al-Ashar slept in great happiness that night. But when he woke next morning, he was terrified to find twenty of the Governor's guards at his door. They seized him, saying: 'You are wanted by our master.'

The men dragged Al-Ashar before the Governor, who asked: 'Whence did you steal all this money and these goods?'

'Noble Governor,' replied Al-Ashar, 'grant me the pledge of mercy, and I will tell you the whole truth.'

The Governor threw him the white handkerchief of pardon, and my brother related to him the story of his adventures, and offered him a handsome share of the spoil. But the Governor seized everything for himself, and, fearing that the Caliph might hear of his action, decided to get rid of my brother by banishing him from the city.

Thus, Al-Ashar was forced to leave Baghdad. But he had not travelled far before he was set upon by a band of highwaymen, who, finding that they could rob him of nothing except his rags, beat him mercilessly and cut off both his ears.

When I heard of my brother's misfortunes, Prince of the Faithful, I set out to search for him and, having found him, brought him back in secret to my house, where I have provided for him ever since.

That is the story of Al-Ashar. I will now tell you the tale of my sixth and last brother, which, as you will readily agree, is even more extraordinary than the other tales.

The Tale of Shakashik
The Barber's Sixth Brother

My sixth brother, he who had both his lips cut off, Prince of the Faithful, is called Shakashik.

In his youth he was very poor. One day, as he was begging in the streets of Baghdad, he passed by a splendid mansion, at the gates of which stood an impressive array of attendants. Upon inquiry my brother was informed that the house belonged to a member of the wealthy and powerful Barmak family. Shakashik approached the door-keepers and solicited alms.

'Go in,' they said, 'and our master will give you all that you desire.'

My brother entered the lofty vestibule and proceeded to a spacious, marble-paved hall, hung with tapestry and overlooking a beautiful garden. He stood bewildered for a moment, not knowing where to turn his steps and then advanced to the far end of the hall. There, among the cushions, reclined a handsome old man with a long beard, whom my brother recognized at once as the master of the house.

'What can I do for you, my friend?' asked the old man, as he rose to welcome my brother.

When Shakashik replied that he was a hungry beggar, the old man expressed the deepest compassion and rent his fine robes, crying: 'Is it possible that there should be a man as hungry as yourself in a city where I am living? It is, indeed, a disgrace that I cannot endure!' Then he comforted my brother, adding: 'I insist that you stay with me and partake of my dinner.'

With this the master of the house clapped his hands and called out to one of the slaves: 'Bring in the basin and ewer.' Then he said to my brother: 'Come forward, my friend, and wash your hands.'

Shakashik rose to do so, but saw neither ewer nor basin. He was bewildered to see his host make gestures as though he were pouring water on his hands from an invisible vessel and then drying them with an invisible towel. When he finished, the host called out to his attendants: 'Bring in the table!'

Numerous servants hurried in and out of the hall, as though they were preparing for a meal. My brother could still see nothing. Yet his host invited him to sit at the imaginary table, saying: 'Honour me by eating of this meat.'

The old man moved his hands about as though he were touching invisible dishes, and also moved his jaws and lips as though he were chewing. Then said he to Shakashik: 'Eat your fill, my friend, for you must be famished.'

My brother began to move his jaws, to chew and swallow, as though he were eating, while the old man still coaxed him, saying: 'Eat, my friend, and note the excellence of this bread and its whiteness.'

'This man,' thought Shakashik, 'must be fond of practical jokes.' So he said: 'It is, sir, the whitest bread I have ever seen, and I have never tasted the like in all my life.'

'This bread,' said the host, 'was baked by a slave-girl whom I bought for five hundred dinars.' Then he called out to one of his slaves: 'Bring in the meat-pudding, and let there be plenty of fat in it!'

Turning to my brother, the old man continued: 'By Allah, my friend, have you ever tasted anything better than this meat-pudding? Now, on my life, you must eat and not be abashed!'

Presently he cried out again: 'Serve up the stewed grouse!' And again he said to Shakashik: 'Eat your fill, my friend, for you must be very hungry.'

My brother moved his jaws, and chewed, and swallowed, while the old man called for one imaginary dish after another, and pressed his guest to eat. Then the host cried out: 'Serve up the chickens stuffed with pistachio-nuts,' and turned to Shakashik, saying: 'Eat, for you have never tasted anything like these chickens!'

'Sir,' replied my brother, 'they are indeed incomparably delicious.'

Thereupon the host moved his fingers as though to pick up a morsel from an imaginary dish, and popped the invisible delicacy into my brother's mouth.

The old man continued to enlarge upon the excellences of the various dishes, while my brother became so ravenously hungry that he would have willingly died for a crust of barley-bread.

'Have you ever tasted anything more delicious,' went on the old man, 'than the spices in these dishes?'

'Never, indeed,' replied Shakashik.

'Eat heartily, then,' said his host, 'and do not be ashamed!'

'I thank you, sir,' answered Shakashik, 'but I have already eaten my fill.'

'Bring in the dessert!' cried the master of the house, and then said to my brother: 'Taste this excellent pastry; eat of these fritters: take this one before the syrup drips out of it!'

Shakashik helped himself to the imperceptible dainty, and, clicking his tongue with delight, remarked upon the abundance of musk in it.

'Yes,' agreed the old man, 'I always insist on a dinar-weight of musk in each fritter, and half that quantity of ambergris.'

My brother continued to move his jaws and lips and to roll his tongue between his cheeks, as though he were enjoying the sumptuous feast.

'Eat of these roasted almonds, and walnuts, and raisins,' said the old man.

'I can eat no more,' replied my brother.

'By Allah,' repeated the host, 'you must eat, and not remain hungry!'

'Sir,' protested Shakashik, 'how can one remain hungry after eating all these dishes?'

My suffering brother considered the manner in which his host was making game of him, and thought: 'By Allah, I will do something that will make him repent of his pranks!'

Presently, however, the old man clapped his hands again and cried: 'Bring in the wine!'

Numerous slaves ran in, moving their hands about as though they were setting wine and cups before their master and his guest. The old man pretended to pour wine into the cups, and to hand one to my brother. 'Take this,' he said, 'and tell me how you like it.'

'Sir,' said Shakashik, 'your generosity overwhelms me!' He lifted the invisible cup to his lips, and made as if to drain it at one gulp.

'Health and joy to you!' exclaimed the old man, as he pretended to pour himself some wine and drink it off. He handed another cup to his guest, and they both continued to act in this fashion until Shakashik, feigning himself drunk, began to roll his head from side to side. Then, taking his bounteous host unawares, he suddenly raised his arm so high that the white of his armpit could be seen, and dealt him a blow on the neck which made the hall echo with the sound. And this he followed by a second blow.

The old man rose in anger and cried: 'What are you doing, vile creature?'

'Sir,' replied my brother, 'you have received your humble slave into your house and loaded him with your generosity; you have fed him with the choicest food and quenched his thirst with the most potent wines. Alas, he became drunk, and forgot his manners! But you are so noble, sir, that you will surely pardon his offence.'

When he heard these words, the old man burst out laughing, and said: 'For a long time I have jested with all types of men, but no one has ever had the patience or the wit to enter into my humours as you have done. Now, therefore, I pardon you, and ask you in truth to eat and drink with me, and to be my companion as long as I live.'

Then the old man ordered his attendants to serve all the dishes which they had consumed in fancy, and when he and my brother had eaten their fill, they repaired to the drinking-chamber, where beautiful young women sang and made music. The old Barmaki gave Shakashik a robe of honour and made him his constant companion.

The two lived in amity for a period of twenty years, until the old man died and the Caliph seized all his property. My brother was forced to fly for his life. He left Baghdad and rode out into the desert, but before long a band of roving bedouin took him prisoner and carried him away to their encampment. Every day their chieftain put him to the torture, and threatened him, saying: 'Pay us your ransom or I will kill you!' Then

my brother would weep and swear to him that he was
no more than a penniless outcast.

Now the chieftain had a beautiful wife. Whenever
her husband was away she would come to my brother
and tempt him with the charms of her body. At first
Shakashik would not yield to her advances, but the art-
ful woman succeeded one day in seducing him. Whilst
they were together the chieftain entered the tent and
found his wife sitting upon my brother's knee.

'Vile wretch,' cried the furious Arab, 'you have cor-
rupted my wife!'

He drew his knife (a blade that might have felled a
camel with one stroke) and, seizing my brother, cut off
his organ and his lips. Then he carried him upon a
camel to a barren hill-side and left him there to perish.

However, Shakashik was rescued by some travellers,
who recognized him and gave him food and drink.
When news of his plight reached me, I journeyed to
him and brought him back to Baghdad. I nursed him
in my own house, and have provided for him ever since.

When he had heard the tale of my sixth brother (continued the barber to the guests), the Caliph Al-Muntasir
Billah burst out laughing and said: 'I can well see, my
silent friend, that you are a man of few words, who
knows neither curiosity nor indiscretion. Yet I must ask
you to leave this city at once and go to live elsewhere.'

Thus, for no conceivable reason, the Caliph banished
me from Baghdad.

I journeyed through far countries and visited many
foreign lands until I heard of Al-Muntasir's death and
the succession of another Caliph. I then returned to
Baghdad, and found that all my brothers had died also.
It was soon after my return that I met this young man,

whom I saved from certain death, and who has so un-
justly accused me of being talkative and officious.

When the barber ended, your majesty (continued the
tailor), we were all convinced that the lame young man
had been the victim of an exceptionally garrulous and
meddlesome barber. We therefore decided to punish
him; so we seized him and locked him in an empty
room. Then we sat in peace, eating and drinking and
making merry until the hour of afternoon prayers.

When I returned home, my wife received me with
angry looks. 'A fine husband you are,' she burst out,
'to enjoy yourself all day while your wife sits moping
alone at home. If you do not take me out at once and
give me a pleasant time, I shall divorce you!'

We went out together and passed the rest of the day
in search of amusement. When we were returning home
in the evening we met this hunchback, whose untimely
death has caused all this company to assemble here.

The King of Basrah was much amused by the tailor's
story, and said: 'The young man's adventure with the
barber certainly surpasses in wonder the story of the
hunchback.' And turning to the Chamberlain and the
tailor, he added: 'Go, seek the barber and bring him
before me. We will then bury the hunchback, for he
has been dead since yesterday.'

The two men hurried to the house where the barber
was still imprisoned. They set him free and brought him
before the King, who found that he was an old man
past his ninetieth year, with dark complexion, long
white beard, and grey, bushy eyebrows; his nose was
long, his ears shrivelled, and his manner lofty. Having
well looked him over, the King burst into a fit of

laughter, and said: 'Silent One, we wish to hear some of your stories.'

'First, your majesty,' replied the barber, 'I would myself know the occasion of this gathering and the reason why the hunchback's body lies before you.'

The King said to the company: 'Tell the barber the story of the hunchback's death, and all that befell him at the hands of the tailor, the doctor, the steward, and the broker.'

When he had heard all, the barber exclaimed: 'By Allah, this is exceedingly strange! Lift the veil from the hunchback's body, and let me examine it.'

They did so; and the barber sat down, placing the hunchback's head upon his knees. After he had scrutinized the face for a while, he burst out laughing and exclaimed: 'Death is one of Allah's mysteries: but the death of this hunchback is a wonder that ought to be recorded for all time!'

The King and all the company were astonished at the barber's words.

'Explain your meaning,' said the King.

'Your majesty,' replied the old man, 'the hunchback s alive!'

So saying, the barber took from his belt a vial containing ointment, with which he rubbed the hunchback's neck. Then, producing a pair of iron forceps from his pocket, he put it down the hunchback's throat and pulled out the piece of fish and the bone. With a violent sneeze the hunchback sprang to his feet. He passed his hands over his face, and said: 'There is no god but Allah, and Mohammed is His Prophet!'

The King and all the company marvelled greatly. 'By Allah,' exclaimed the King, 'I have never in all my life heard of an incident more strange than this!' Then, turning to the captains of his troops, he added: 'Have any of you, good Moslems, ever seen a dead man come to life in this fashion? Had not Allah sent him this barber, our hunchback would have now been counted among the dead.'

And all those present said: 'By Allah, it is a rare marvel!'

The King ordered that the incident be recorded on parchment and that the scroll be kept in the royal library. He bestowed robes of honour upon the Jew, the Christian, the steward, the tailor, the hunchback, and the barber. He appointed the tailor to his court, and endowed him with a large annuity, and reconciled him with the hunchback, who again became the King's drinking companion. The barber also he appointed to his court, and conferred upon him many honours, and made him a favourite companion. And they all lived happily until they were visited by the Destroyer of all earthly pleasures, the Annihilator of men.

THE DONKEY

IT is related that a pair of tricksters once saw a simpleton leading a donkey by its halter along a deserted road. 'I will steal that beast,' said one of them to his companion, 'and make an ass of its master. Follow me and you shall see.'

He went up behind the simpleton without a sound, and, deftly loosing the halter from the donkey, placed it round his own neck. He then jogged along as though nothing had happened.

When his friend had safely made off with the beast, the thief abruptly halted and would not yield to the repeated jerks of the rope. Looking over his shoulder, the simpleton was utterly confounded to see his donkey transformed into a human being.

'Who in heaven's name are you?' he cried.

'Sir,' replied the thief, 'I am your donkey; but my story is marvellously strange. It all happened one day when I returned home very drunk, as was my custom. My pious old mother received me with an indignant rebuke and pleaded with me against my evil ways. But I took up my staff and beat her. Whereupon she invoked Allah's vengeance and I was instantly transformed into the donkey which has faithfully served you all these years. To-day the old woman must have taken pity on me and prayed to Allah to change me back into human shape.'

'There is no strength nor help save in Allah!' cried the simpleton. 'I beg you to pardon the treatment you have received at my hands and all the hardships you have endured in my service.'

He set the robber free, and returned home in a pitiful state of bewilderment and dejection.

'What has happened to you, and where is your donkey?' asked his wife.

When he had related to her the strange story, the woman began to wring her hands, crying: 'The wrath of Allah will be upon us now for having used a human being so brutally.' And she fell down penitently on her knees, reciting verses from the Koran.

For several days afterwards the simpleton stayed idle at home. At length his wife counselled him to go and buy another donkey in order that he might resume his work. So he went off to the market-place, and, as he was inspecting the animals put up for sale, he was astounded to see his own donkey amongst them. Having identified the beast beyond all doubt, the simpleton whispered in its ear:

'The Devil take you for an incorrigible wretch! Have you been drinking and beating your mother again? By Allah, I will not buy you a second time!'

THE FISHERMAN AND
THE JINNEE

ONCE upon a time there was a poor fisherman who had a wife and three children to support.

He used to cast his net four times a day. It chanced that one day he went down to the sea at noon and, reaching the shore, set down his basket, rolled up his shirt-sleeves, and cast his net far out into the water. After he had waited for it to sink, he pulled on the cords with all his might; but the net was so heavy that he could not draw it in. So he tied the rope ends to a wooden stake on the beach and, putting off his clothes, dived into the water and set to work to bring it up. When he had carried it ashore, however, he found in it a dead donkey.

'By Allah, this is a strange catch!' cried the fisherman, disgusted at the sight. After he had freed the net and wrung it out, he waded into the water and cast it again, invoking Allah's help. But when he tried to draw it in he found it even heavier than before. Thinking that he had caught some enormous fish, he fastened the ropes to the stake and, diving in again, brought up the net. This time he found a large earthen vessel filled with mud and sand.

Angrily the fisherman threw away the vessel, cleaned his net, and cast it for the third time. He waited patiently, and when he felt the net grow heavy he hauled it in, only to find it filled with bones and broken glass. In despair, he lifted his eyes to heaven and cried: 'Allah knows that I cast my net only four times a day. I have already cast it for the third time and caught no fish at all. Surely He will not fail me again!'

With this the fisherman hurled his net far out into the sea, and waited for it to sink to the bottom. When at length he brought it to land he found in it a bottle made of yellow copper. The mouth was stopped with lead and bore the seal of our master Solomon son of David. The fisherman rejoiced, and said: 'I will sell this in the market of the coppersmiths. It must be worth ten pieces of gold.' He shook the bottle and, finding it heavy, thought to himself: 'I will first break the seal and find out what is inside.'

The fisherman removed the lead with his knife and again shook the bottle; but scarcely had he done so, when there burst from it a great column of smoke which spread along the shore and rose so high that it almost touched the heavens. Taking shape, the smoke resolved itself into a jinnee of such prodigious stature that his head reached the clouds, while his feet were planted on the sand. His head was a huge dome and his mouth as wide as a cavern, with teeth ragged like broken rocks. His legs towered like the masts of a ship, his nostrils were two inverted bowls, and his eyes, blazing like torches, made his aspect fierce and menacing.

The sight of this jinnee struck terror to the fisherman's heart; his limbs quivered, his teeth chattered together, and he stood rooted to the ground with parched tongue and staring eyes.

'There is no god but Allah and Solomon is His Prophet!' cried the jinnee. Then, addressing himself to the fisherman, he said: 'I pray you, mighty Prophet, do not kill me! I swear never again to defy your will or violate your laws!'

'Blasphemous giant,' cried the fisherman, 'do you presume to call Solomon the Prophet of Allah? Solomon has been dead these eighteen hundred years, and we are now approaching the end of Time. But what is your history, pray, and how came you to be imprisoned in this bottle?'

On hearing these words the jinnee replied sarcastically: 'Well, then; there is no god but Allah! Fisherman, I bring you good news.'

'What news?' asked the old man.

'News of your death, horrible and prompt!' replied the jinnee.

'Then may heaven's wrath be upon you, ungrateful wretch!' cried the fisherman. 'Why do you wish my death, and what have I done to deserve it? Have I not brought you up from the depths of the sea and released you from your imprisonment?'

But the jinnee answered: 'Choose the manner of your death and the way that I shall kill you. Come, waste no time!'

'But what crime have I committed?' cried the fisherman.

'Listen to my story, and you shall know,' replied the jinnee.

'Be brief, then, I pray you,' said the fisherman, 'for you have wrung my soul with terror.'

'Know,' began the giant, 'that I am one of the rebel jinn who, together with Sakhr the Jinnee, mutinied against Solomon son of David. Solomon sent against me his Vizier, Asaf ben Berakhya, who vanquished me despite my supernatural power and led me captive before his master. Invoking the name of Allah, Solomon adjured me to embrace his faith and pledge him absolute obedience. I refused, and he imprisoned me in this bottle, upon which he set a seal of lead bearing the Name of the Most High. Then he sent for several of his faithful jinn, who carried me away and cast me into the middle of the sea. In the ocean depths I vowed: "I will bestow eternal riches on him who sets me free!" But a hundred years passed away and no one freed me. In the second hundred years of my imprisonment I said: "For him who frees me I will open up the buried treasures of the earth!" And yet no one freed me. Whereupon I flew into a rage and swore: "I will kill the man who sets me free, allowing him only to choose the manner of his death!" Now it was you who set me free; therefore prepare to die and choose the way that I shall kill you.'

'O wretched luck, that it should have fallen to my lot to free you!' exclaimed the fisherman. 'Spare me, mighty jinnee, and Allah will spare you; kill me, and so shall Allah destroy you!'

'You have freed me,' repeated the jinnee. 'Therefore you must die.'

'Chief of the jinn,' cried the fisherman, 'will you thus requite good with evil?'

'Enough of this talk!' roared the jinnee. 'Kill you I must.'

At this point the fisherman thought to himself: 'Though I am but a man and he is a jinnee, my cunning may yet overreach his malice.' Then, turning to his adversary, he said: 'Before you kill me, I beg you in the Name of the Most High engraved on Solomon's seal to answer me one question truthfully.'

The jinnee trembled at the mention of the Name, and, when he had promised to answer truthfully, the fisherman asked: 'How could this bottle, which is scarcely large enough to hold your hand or foot, ever contain your entire body?'

'Do you dare doubt that?' roared the jinnee indignantly.

'I will never believe it,' replied the fisherman, 'until I see you enter this bottle with my own eyes!'

Upon this the jinnee trembled from head to foot and dissolved into a column of smoke, which gradually wound itself into the bottle and disappeared inside. At once the fisherman snatched up the leaden stopper and thrust it into the mouth of the bottle. Then he called out to the jinnee: 'Choose the manner of your death and the way that I shall kill you! By Allah, I will throw you back into the sea, and keep watch on this shore to warn all men of your treachery!'

When he heard the fisherman's words, the jinnee struggled desperately to escape from the bottle, but was prevented by the magic seal. He now altered his tone and, assuming a submissive air, assured the fisherman that he had been jesting with him and implored him to let him out. But the fisherman paid no heed to the jinnee's entreaties, and resolutely carried the bottle down to the sea.

'What are you doing with me?' whimpered the jinnee helplessly.

'I am going to throw you back into the sea!' replied the fisherman. 'You have lain in the depths eighteen hundred years, and there you shall remain till the Last Judgement! Did I not beg you to spare me so that Allah might spare you? But you took no pity on me, and He has now delivered you into my hands.'

'Let me out,' cried the jinnee in despair, 'and I will give you fabulous riches!'

'Perfidious jinnee,' retorted the fisherman, 'you justly deserve the fate of the King in the tale of "Yunan and the Doctor".'

'What tale is that?' asked the jinnee.

The Tale of King Yunan and Duban the Doctor

IT is related (began the fisherman) that once upon a time there reigned in the land of Persia a rich and mighty king called Yunan. He commanded great armies and had a numerous retinue of followers and courtiers. But he was afflicted with a leprosy which baffled his physicians and defied all cures.

One day a venerable old doctor named Duban came to the King's capital. He had studied books written in Greek, Persian, Latin, Arabic, and Syriac, and was deeply versed in the wisdom of the ancients. He was master of many sciences, knew the properties of plants and herbs, and was above all skilled in astrology and medicine. When this physician heard of the leprosy with which Allah had plagued the King and of his doctors' vain endeavours to cure him, he put on his finest robes and betook himself to the royal palace. After he had kissed the ground before the King and called down blessings upon him, he told him who he was and said: 'Great King, I have heard about the illness with which you are afflicted and have come to heal you. Yet will I give you no potion to drink, nor any ointment to rub upon your body.'

The King was astonished at the doctor's words, and asked: 'How will you do that? By Allah, if you cure me

I will heap riches upon you, and your children's children after you. Anything you wish for shall be yours and you shall be my companion and my friend.'

Then the King gave him a robe of honour and other presents, and asked: 'Is it really true that you can heal me without draught or ointment? When is it to be? What day, what hour?'

'To-morrow, if the King wishes,' he replied.

The doctor took leave of the King, and hastening to the centre of the town rented for himself a house, to which he carried his books, his drugs, and his other medicaments. Then he distilled balsams and elixirs, and these he poured into a hollow polo-stick.

Next morning he went to the royal palace and, kissing the ground before the King, requested him to ride to the field and play a game of polo with his friends. The King rode out with his viziers and his chamberlains, and when he had entered the playing-field the doctor handed him the hollow club and said: 'Take this and grasp it firmly. Strike the ball with all your might until the palm of your hand and the rest of your body begin to perspire. The cure will penetrate your palm and course through the veins and arteries of your body. When it has done its work, return to the palace, wash yourself, and go to sleep. Thus shall you be cured; and peace be with you.'

The King took hold of the club and, gripping it firmly, struck the ball and galloped after it with the other players. Harder and harder he struck the ball as he dashed up and down the field, until his palm and all his body perspired. When the doctor saw that the cure had begun its work, he ordered the King to return to the palace. The slaves hastened to make ready the royal bath and hurried to prepare the linens and the towels.

The King bathed, put on his night-clothes, and went to sleep.

Next morning the physician went to the palace. When he was admitted to the King's presence he kissed the ground before him and wished him peace. The King hastily rose to receive him; he threw his arms round his neck and seated him by his side.

For when the King left the bath the previous evening, he looked upon his body and rejoiced to find no trace of the leprosy: his skin had become as pure as virgin silver.

The King regaled the physician sumptuously all day. He bestowed on him robes of honour and other gifts, and when evening came, gave him two thousand pieces of gold and mounted him on his own favourite horse. And so enraptured was the King by the consummate skill of his doctor that he kept repeating to himself: 'This wise physician has cured me without draught or ointment. By Allah, I will load him with honours and he shall henceforth be my companion and trusted friend.' And that night the King lay down to sleep in perfect bliss, knowing that he was clean in body and rid at last of his disease.

Next morning, as soon as the King sat down upon his throne, with the officers of his court standing before him and his lieutenants and viziers seated on his right and left, he called for the physician, who went up to him and kissed the ground before him. The King rose and seated the doctor by his side. He feasted him all day, gave him a thousand pieces of gold and more robes of honour, and conversed with him till nightfall.

Now among the King's viziers there was a man of repellent aspect, an envious, black-souled villain, full of spite and cunning. When this Vizier saw that the King had made the physician his friend and lavished on him high dignities and favours, he became jealous and began to plot the doctor's downfall. Does not the proverb say: 'All men envy, the strong openly, the weak in secret?'

So, on the following day, when the King entered the council-chamber and was about to call for the physician, the Vizier kissed the ground before him and said: 'My bounteous master, whose munificence extends to all men, my duty prompts me to forewarn you against an evil which threatens your life; nor would I be anything but a base-born wretch were I to conceal it from you.'

Perturbed at these ominous words, the King ordered him to explain his meaning.

'Your majesty,' resumed the Vizier, 'there is an old proverb which says: "He who does not weigh the consequences of his acts shall never prosper." Now I have seen the King bestow favours and shower honours upon his enemy, on an assassin who cunningly seeks to destroy him. I fear for the King's safety.'

'Who is this man whom you suppose to be my enemy?' asked the King, turning pale.

'If you are asleep, your majesty,' replied the Vizier, 'I beg you to awake. I speak of Duban, the doctor.'

'He is my friend,' replied the King angrily, 'dearer to me than all my courtiers; for he has cured me of my leprosy, an evil which my physicians had failed to remove. Surely there is no other physician like him in the whole world, from East to West. How can you say these monstrous things of him? From this day I will appoint him my personal physician, and give him every month a thousand pieces of gold. Were I to bestow on him the half of my kingdom, it would be but a small reward for his service. Your counsel, my Vizier, is the prompting of jealousy and envy. Would you have me

kill my benefactor and repent of my rashness, as King
Sindbad repented after he had killed his falcon?'

The Tale of King Sindbad
and the Falcon

ONCE upon a time (went on King Yunan) there was
a Persian King who was a great lover of riding and
hunting. He had a falcon which he himself had trained
with loving care and which never left his side for a
moment; for even at night-time he carried it perched
upon his fist, and when he went hunting took it with
him. Hanging from the bird's neck was a little bowl of
gold from which it drank. One day the King ordered
his men to make ready for a hunting expedition, and,
taking with him his falcon, rode out with his courtiers.
At length they came to a valley where they laid the
hunting nets. Presently a gazelle fell into the snare, and
the King said: 'I will kill the man who lets her escape!'

They drew the nets closer and closer round the beast.
On seeing the King the gazelle stood on her haunches
and raised her forelegs to her head as if she wished to
salute him. But as he bent forward to lay hold of her,
she leapt over his head and fled across the field. Looking round, the King saw his courtiers winking at one
another.

'Why are they winking?' he asked his Vizier.

'Perhaps because you let the beast escape,' ventured
the other, smiling.

'On my life,' cried the King, 'I will chase this gazelle
and bring her back!'

At once he galloped off in pursuit of the fleeing

animal, and when he had caught up with her, his falcon swooped upon the gazelle, blinding her with his beak, and the King struck her down with a blow of his sword. Then dismounting he flayed the animal and hung the carcass on his saddle-bow.

It was a hot day and the King, who by this time had become faint with thirst, went to search for water. Presently, however, he saw a huge tree, down the trunk of which water was trickling in great drops. He took the little bowl from the falcon's neck and, filling it with this water, placed it before the bird. But the falcon knocked the bowl with its beak and toppled it over. The King once again filled the bowl and placed it before the falcon, but the bird knocked it over a second time. Upon this the King became very angry, and, filling the bowl a third time, set it down before his horse. But the falcon sprang forward and knocked it over with its wings.

'Allah curse you for a bird of ill omen!' cried the King. 'You have prevented yourself from drinking and the horse also.'

So saying, he struck the falcon with his sword and cut off both its wings. But the bird lifted its head as if to say: 'Look into the tree!' The King raised his eyes and saw in the tree an enormous serpent spitting its venom down the trunk.

The King was deeply grieved at what he had done, and, mounting his horse, hurried back to the palace. He threw his kill to the cook, and no sooner had he sat down, with the falcon still perched on his fist, than the bird gave a convulsive gasp and dropped down dead.

The King was stricken with sorrow and remorse for having so rashly killed the bird which had saved his life.

When the Vizier heard the tale of King Yunan, he said: 'I assure your majesty that my counsel is prompted by no other motive than my devotion to you and my concern for your safety. I beg leave to warn you that, if you put your trust in this physician, it is certain that he will destroy you. Has he not cured you by a device held in the hand? And might he not cause your death by another such device?'

'You have spoken wisely, my faithful Vizier,' replied the King. 'Indeed, it is quite probable that this physician has come to my court as a spy to destroy me. And since he cured my illness by a thing held in the hand, he might as cunningly poison me with the scent of a perfume. What should I do, my Vizier?'

'Send for him at once,' replied the other, 'and when he comes, strike off his head. Only thus shall you be secure from his perfidy.'

Thereupon the King sent for the doctor, who hastened to the palace with a joyful heart, not knowing what lay in store for him.

'Do you know why I have sent for you?' asked the King.

'Allah alone knows the unspoken thoughts of men,' replied the physician.

'I have brought you here to kill you,' said the King.

The physician was thunderstruck at these words, and cried: 'But why should you wish to kill me? What crime have I committed?'

'It has come to my knowledge,' replied the King, 'that you are a spy sent here to cause my death. But you shall be the first to die.'

Then he called out to the executioner, saying: 'Strike off the head of this traitor!'

D

'Spare me, and Allah will spare you!' cried the unfortunate doctor. 'Kill me, and so shall Allah kill you!'

But the King gave no heed to his entreaties. 'Never will I have peace again,' he cried, 'until I see you dead. For if you cured me by a thing held in the hand, you will doubtless kill me by the scent of a perfume, or by some other foul device.'

'Is it thus that you repay me?' asked the doctor. 'Will you thus requite good with evil?'

But the King said: 'You must die; nothing can now save you.'

When he saw that the King was determined to put him to death, the physician wept, and bitterly repented the service he had done him. Then the executioner came forward, blindfolded the doctor, and, drawing his sword, held it in readiness for the King's signal. But the doctor continued to wail, crying: 'Spare me, and Allah will spare you! Kill me, and so shall Allah kill you!'

Moved by the old man's lamentations, one of the courtiers interceded for him with the King, saying: 'Spare the life of this man, I pray you. He has committed no crime against you, but rather has he cured you of an illness which your physicians have failed to remedy.'

'If I spare this doctor,' replied the King, 'he will use his devilish art to kill me. Therefore he must die.'

Again the doctor cried: 'Spare me, and Allah will spare you! Kill me, and so shall Allah kill you!' But when at last he saw that the King was fixed in his resolve, he said: 'Your majesty, if you needs must kill me, I beg you to grant me a day's delay, so that I may go to my house and wind up my affairs. I wish to say farewell to my family and my neighbours, and instruct them to arrange for my burial. I must also give away my books of medicine, of which there is one, a work of unparalleled virtue, which I would offer to you as a parting gift, that you may preserve it among the treasures of your kingdom.'

'What may this book be?' asked the King.

'It holds secrets and devices without number, the least of them being this: that if, after you have struck off my head, you turn over three leaves of this book and read the first three lines upon the left-hand page, my severed head will speak and answer any questions you may ask it.'

The King was astonished to hear this, and at once ordered his guards to escort the physician to his house. That day the doctor put his affairs in order, and next morning returned to the King's palace. There had already assembled the viziers, the chamberlains, the nabobs, and all the chief officers of the realm, so that with their coloured robes the court seemed like a garden full of flowers.

The doctor bowed low before the King; in one hand he held an ancient book, and in the other a little bowl filled with a strange powder. Then he sat down and said: 'Bring me a platter!' A platter was instantly brought in, and the doctor sprinkled the powder on it, smoothing it over with his fingers. After that he handed the book to the King and said: 'Take this book and set it down before you. When my head has been cut off, place it upon the powder to staunch the bleeding. Then open the book.'

The King ordered the executioner to behead the physician. He did so. Then the King opened the book, and, finding the pages stuck together, put his finger to his mouth and turned over the first leaf. After much difficulty he turned over the second and the third, moistening his finger with his spittle at every page, and tried to read. But he could find no writing there.

'There is nothing written in this book,' cried the King.

'Go on turning,' replied the severed head.

The King had not turned six pages when the venom (for the leaves of the book were poisoned) began to work in his body. He fell backward in an agony of pain, crying: 'Poisoned! Poisoned!' and in a few moments breathed his last.

'Now, treacherous jinnee,' continued the fisherman, 'had the King spared the physician, he in turn would have been spared by Allah. But he refused, and Allah brought about the King's destruction. And as for you, if you had been willing to spare me, Allah would have been merciful to you, and I would have spared your life. But you sought to kill me; therefore I will throw you back into the sea and leave you to perish in this bottle!'

'Let me out! Let me out, in the name of Allah!' cried the jinnee. 'Do not be angry with me, I pray you. If I have done you evil, repay me with good and, as the saying goes, punish me with kindness. Do not do as Umamah did to Atikah!'

'What is their story?' asked the fisherman.

'This bottle is no place to tell stories in!' cried the jinnee, writhing with impatience. 'Let me out, and I will tell you all that passed between them.'

'Never!' replied the fisherman. 'I will throw you into the sea, and you shall remain imprisoned in your bottle till the end of Time!'

'Let me out! Let me out!' cried the jinnee in despair.

I swear that I will never harm you, and promise to render you a service that will enrich you!'

At length the fisherman accepted the jinnee's pledge, and after he had made him swear by the Most High Name, opened the bottle with trembling hands.

At once the smoke burst out and in a twinkling took the shape of a gigantic jinnee, who with a triumphant kick sent the bottle flying into the sea. When the fisherman saw the bottle disappear beneath the water, he was so overcome with terror that he wetted his drawers. 'This is a bad sign,' he thought, but quickly putting on a defiant air he cried: 'Mighty jinnee, Allah has said in his sacred book: "Be true to your promises, or We will call you to account." You have both promised and sworn that you would not deal treacherously with me. Therefore, if you break your pledge Allah will punish you; for He is a jealous God, and, though He may be slow in retribution, He does not forget. Remember that I said to you, as the physician said to the King: "Spare me, and Allah will spare you!"'

At this the jinnee fell into convulsions of laughter, and cried: 'Follow me!'

Still dreading the jinnee's intent, the fisherman walked on behind him until they left the city. They climbed a mountain and at length descended into a vast and barren valley in the middle of which there was a lake. At the shore of this lake the jinnee halted and bade the fisherman cast his net. The fisherman saw white fish and red fish, blue fish and yellow fish, sporting in the water. Marvelling at the sight, he cast his net into the lake, and, when he drew it in, rejoiced to find in it four fish, each of a different colour.

'Take these fish to the King's palace,' said the jinnee, 'and he will give you gold. In the meantime, I must beg

you to pardon the scant courtesy I have shown you;
for I have dwelt so long at the bottom of the sea that I
have forgotten my manners. Come and fish in this lake
each day – but only once a day. And now, farewell!'

So saying, the jinnee stamped his feet against the
earth, which instantly opened and swallowed him up.

The fisherman went back to his house, marvelling at
all that had befallen him. He filled an earthen bowl with
water and, placing the fish in it, carried it upon his head
to the King's palace, as the jinnee had bidden him.
When he had gained admission to the King's presence
and offered him the fish, the King, who had never seen
their like in size or colour, marvelled greatly and ordered
his Vizier to take them to the black cook-maid. This
slave-girl had been sent to the King as a present three
days before by Caesar, and the King had as yet had
no opportunity to test her culinary skill. So the Vizier
took the four fish to the slave-girl and ordered her to
fry them, saying: 'The King has reserved you, pretty
negress, for a great occasion. Let us have proof to-day
of your accomplishments.'

The King ordered the Vizier to give the fisherman
four hundred pieces of gold. The fisherman received
the coins in the lap of his skirt, and departed in a transport of joy. He bought bread, meat, and other necessities, and hurried home to his wife and children.

Meanwhile the slave-girl cleaned the fish, put them
in the frying-pan, and left them over the fire. When
they were well cooked on one side, she turned them
over; but scarcely had she done so when the wall of
the kitchen suddenly opened and through it entered
a beautiful young girl. Her eyes were darkened with
kohl, her cheeks were smooth and fresh, and her breasts
round and shapely. She wore jewelled rings on her

fingers and gold bracelets round her wrists, and her hair was wrapped in a blue-fringed kerchief of the rarest silk.

The girl came forward and, thrusting into the frying-pan a wand she carried in her hand, said: 'Fish, fish, are you still faithful?'

At the sight of this apparition the slave fainted away, and the young girl repeated her question a second and a third time. Then the four fishes lifted their heads from the pan and replied in unison: 'Yes, yes, we are faithful!'

Upon this the young girl overturned the pan and went out the way she had come, the wall of the kitchen closing behind her. When the slave-girl came to her senses, she found the fish burnt to cinders. She set up a great screaming, and hurried to tell the Vizier all that had happened. Amazed at her story, the Vizier sent at once for the fisherman and ordered him to bring four other fish of the same kind. So the fisherman went to the lake, and casting his net, caught four more fish. These he took to the Vizier, who carried them to the slave-girl, saying: 'Rise now and fry these in my presence.'

The slave cleaned the fish and put them in the frying-pan; but scarcely had she done so when the wall opened as before and the girl reappeared, dressed in the same way and still holding the wand in her hand. She thrust the end of the wand into the pan and said: 'Fish, fish, are you still faithful?'

The four fishes raised their heads and replied: 'Yes, yes, we are faithful!' And the girl overturned the pan with her wand and vanished through the wall.

'The King must be informed of this!' cried the Vizier, and hurrying to his master, recounted to him all that he had seen.

'I must see this myself,' said the King in astonishment. He sent for the fisherman and ordered him to bring four more fish. The fisherman again hastened to the lake and promptly returned with the fish, for which he received four hundred pieces of gold. Then the King commanded his Vizier to cook the fish in his presence.

'I hear and obey,' replied the Vizier. He cleaned the fish and set the pan over the fire; but scarcely had he thrown them in when the wall opened and there appeared a great Negro, as ugly as a bull and taller than a warrior of the tribe of Aad. He held a green twig in his hand, and as soon as he set eyes on the pan, roared out: 'Fish, fish, are you still faithful?'

The four fishes lifted their heads and replied: 'Yes, yes, we are faithful!' Then the Negro overturned the pan with his twig and disappeared through the chasm in the wall, leaving the four fishes burnt to black cinders.

Confounded at the spectacle, the King cried: 'By Allah, I must find the answer to this riddle! No doubt these fishes have some strange history.'

He sent again for the fisherman, and asked him whence he had brought the fish.

'From a lake between four hills,' replied the fisherman, 'beyond the mountain which overlooks this city.'

'How many days' journey is it?' asked the King.

'It is barely half an hour's walk, your majesty,' he answered.

The King set out for the lake at the head of his troops, taking with him the bewildered fisherman, who led the way, muttering curses at the jinnee as he went. At length they came to the mountain and, climbing to the top, descended into a great desert which they had never seen before. They all marvelled at the mountains, the lake, and the fish of different colours which swam in it.

The King asked the troops if any of them had ever seen a lake in that place, and when they all replied that they had not, he said: 'By Allah, I will never again enter my city or sit upon my throne until I have solved the mystery of this lake and these coloured fishes.'

He ordered his troops to pitch their tents for the night, and, summoning his Vizier, who was a wise counsellor and a man of deep learning, said to him: 'Know that I have decided to go out this night and search for the answer to the mystery of the lake and the fishes. I wish you to stand guard at the door of my tent and tell anyone who may wish to see me that I am ill and that no one is to be admitted to my presence. Above all, you must keep my plan secret.'

At nightfall the King disguised himself, girt on his sword, and slipped out from the camp unnoticed by his guards. All that night and throughout the following day he journeyed on, stopping only to rest awhile in the midday heat. Early next morning he sighted a black building in the distance. He rejoiced and thought: 'There perhaps I shall find someone who can tell me the history of the lake and the fishes.'

Drawing nearer, he found that this was a towering palace built of black stone sheeted with iron. He went up to the great double door, one half of which was wide open, and knocked gently, once, twice, and again, but heard no answer. The fourth time he knocked hard, but still received no reply. Supposing the palace to be deserted, he summoned up his courage and entered, calling out at the top of his voice: 'People of this house, have you any food for a weary traveller?' This he repeated again and again, and getting no answer, walked through the long vestibule to the centre of the building. The hall was richly carpeted and hung with fine curtains and splendid tapestries. In the middle of the inner court a beautiful fountain resting on four lions of red gold spurted forth a jewelled spray, and about the fountain fluttered doves and pigeons under a golden net stretched above the courtyard.

The King marvelled greatly at the splendour of all that he beheld, but grieved to find no one in the palace who could explain to him the mystery. As he was loitering pensively about the court, however, he suddenly heard a low, mournful voice which seemed to issue from a heart laden with grief. The King hastened in the direction from which the sound proceeded, and presently came to a doorway concealed behind a curtain. Lifting the curtain, he saw a handsome youth, dressed in a gold-embroidered robe of Egyptian silk, lying on a bed in a great marble hall. His brow was as white as a lily, and on his cheek was a mole like a speck of black amber.

The King rejoiced to see the young man, and greeted him, saying: 'Peace be with you!' But the youth, whose eyes were sore with weeping, remained motionless on the bed and returned the King's greeting in a faint voice, saying: 'Pardon me, sir, for not rising.'

'Pray tell me the story of the lake and the fishes,' said the King, 'and the reason of your tears and your solitary sojourn in this palace.'

At these words the youth wept even more bitterly and replied: 'How can I refrain from weeping, condemned as I am to this unnatural state?'

So saying, he stretched out his hand and lifted the skirt of his robe. The King was astonished to see that the lower half of his body was all of stone, while the upper half, from his waist to the hair upon his head, remained that of a living man.

'The story of the fishes,' said the youth, 'is indeed a strange story. If it were written with a needle on the corner of an eye, it would yet serve as a lesson to those who seek wisdom.'

Upon this the youth proceeded to recount:

The Tale of the Enchanted King

KNOW that my father was the King of an illustrious city which once flourished around this palace. His name was Mahmoud and he was lord of the Black Islands, which are now four mountains. He reigned for seventy years, and on his death I succeeded to the throne of his kingdom. I took in marriage my cousin, the daughter of my uncle, who loved me so passionately that she could not bear to part from me even for a moment. I lived happily with her for five years. It chanced one day, however, that my wife left the palace to visit the baths and was absent so long that I grew anxious for her safety. But I strove to dismiss these fears from my mind, and, entering my chamber, lay down to sleep upon my couch, bidding two of my slave-girls to fan me. One sat at my head and the other at my feet; and as I lay with my eyes closed, I heard one say to the other: 'How unfortunate is the young King our master, Massoudah, and how pitiful it is that he should have married our mistress, that shameless woman, that black-souled whore!'

'Allah's curse upon all adulteresses!' replied the other. 'This harlot who revels away her nights in the beds of thieves and cut-throats is a thousandfold too vile to be the wife of our master.'

'And yet he must be blind not to see it,' said the first slave.

'But how should he suspect her?' returned the other, 'when every night she mixes in his cup a potent drug which so benumbs his senses that he sleeps like the dead till morning? How can he know what she does and where she goes? After he has gone to sleep, she dresses and goes out of the palace. She returns at daybreak, and wakes her husband by the fume of an aromatic incense.'

When I heard these words the world darkened before my eyes and I was dazed with horror. At dusk my wife returned to the palace, and we sat for an hour eating and drinking together as was our custom every evening. At length I asked for the final cup which I drank every night before retiring. When she handed it to me, I lifted the cup to my lips, but instead of drinking, poured it hastily into the folds of my garments. Then I lay down on my bed and pretended to fall asleep.

Presently I heard her say: 'Sleep, and may you never wake again! O how I abhor you! My soul sickens at the sight of you!' After this she dressed, perfumed herself, girt on my sword, and left the palace. At once I rose and followed her. She stealthily threaded her way through the streets of the town, and, reaching the city gates, mumbled a magic charm. Suddenly the heavy locks fell to the ground and the gates swung wide open. Without a sound I followed her out of the city until she came to a desolate waste-land strewn with garbage heaps, and entered a ruined hovel surmounted by a dome. I climbed up to the roof and crouched over a chink in the ceiling. I saw her draw near to a pitch-black, thick-lipped Negro. His skin was covered with sores and he lay in tattered rags upon a mat of mouldering reeds.

Then I saw my wife, the daughter of my uncle, throw

herself at his feet and kiss the ground before him. The Negro raised his head and growled: 'Execrable whore, why are you so late? All my black friends were in my house this evening, drinking, and enjoying their women. But I could not share in the merriment because you were not here.'

'Master, flower of my heart,' she answered, 'have you forgotten that I am married to that cousin of mine, whom I detest with all my soul? Had you permitted me, I would long ago have levelled this city to the ground and scattered its stones as far as the Mountain of Kaf, leaving only the cries of the owl and the raven to echo among its ruins!'

'Foulest of white whores,' replied the slave, 'do you dare trifle with me? I swear by the honour and chivalry of my tribe that, if you fail me once more, I will cast you off and never lay my body over yours again!'

When I heard these exchanges and witnessed with my own eyes what passed between them, the world black-ened before me. Then I saw my wife, the daughter of my uncle, weep and humble herself before the black slave, saying: 'Light of my eyes, treasure of my heart, I care for none but you. Do not send me away, I beg you!'

When at length her lover was pacified, she rose, un-robed herself, and stood before him quite naked. Then she said: 'My lord, have you no refreshment for your slave?'

'In the pot,' he replied, 'you will find a stew of rats' bones, and there is some barley-water in the can which you may drink.'

As soon as she had finished her meal, she washed her hands and nestled close to the Negro on his bed of filth. Seeing all this I could control my rage no longer, and, jumping down from the roof, snatched the sword from my wife's belt and struck the negro through the neck. A loud gasp convulsed his body. Thinking that the blow had killed him, I rushed out of the house and ran straight to the palace, where I tucked myself in bed and lay still. By and by my wife returned and lay down quietly beside me.

The next day I saw that my wife had cut off her tresses and dressed herself in deep mourning. 'Son of my uncle,' she said, 'do not be angry with me for wearing these garments. I have just heard that my mother has died, that my father has lost his life in the holy war, that one of my brothers has been bitten to death by a serpent, and the other killed by the fall of a house. It is but right that I should weep and mourn.'

Showing no sign of anger, I replied: 'Do as you think fit. I shall not prevent you.'

She went in mourning for a whole year, and at the end of this time she had a dome built in the grounds of the palace. She called it the House of Grief, and to this monument she had the Negro carried: for he was still alive, though crippled and bereft of speech, and no longer able to gratify his mistress's lust. He still drank deep, and every day, early and late, my wife took to him wine and stews and broths, and fell to wailing under the dome. All this I suffered patiently.

One day, however, I entered upon her unawares and found her weeping and beating her face in a most violent fashion. Unable to contain my fury, I drew my sword and was about to strike her, when she sprang to her feet and, as it seemed, suddenly realizing that it was I who had wounded her lover, muttered some mysterious charm and cried: 'Now, Powers of Magic, let half his body be turned to stone!'

At that moment I became as you now see me, neither alive nor dead. Then she bewitched my entire kingdom, turning its four islands into mountains with a lake in their midst and transforming all my subjects – Moslems, Jews, Christians, and heathens – into fishes of four different colours. Nor was she satisfied with this, for every day she comes to torture me; she gives me a hundred lashes with a leather thong and puts a shirt of hair-cloth upon my wounds, all over the living part of my body.

When he had heard the young man's story, the King said to him: 'By Allah, your tale has added a heavy sorrow to my sorrows. But where is this enchantress now?'

'With the Negro in the monument, which you can see from the door of this hall,' replied the youth.

'By Allah,' cried the King, 'I will do you a service that shall be long remembered, a deed that shall be recorded for all time!'

At midnight the King rose, undressed, and, on the striking of the secret hour of sorcery, stole away towards the monument with his sword unsheathed in his hand. Inside he saw lighted lamps and candles, and braziers in which incense was burning. Without a sound he approached the Negro and struck him a mighty blow with his sword. The slave fell dead upon the instant, and the King, after stripping him of his clothes, carried the body upon his shoulders and threw it down a deep well in the grounds of the palace. Then he returned to the monument, put on the Negro's clothes, and sat down with his sword hidden in the folds of his garment.

Shortly afterwards the young enchantress entered her husband's chamber and, uncovering his body, gave him a hundred lashes. When he cried: 'Enough, for pity's sake!' she replied: 'Do you dare speak of pity? Did you show pity to my lover?' After she had wrapped him in a shirt of hair-cloth and put on him his other garments, she went off to the monument, taking with her a cup of wine and a bowl of hot soup. As soon as she entered, she said, weeping: 'Speak to me, my master! Let me hear your voice!'

Rolling his tongue in his mouth so that he should sound like a Negro, the King replied in a low voice: 'There is no power nor majesty save in Allah!'

When she heard the voice of her supposed lover, who had for so long been silent, the young witch uttered a joyful scream and fainted away. But soon recovering herself, she cried: 'Praise to the Highest! My master is restored!'

'Wretch,' said the King in the same low voice, 'you are not worthy that I should speak to you!'

'Why, what have I done?' she asked.

'You have deprived me of all sleep,' he answered. 'Day after day you whip that husband of yours, so that his cries keep me awake all night. Had you had more thought for my comfort, I would have recovered long ago.'

'If it be your wish,' she replied, 'I will instantly restore him.'

'Do so,' said the King, 'and let us have some peace.'

'I hear and obey,' answered the witch, and, leaving the monument, hastened to the hall where the young man was lying. There she took a bowl filled with water and, bending over it, murmured some magic words. The water began to seethe and bubble as if in a heated cauldron; and sprinkling it upon her husband she said: 'Now, Powers of Magic, return him to his natural state!'

A quiver passed through the young man's body and,

he sprang to his feet, shouting for joy, and crying: 'There is no god but Allah, and Mohammed is His Prophet!'

'Go!' shrieked his wife, 'and never return, or I will kill you!'

The young man hurried from her presence, and she came back to the monument, saying: 'Rise up, my master, that I may look upon you!'

In a feeble voice the King replied: 'You have remedied but one part of the evil. The root cause still remains.'

'What may that be, my master?' she asked.

'The people of this enchanted city and the Four Islands,' he replied. 'Night after night, when the hour strikes midnight, the fish raise their heads from the lake and call down curses upon us both. I shall not be cured until they are delivered. Free them, and return to help me from my bed, for by that act I shall be restored to health.'

Still taking him for her lover, she answered joyfully: 'I hear and obey!'

She rose and, going out of the palace, hastened towards the lake. At the shore she took a few drops of water in her palm and muttered an incantation. The spell was broken. The fish wriggled in the water and, raising their heads, changed back into human shape; the lake was transformed into a prosperous city, where people were buying and selling in the market-place; and the mountains became four islands.

Then the witch ran back to the palace and, hurrying to the King, said: 'Give me your hand, my master, and let me help you to your feet.'

'Come closer,' he murmured.

When she had drawn near, the King lifted his sword and thrust it into her breast, until the blade passed through to her back. Then he struck her down and chopped her body to pieces.

The King found the young man waiting for him at the palace gates. He congratulated him on his deliverance, and the youth kissed his hand and thanked him with all his heart. Then the King asked: 'Do you wish to stay in your own city or will you return with me to my kingdom?'

'Sir,' replied the youth, 'do you know how far your kingdom is from here?'

'Why, it is but two and a half days' journey,' answered the King.

The young man laughed and said: 'If you are dreaming, your majesty, then you must wake. Know that you are at least a year's journey from your capital. If you came here in two days and a half, that was because my kingdom was enchanted. ... But I will never leave you again, even for a moment.'

The King rejoiced and cried: 'Praise be to Allah, who has brought us together! Henceforth you shall be my son, for I have not been blessed with an heir of my own.'

The King and the young man embraced one another and rejoiced exceedingly.

Returning to the palace, the young King told his courtiers of his intention to set out on a long journey. When all preparations were completed, the two Kings set forth from the Black Islands together with fifty slaves and fifty mules laden with priceless treasure. They journeyed for a whole year, and when at last they came in sight of the King's capital, the Vizier and the troops, who had abandoned all hope of his return, went out to meet their master and gave him a tumultuous welcome.

The King seated himself upon his throne in his own

palace, and, summoning the Vizier and his other courtiers, recounted to them his adventure from beginning to end. Then he bestowed gifts on all who were present and said to the Vizier: 'Send for the fisherman who brought us the coloured fishes.'

When the fisherman, who had been the means of delivering the enchanted city, was admitted to his presence, the King vested him with a robe of honour and questioned him about his manner of life and whether he had any children. The fisherman replied that he had one son and two daughters. The King took one of the daughters in marriage and the young Prince wedded the other, while the fisherman's son was appointed Keeper of the Royal Treasury. The Vizier became Sultan of the Black Islands, and departed thither with fifty slaves and robes of honour for all the courtiers of that kingdom.

The King and the young Prince lived happily ever afterwards. The fisherman became the richest man of his day, and his daughters were the wives of kings till the end of their lives.

THE YOUNG WOMAN AND
HER FIVE LOVERS

ONCE upon a time, in a certain city, there lived a rich and beautiful young woman whose husband was a great traveller. It so chanced that he once journeyed to a distant land and was absent so long that at last his wife succumbed to the temptations of the flesh and fell in love with a handsome youth who himself loved her tenderly.

One day the youth was engaged in a savage brawl and a complaint was lodged against him with the Governor of that city, who had him thrown into prison. The young woman was deeply grieved at the news of her lover's arrest. Without losing a moment she put on her finest robes and hurried to the Governor's house.

She greeted the Governor and handed him a petition which read: 'My noble master, the young man So-and-so, whom you have arrested and thrown into prison, is my brother and my sole support. He is the victim of a villainous plot, for those who testified against him were false witnesses. I hereby beseech you to consider the justice of my cause and to order his release.'

When he had read the petition the Governor lifted his eyes to the young woman and was so smitten with her seductive looks that he fell in love with her at sight. 'Wait in the harem of my house,' he said, 'whilst I write out an order for your brother's release. I will join you there presently.'

The young woman, who lacked neither cunning nor knowledge of the ways of men, at once perceived the Governor's intent and answered: 'You will be welcome, sir, at my own house, but custom forbids me to enter a stranger's dwelling.'

'And where is your house?' asked the old man, transported with joy.

'At such-and-such a place,' she replied. 'I will expect you there this evening.'

Taking leave of the enamoured Governor, the young woman went to the Cadi's house. 'Consider, sir, I pray you, the wrong that has been done me,' she began, 'and Allah will reward you.'

'Who has dared to wrong you?' asked the Cadi indignantly.

'Sir,' she answered, 'my brother, the sole pillar of my house, has on false witness been imprisoned by the Governor. I beg you to intercede on his behalf.'

But as soon as the Cadi had set eyes on the young woman his heart had begun to throb with a violent longing for her, and he said: 'I shall instantly request the Governor to set your brother free. Meanwhile, wait for me in my harem. I will join you there presently.'

'My pious master,' she replied, 'it is more fitting that I should wait for you in my own house, where there are neither slaves nor maidservants to intrude upon our privacy.'

'And where is your house?' asked the Cadi eagerly.

'In such-and-such a place,' she answered. 'I will expect you there this evening.'

The young woman then hastened to the Vizier's

house. She handed him her petition and implored him to release the youth from prison. Captivated by her beauty, the Vizier promised to do as she desired and pressed her to accompany him to his sleeping chamber. But the young woman put off his advances with winning grace, saying: 'I shall be delighted to receive you at my own house this evening.'

'And where is your house?' asked the Vizier.

'In such-and-such a place,' she replied.

Then she made her way to the royal palace and sought an audience with the King. She kissed the ground before him and begged him on her knees to order the youth's release. But as soon as his eyes fell upon the young woman, the King was seized with a passionate desire to lie with her.

'I will at once send for the Governor and order him to free your brother,' he said. 'Meanwhile, wait for me in my private chamber.'

'Your majesty,' she answered, 'a helpless woman cannot but obey the command of a mighty king. If this be indeed your majesty's wish, I shall regard it as a mark of high favour; but if the King will graciously consent to vouchsafe me a visit at my own house this evening, he will do me an even greater honour.'

'It shall be as you wish,' replied the King.

After directing him to her house, the young woman left the royal presence, and went to look for a carpenter's shop. When she had found one she said to the carpenter: 'Make me a large cupboard with four compartments, one above the other. To each compartment let there be a separate door fitted with a stout lock, and have it delivered at my house, at such-and-such a place, early this evening. What will be your charge?'

'Four dinars,' answered the carpenter. 'But if you

will consent, sweet lady, to step into the backroom of my shop, I will ask no payment at all.'

'In that case,' said the young woman, 'you will be welcome at my own house this evening. ... But I have just remembered that I require five compartments in that cupboard and not four.'

'I hear and obey,' replied the carpenter, beaming with joy.

He set to work at once whilst the young woman waited in his shop. In a few hours a large cupboard with five compartments was completed, and his fair customer hired a porter and had it carried to her house, where she stood it in the reception hall.

She next took four strangely fashioned garments to a dyer, and after having them each dyed a different colour, returned home and made ready for the evening. She prepared meat and drink, arranged fruit and flowers, and burned incense in the braziers. At sunset she arrayed herself in splendid robes, putting on her richest jewels and sweetest perfumes, and sat waiting for her distinguished guests.

The first to arrive was the Cadi. She bowed low before him and, taking him by the hand, led him to a couch. No sooner had they seated themselves than the Cadi began to dally with her, and it was not long before he was roused to a frenzy of passion. But when he was about to throw himself upon her, the young woman said: 'First take off your clothes and turban. You will be more comfortable in this light robe and bonnet.'

Burning with desire, the Cadi promptly cast aside his clothes, and had scarcely put on the curious yellow robe and bonnet which his hostess handed him, when there was heard a knocking at the door.

'Who may that be?' asked the Cadi, wincing with impatience.

'By Allah, that must be my husband!' she exclaimed in great agitation.

'What is to be done? Where shall I go?' cried the Cadi.

'Have no fear,' she replied. 'I will hide you in this cupboard.'

The young woman took the Cadi by the hand, and, pushing him into the lowest compartment of the cupboard, locked the door upon him. Then she went to open for her next visitor.

This proved to be the Governor. The young woman kissed the ground before him and said: 'Pray regard this dwelling as your own. The night is still young; take off your robes and put on this night-shirt.'

Delighted at the suggestion, the Governor quickly stripped himself of his heavy robes and slipped on an ill-cut garment of red cloth, while his hostess swathed his head in an old rag of many colours.

'First,' said the young woman, as the Governor made ready to begin the amorous sport, 'you must write me an order for my brother's release.'

The Governor instantly wrote out the order, and, setting his seal upon it, handed it to her. Then they dallied with each other, but as he was on the point of mounting her, there came a knocking at the door.

'That must be my husband!' exclaimed the young woman in terror.

'What is to be done?' cried the Governor, greatly perturbed.

'Climb up into that cupboard and stay there until I get rid of him,' said the young woman, as she bundled him into the second compartment and locked the door upon him. Then she went to open for her third visitor.

This was the Vizier. She kissed the ground before him and gave him a courteous welcome. 'Sir,' she said, 'you do me great honour by stepping into this humble house.' Then she begged him to take off his clothes and turban, saying: 'Pray put on this light shirt and bonnet. They are better fitted for a night of revelry and merry-making.'

When the Vizier had put off his ministerial vestments, his hostess helped him into a blue shirt and a long, red night-cap. But just as he was about to enjoy her, the King arrived. And the young woman made the worthy Vizier climb up into the third compartment of the cupboard, and locked the door upon him.

When the King entered the young woman kissed the ground before him, saying: 'Your slave lacks words to thank your majesty for this honour.'

Having invited him to sit down, she soon prevailed upon him to take off his costly robes and to put on a tattered old shirt scarcely worth ten dirhams. When the King was on the point of achieving his desire, however, a violent knocking at the door sent him scampering into the fourth compartment of the cupboard. Then she went to open for the carpenter.

'Pray, what kind of cupboard is this you have made me?' snapped the young woman at the carpenter as he stepped into the reception hall. 'Why, the top compartment is so small that it is quite useless.'

'It is a very large compartment,' protested the fat carpenter. 'It could hold me and three others of my size.'

'Try then,' she said. And when the carpenter had climbed up into the fifth compartment of the cupboard, the door was locked upon him.

The young woman took the Governor's order to the

superintendent of the prison, and rejoiced to see her lover free at last. She told him all that had happened, adding: 'We must now leave this city and go to live in a distant land.' Then they hurried back to the house, packed up all their valuables, and set out for another kingdom.

Not daring to utter a sound, the five men stayed in the cupboard without food or drink for three days; and for three days they resolutely held their water. The carpenter, however, was the first to give in; and his piss fell on the King below him. Then the King pissed on the Vizier; and the Vizier pissed on the Governor; and the Governor pissed on the Cadi.

'Filth! Filth!' shouted the Cadi. 'Has not our punishment been cruel enough? Must we be made to suffer in this vile fashion also?'

The Governor and the Vizier were the next to speak, and the three recognized each other's voice.

'Allah's curse be upon this woman!' exclaimed the Vizier. 'She has locked all the senior officers of the kingdom in this cupboard. Thank Allah the King has been spared!'

'Hold your tongue!' muttered the King. 'I am here too. And if I am not mistaken, I must have been the first to fall into the snares of this impudent whore.'

'And to think that I made her this cupboard with my own hands!' groaned the carpenter from the top compartment.

It was not long, however, before the neighbours, who had noticed that the house was deserted, began to suspect foul play. They all crowded around the door debating what action they should take.

'Let us break down the door,' urged one, 'and find out if there is anyone at home.'

'We must investigate the matter,' said another, 'lest the Governor or the King himself should learn of it and have us thrown into prison for failing to do our duty.'

The neighbours forced open the door, and on entering the hall what should they find but a large wooden cupboard echoing with the groans of famished men!

'There must be a jinnee in this cupboard!' exclaimed one of the neighbours.

'Let us set fire to it!' cried another.

'Good people,' howled the Cadi from within, 'in Allah's name do not burn us alive!'

But they gave no heed to his cries, and said to each other: 'The jinn have been known to assume human shape and speak with men's voices.'

Seeing that they were still in doubt, the Cadi intoned aloud some verses from the Koran and entreated them to draw closer. They came near, and in a few words he related to them all that had happened. The neighbours promptly called in a carpenter, who forced the locks, and delivered from the cupboard five men rigged out in fancy costume.

The luckless lovers burst out laughing when they saw each other, and, putting on their clothes, departed, each to his own house.

SINDBAD THE SAILOR AND
SINDBAD THE PORTER

ONCE upon a time, in the reign of the Caliph Haroun al-Rashid, there lived in the city of Baghdad a poor man who earned his living by carrying burdens upon his head. He was called Sindbad the Porter.

One day, as he was staggering under a heavy load in the sweltering heat of the summer sun, he passed by a merchant's house that stood in a pleasant, shaded spot on the roadside. The ground before it was well swept and watered; and Sindbad, seeing a broad wooden bench just outside the gates, put down his load and sat there to rest awhile and to wipe away the sweat which trickled down his forehead. A cool and fragrant breeze blew through the doorway, and from within came the melodious strains of the lute and voices singing. They mingled with the choirs of birds warbling hymns to Allah in various tongues and tunes: curlews and pigeons, merles and bulbuls and turtle-doves.

Moved with great joy, he went up to the door and, looking within, saw in the centre of the noble court-yard a beautiful garden, around which stood numerous slaves and eunuchs, and such an array of attendants as can be found only in the courts of illustrious kings. And all about the place floated the aroma of the choicest meats and wines.

Still marvelling at the splendour of what he saw,

Sindbad lifted up his burden and was about to go his way when there came from within a handsome and well-dressed little page, who took him by the hand, saying: 'Pray come in; my master wishes to speak with you.'

The porter politely declined; but the lad would take no refusal. So Sindbad left his burden in the vestibule with the door-keeper and followed the page into the house.

He was conducted into a magnificent and spacious hall, where an impressive company of nobles and mighty sheikhs were seated according to rank at tables spread with the daintiest meats and richest wines, and gaily decked with flowers and fruit. On one side of the hall sat beautiful slave-girls who sang and made music; and to the fore reclined the host, a venerable old man whose beard was touched with silver. Bewildered at the grandeur and majesty of all that he beheld, the porter thought to himself: 'By Allah, this must either be a corner of Paradise or the palace of some mighty king!'

Sindbad courteously greeted the distinguished assembly and, kissing the ground before them, wished them joy and prosperity. He then stood in silence with eyes cast down.

The master of the house welcomed him kindly and bade him draw near and be seated. He ordered his slaves to set before the porter a choice of delicate foods and pressed him to eat. After pronouncing the blessing Sindbad fell to, and when he had eaten his fill washed his hands and thanked the old sheikh for his hospitality.

'You are welcome to this house, my friend,' said the host, 'and may this day bring you joy. We would gladly know your name and calling.'

'My name is Sindbad,' he answered, 'by trade a porter.'

'How strange a chance!' smiled the old man. 'For my name, too, is Sindbad. They call me Sindbad the Sailor, and marvel at my strange history. Presently, my brother, you shall hear the tale of my fortunes and all the hardships that I suffered before I rose to my present state and became the lord of this mansion where we are now assembled. For only after long toil, fearful ordeals, and dire peril did I achieve this fame. Seven voyages I made in all, each a story of such marvel as confounds the reason and fills the soul with wonder. All that befell me had been pre-ordained; and that which the moving hand of Fate has written no mortal power can revoke.'

The First Voyage of Sindbad the Sailor

KNOW, my friends, that my father was the chief merchant of this city and one of its richest men. He died whilst I was still a child, leaving me great wealth and many estates and farm-lands. As soon as I came of age and had control of my inheritance, I took to extravagant living. I clad myself in the costliest robes, ate and drank sumptuously, and consorted with reckless prodigals of my own age, thinking that this mode of life would endure for ever.

It was not long before I awoke from my heedless folly to find that I had frittered away my entire fortune. I was stricken with horror and dismay at the gravity of my plight, and bethought myself of a proverb of our master Solomon son of David (may peace be upon them both!) which my father often used to cite: 'The day of death is better than the day of birth, a live dog is better than a dead lion, and the grave is better than poverty.' I sold the remainder of my lands and my

household chattels for the sum of three thousand dirhams, and, fortifying myself with hope and courage,
resolved to travel abroad and trade in foreign lands.

I bought a large quantity of merchandise and made
preparations for a long voyage. Then I set sail together
with a company of merchants in a river-ship bound for
Basrah. There we put to sea and, voyaging many days
and nights from isle to isle and from shore to shore,
buying and selling and bartering wherever the ship
anchored, we came at length to a little island as fair as
the Garden of Eden. Here the captain of our ship cast
anchor and put out the landing-planks.

The passengers went ashore and set to work to light
a fire. Some busied themselves with cooking and washing, some fell to eating and drinking and making merry,
while others, like myself, set out to explore the island.
Whilst we were thus engaged we suddenly heard the
captain cry out to us from the ship: 'All aboard, quickly!
Abandon everything and run for your lives! The mercy
of Allah be upon you, for this is no island but a gigantic
whale floating on the bosom of the sea, on whose back
the sands have settled and trees have grown since the
world was young! When you lit the fire it felt the heat
and stirred. Make haste, I say; or soon the whale will
plunge into the sea and you will all be lost!'

Hearing the captain's cries, the passengers made for
the ship in panic-stricken flight, leaving behind their
cooking-pots and other belongings. Some reached the
ship in safety, but others did not; for suddenly the island
shook beneath our feet and, submerged by mountain-
ous waves, sank with all that stood upon it to the
bottom of the roaring ocean.

Together with my unfortunate companions I was en-
gulfed by the merciless tide; but Providence came to

my aid, casting in my way a great wooden trough which
had been used by the ship's company for washing. Im-
pelled by that instinct which makes all mortals cling to
life, I held fast to the trough and, bestriding it firmly,
paddled away with my feet as the waves tossed and buf-
feted me on every side. Meanwhile the captain hoisted
sail and set off with the other passengers. I followed
the ship with my eyes until it vanished from sight, and
I resigned myself to certain death.

Darkness soon closed in upon the ocean. All that
night and throughout the following day I drifted on,
lashed by the wind and the waves, until the trough
brought me to the steep shores of a densely wooded
island, where trees hung over the sea.

I caught hold of one of the branches, and with its aid
managed to clamber ashore after fighting so long for
my life. Finding myself again on dry land, I realized
that I had lost the use of my legs, and my feet began
to smart with the bites of fish.

Worn out by anguish and exertion, I sank into a
death-like slumber; and it was not until the following
morning when the sun rose that I came to my senses.
But my feet were so sore and swollen that I could move
about only by crawling on my knees. By good fortune,
however, the island had an abundance of fruit-trees,
which provided me with sustenance, and many springs
of fresh water; so that after a few days my body was
restored to strength and my spirit revived. I cut myself
a staff from the branch of a tree, and with its aid set out
to explore the island and to admire the many goodly
things which Allah had planted on its soil.

One day, as I was roaming about the beach in an unfamiliar part of the island, I caught sight of a strange
object in the distance which appeared to be some wild

beast or sea-monster. As I drew nearer and looked more closely at it, I saw that it was a noble mare of an uncommonly high stature haltered to a tree. On seeing me the mare gave an ear-splitting neigh which made me take to my heels in terror. Presently there emerged from the ground a man, who pursued me, shouting: 'Who are you and whence have you come? What are you doing here?'

'Sir,' I replied, 'I am a luckless voyager, abandoned in the middle of the sea; but it was Allah's will that I should be rescued from the fury of the waves and cast upon this island.'

The stranger took me by the hand and bade me follow him. He led me to a subterranean cavern, and, after asking me to be seated, he placed some food before me and invited me to eat. When I had eaten my fill he questioned me about the fortunes of my voyage, and I related to him all that had befallen me from first to last.

'But, pray tell me, sir,' I inquired, as my host marvelled at my adventure, 'what is the reason of your vigil here and for what purpose is this mare tethered on the beach?'

'Know,' he replied, 'that I am one of the many grooms of King Mahrajan. We have charge of all his horses and are stationed in different parts of this island. Each month, on the night of the full moon, we tether all the virgin mares on the beach and hide in shelters near by. Presently the sea-horses scent the mares and, emerging from the water, leap upon the beasts and cover them. Then they try to drag them away into the sea. But this they fail to do, as the mares are securely roped. With angry cries the sea-horses attack the mares and kick them with their hind legs. At this point we

E

rush from our hiding-places and drive the sea-horses back into the water. The mares then conceive and bear colts and fillies of inestimable worth. To-night,' he added, 'when we have completed our task, I shall take you to our King and show you our city. Allah be praised for this happy encounter; for had you not chanced to meet us you would have surely come to grief in the solitude of these wild regions.'

I thanked him with all my heart and called down blessings upon him. Whilst we were thus engaged in conversation we heard a dreadful cry in the distance. The groom quickly snatched up his sword and buckler and rushed out, shouting aloud and banging his sword on his shield. Thereupon several other grooms came out from their hiding-places, brandishing their spears and yelling at the top of their voices. The sea-horse, who had just covered the mare, took fright at this tumult and plunged, like a buffalo, headlong into the sea, where he disappeared beneath the water.

As we sat on the ground to recover our breath, the other grooms, each leading a mare, approached us. My companion explained to them the circumstances of my presence, and, after exchanging greetings, we rode to the city of King Mahrajan.

As soon as the King was informed of my arrival he summoned me to his presence. He marvelled at my story, saying: 'By Allah, my son, your preservation has been truly miraculous. Praise be to the Highest for your deliverance!'

Thenceforth I rose rapidly in the King's favour and soon became a trusted courtier. He vested me with robes of honour and appointed me Comptroller of Shipping at the port of his kingdom. And during my sojourn in that realm I earned the gratitude of the poor and the humble for my readiness to intercede for them with the King.

There I witnessed many prodigies and met travellers from different foreign lands. One day I entered the King's chamber and found him entertaining a company of Indians. I exchanged greetings with them and questioned them about their country. In the course of conversation I was astonished to learn that there were no fewer than seventy-two different castes in India. The noblest of these castes is known as Shakiriyah, and its members are renowned for piety and fair dealing. Another caste are the Brahmins. They are skilled breeders of camels, horses, and cattle, and though they abstain from wine, they are a merry and pleasure-loving people.

Not far from the King's dominions there is a little island where at night is heard a mysterious beating of drums and clash of tambourines. Travellers and men from neighbouring isles told me that its inhabitants were a shrewd and diligent race.

In those distant seas I once saw a fish two hundred cubits in length, and another with a head that resembled an owl's. This I saw with my own eyes, and many other things no less strange and wondrous.

Whenever I walked along the quay I talked with the sailors and travellers from far countries, inquiring whether any of them had heard tell of the city of Baghdad and how far off it lay; for I never lost hope that I should one day find my way back to my native land. But there was none who knew of that city; and as the days dragged by, my longing for home weighed heavy upon my heart.

One day, however, as I stood on the wharf, leaning upon my staff and gazing out to sea, a ship bearing a large company of merchants came sailing into the harbour. As soon as it was moored, the sails were furled and landing-planks put out. The crew began to unload the cargo, and I stood by entering up the merchandise in my register. When they had done, I asked the captain if all the goods had now been brought ashore.

'Sir,' he replied, 'in the ship's hold I still have a few bales which belonged to a merchant who was drowned at an early stage of our voyage. We shall put them up for sale and take the money to his kinsmen in Baghdad, the City of Peace.'

'What was the merchant's name?' I demanded.

'Sindbad,' he answered.

I looked more closely into his face, and, recognizing him at once, uttered a joyful cry.

'Why!' I exclaimed, 'I am Sindbad, the self-same owner of these goods, who was left to drown with many others when the great whale plunged into the sea. But through the grace of Allah I was cast by the waves onto the shores of this island, where I found favour with the King and became Comptroller at this port. I am the true owner of these goods, which are my only possessions in this world.'

'By Allah,' cried the captain, 'is there no longer any faith or honesty in man? I have but to mention a dead man's goods and you claim them for your own! Why, we saw Sindbad drown before our very eyes. Dare you lay claim to his property?'

'I pray you, captain,' I rejoined, 'listen to my story and you shall soon learn the whole truth.' I then recounted to him all the details of the voyage from the day we set sail from Basrah till we cast anchor off the treacherous island, and reminded him of a certain matter that had passed between us.

The captain and the passengers now recognized me, and all congratulated me on my escape, saying: 'Allah has granted you a fresh span of life!'

At once my goods were brought ashore and I rejoiced to find the bales intact and sealed as I had left them. I selected some of the choicest and most precious articles as presents for King Mahrajan, and had them carried by the sailors to the royal palace, where I laid them at his feet. I informed the King of the unexpected arrival of my ship and the happy recovery of all my goods. He marvelled greatly at this chance, and, in return for my presents, bestowed upon me priceless treasures.

I sold my wares at a substantial profit and re-equipped myself with the finest produce of that island. When all was ready for the homeward voyage I presented myself at the King's court, and, thanking him for the many favours he had shown me, begged leave to return to my land and people.

Then we set sail, trusting in Allah and propitious Fortune; and after voyaging many days and nights we at length safely arrived in Basrah.

I spent but a few days in that town and then, loaded with treasure, set out for Baghdad, the City of Peace. I was overjoyed to be back in my native city, and hastening to my old street entered my own house, where by and by all my friends and kinsmen came to greet me.

I bought fine houses and rich farm-lands, concubines and eunuchs and black slaves, and became richer than I had ever been before. I kept open house for my old companions, and, soon forgetting the hardships of my voyage, resumed with new zest my former mode of living.

That is the story of the first of my adventures. To-morrow, if Allah wills, I shall relate to you the tale of my second voyage.

The day was drawing to its close, and Sindbad the Sailor invited Sindbad the Porter to join the guests in the evening meal. When the feast was finished he gave him a hundred pieces of gold, saying: 'You have de-lighted us with your company this day.'

The porter thanked him for his generous gift and de-parted, pondering over the vicissitudes of fortune and marvelling at all that he had heard.

Next morning he went again to the house of his bene-factor, who received him courteously and seated him by his side. Presently the other guests arrived, and when they had feasted and made merry, Sindbad the Sailor began:

The Second Voyage of Sindbad the Sailor

For some time after my return to Baghdad I con-tinued to lead a gay and care-free life, but it was not long before I felt an irresistible longing to travel again about the world and to visit distant cities and islands in quest of profit and adventure. So I bought a great store of merchandise and, making preparations for departure, sailed down the Tigris to Basrah. There I embarked, together with a band of merchants, in a fine new vessel, well-equipped and manned by a sturdy crew, which set sail the same day.

Aided by a favourable wind, we voyaged for many days and nights from port to port and from island to island, selling and bartering our goods, and haggling with merchants and officials wherever we cast anchor. At length Destiny carried our ship to the shores of an uninhabited island, rich in fruit and flowers, and jubilant with the singing of birds and the murmur of crystal streams.

Here passengers and crew went ashore, and we all set off to enjoy the delights of the island. I strolled through the green meadows, leaving my companions far behind, and sat down in a shady thicket to eat a simple meal by a spring of water. Lulled by the soft and fragrant breeze which blew around me, I lay upon the grass and presently fell asleep.

I cannot tell how long I slept, but when I awoke I saw none of my fellow-travellers, and soon realized that the ship had sailed away without anyone noticing my absence. I ran in frantic haste towards the sea, and on reaching the shore saw the vessel, a white speck upon the vast blue ocean, dissolving into the far horizon.

Broken with terror and despair, I threw myself upon the sand, wailing: 'Now your end has come, Sindbad! The jar that drops a second time is sure to break!' I cursed the day I bade farewell to the joys of a contented life and bitterly repented my folly in venturing again upon the hazards and hardships of the sea, after having so narrowly escaped death in my first voyage.

At length resigning myself to my doom, I rose and, after wandering about aimlessly for some time, climbed into a tall tree. From its top I gazed long in all directions, but could see nothing save the sky, the trees, the birds, the sands, and the boundless ocean. As I scanned the interior of the island more closely, however, I gradually became aware of some white object looming in the distance. At once I climbed down the tree and made my way towards it. Drawing nearer, I found to my astonishment that it was a white dome of extraordinary dimensions. I walked all round it, but could find no door or entrance of any kind; and so smooth and slippery was its surface that any attempt to climb it would have been fruitless. I walked round it again, and, making a mark in the sand near its base, found that its circumference measured more than fifty paces.

Whilst I was thus engaged the sun was suddenly hidden from my view as by a great cloud and the world grew dark around me. I lifted up my eyes towards the sky, and was confounded to see a gigantic bird with enormous wings which, as it flew through the air, screened the sun and hid it from the island.

The sight of this prodigy instantly called to my mind a story I had heard in my youth from pilgrims and adventurers – how in a far island dwelt a bird of monstrous size called the roc, which fed its young on elephants; and at once I realized that the white dome was no other than a roc's egg. In a twinkling the bird alighted upon the egg, covering it completely with its wings and stretching out its legs behind it on the ground. And in this posture it went to sleep. (Glory to Him who never sleeps!)

Rising swiftly, I unwound my turban from my head, then doubled it and twisted it into a rope with which I securely bound myself by the waist to one of the great talons of the monster. 'Perchance this bird,' I thought, 'will carry me away to a civilized land; wherever I am set down, it will surely be better than a solitary island.'

I lay awake all night, fearing to close my eyes lest the bird should fly away with me while I slept. At daybreak the roc rose from the egg, and, spreading its wings, took to the air with a terrible cry. I clung fast to its talon as it winged its flight through the void and soared higher and higher until it almost touched the heavens. After some time it began to drop, and sailing swiftly downwards came to earth on the brow of a steep hill.

Trembling with fear, I hastened to untie my turban before the roc became aware of my presence. Scarcely had I released myself when the monster darted off towards a great black object lying near and, clutching it in its fearful claws, took wing again. As it rose in the air I was astonished to see that this was a serpent of immeasurable length; and with its prey the bird vanished from sight.

Looking around, I found myself on a precipitous hillside overlooking an exceedingly deep and vast valley. On all sides towered craggy mountains whose beetling summits no man could ever scale. I was stricken with fear and repented my rashness. 'Would I had remained in that island!' I thought to myself. 'There at least I lacked neither fruit nor water, while these barren steeps offer nothing to eat or drink. No sooner do I escape from one peril than I find myself in another more grievous. There is no strength nor help save in Allah!'

When I had made my way down the hill I marvelled to see the ground thickly covered with the rarest diamonds, so that the entire valley blazed with a glorious light. Here and there among the glittering stones, however, coiled deadly snakes and vipers, dread keepers of the fabulous treasure. Thicker and longer than giant palm-trees, they could have swallowed whole elephants at one gulp. They were crawling back into their sunless dens, for by day they hid themselves from their enemies the rocs and the eagles, and moved about only at night.

Overwhelmed with horror, and oblivious of hunger

and fatigue, I roamed the valley all day searching with infinite caution for a shelter where I might pass the night. At dusk I came upon a narrow-mouthed cave, into which I crawled, blocking its entrance from within by a great stone. I thought to myself: 'Here I shall be safe this night. When to-morrow comes, let Destiny do its worst.'

Scarcely had I advanced a few steps, when I saw at the far end of the cave an enormous serpent coiled in a great knot round its eggs. My hair stood on end and I was transfixed with terror. Seeing no way of escape, however, I put my trust in Allah and kept vigil all night. At daybreak I rolled back the stone and staggered out of the cave, reeling like a drunken man.

As I thus stumbled along I noticed a great joint of flesh come tumbling down into the valley from rock to rock. Upon closer inspection I found this to be a whole sheep, skinned and drawn. I was deeply perplexed at the mystery, for there was not a soul in sight; but at that very moment there flashed across my mind the memory of a story I had once heard from travellers who had visited the Diamond Mountains – how men obtained the diamonds from this treacherous and inaccessible valley by a strange device. Before sunrise they would throw whole carcasses of sheep from the top of the mountains, so that the gems on which they fell penetrated the soft flesh and became embedded in it. At midday rocs and mighty vultures would swoop down upon the mutton and carry it away in their talons to their nests in the mountain heights. With a great clamour the merchants would then rush at the birds and force them to drop the meat and fly away, after which it would only remain to look through the carcasses and pick out the diamonds.

As I recalled this story a plan of escape formed in my mind. I selected a great quantity of priceless stones and hid them all about me, filling my pockets with them and pressing them into the folds of my belt and garments. Then I unrolled my turban, stuffed it with more diamonds, twisted it into a rope as I had done before, and, lying down below the carcass, bound it firmly to my chest. I had not remained long in that position when I suddenly felt myself lifted from the ground by the talons of a huge vulture which had tightly closed upon the meat. The bird climbed higher and higher, and finally alighted upon the top of a mountain. As soon as it began to tear at the flesh there arose from behind the neighbouring rocks a great tumult, at which the bird took fright and flew away. At once I freed myself and sprang to my feet, with face and clothes all bloody.

I saw a man come running to the spot and stop in alarm as he saw me. Without uttering a word he cautiously bent over the carcass to examine it, eyeing me suspiciously all the while; but finding no diamonds, he wrung his hands and lifted up his arms, crying: 'O heavy loss! Allah, in whom alone dwell all power and majesty, defend us from the wiles of the Evil One!'

Before I could explain my presence the man, shaking with fear, turned to me and asked: 'Who are you, and how came you here?'

'Do not be alarmed, sir,' I replied, 'I am no evil spirit, but an honest man, a merchant by profession. My story is an extraordinary one, and the adventure which has brought me to these mountains surpasses in wonder all the marvels that men have seen or heard of. But first, pray accept some of these diamonds, which I myself gathered in the fearful valley below.'

I took some splendid jewels from my pocket and

offered them to him, saying: 'These will bring you all the riches you can desire.'

The owner of the bait was overjoyed at the unexpected gift; he warmly thanked me and called down blessings upon me. Whilst we were thus talking, several other merchants came up from the mountain-side. They crowded round us, listening in amazement to my story, and congratulated me, saying: 'By Allah, your escape was a miracle; for no man has ever set foot in that valley and returned alive. Allah alone be praised for your salvation.'

The merchants then led me to their tent. They gave me food and drink and there I slept soundly for many hours. Early next day, we set out from our tent and, journeying over a vast range of mountains, came at length to the seashore. After a short voyage we arrived in a pleasant, densely wooded island, covered with trees so huge that beneath one of them a hundred men could shelter from the sun. It is from these trees that the aromatic substance known as camphor is extracted. The trunks are hollowed out, and the sap oozes drop by drop into vessels which are placed beneath, soon curdling into a crystal gum.

In that island I saw a gigantic beast called the karkadan, or rhinoceros, which grazes in the fields like a cow or buffalo. Taller than a camel, it has a single horn in the middle of its forehead, and upon this horn Nature has carved the likeness of a man. The karkadan attacks the elephant and, impaling it upon its horn, carries it aloft from place to place until its victim dies. Before long, however, the elephant's fat melts in the heat of the sun and, dripping down into the karkadan's eyes, puts out its sight; so that the beast blunders helplessly along and finally drops dead. Then the roc swoops down upon both animals and carries them off to its nest in the high mountains. I also saw many strange breeds of buffalo in that island.

I sold a part of my diamonds for a large sum, and exchanged more for a vast quantity of merchandise. Then we set sail, and, trading from port to port and from island to island, at length safely arrived in Basrah. After a few days' sojourn there I set out upstream to Baghdad, the City of Peace.

Loaded with precious goods and the finest of my diamonds, I hastened to my old street and entering my own house, rejoiced to see my friends and kinsfolk. I gave them gold and presents, and distributed alms among the poor of the city.

I soon forgot the perils and hardships of my travels, and took again to sumptuous living. I ate well, dressed well, and kept open house for innumerable gallants and gay companions.

From far and near men came to hear me speak of my adventures and to learn from me the news of foreign lands. All were astounded at the dangers I had escaped and wished me joy of my return. Such was my second voyage.

To-morrow, my friends, if Allah wills, I shall relate to you the extraordinary tale of my third voyage.

The famous mariner ended. The guests marvelled at his story.

When the evening feast was over, Sindbad the Sailor gave Sindbad the Porter a hundred pieces of gold, which he took with thanks and many blessings, and departed, lost in wonderment at all he had heard.

Next day the porter rose and, after reciting his morning prayers, went to the house of his illustrious friend, who received him kindly and seated him by his side. And when all the guests had assembled, Sindbad the Sailor began:

The Third Voyage of Sindbad the Sailor

KNOW, my friends, that for some time after my return I continued to lead a happy and tranquil life, but I soon grew weary of my idle existence in Baghdad and once again longed to roam the world in quest of profit and adventure. Unmindful of the dangers of ambition and worldly greed, I resolved to set out on another voyage. I provided myself with a great store of goods and, taking them down the Tigris, set sail from Basrah, together with a band of honest merchants.

The voyage began prosperously. We called at many foreign ports, trading profitably with our merchandise. One day, however, whilst we were sailing in mid-ocean, we heard the captain of our ship, who was on deck scanning the horizon, suddenly burst out in a loud lament. He beat himself about the face, tore his beard, and rent his clothes.

'We are lost!' he cried, as we crowded round him. 'The treacherous wind has driven us off our course towards that island which you see before you. It is the Isle of the Zughb, where dwell a race of dwarfs more akin to apes than men, from whom no voyager has ever escaped alive!'

Scarcely had he uttered these words when a multitude of ape-like savages appeared on the beach and began to swim out towards the ship. In a few moments they were upon us, thick as a swarm of locusts. Barely four spans in height, they were the ugliest of living creatures, with little gleaming yellow eyes and bodies thickly covered with black fur. And so numerous were they that we did not dare to provoke them or attempt to drive them away, lest they should set upon us and kill us to a man by force of numbers.

They scrambled up the masts, gnawing the cables with their teeth and biting them to shreds. Then they seized the helm and steered the vessel to their island. When the ship had run ashore, the dwarfs carried us one by one to the beach, and, promptly pushing off again, climbed on board and sailed away.

Disconsolately we set out to search for food and water, and by good fortune came upon some fruit-trees and a running stream. Here we refreshed ourselves, and then wandered about the island until at length we saw far off among the trees a massive building, where we hoped to pass the night in safety. Drawing nearer, we found that it was a towering palace surrounded by a lofty wall, with a great ebony door which stood wide open. We entered the spacious courtyard, and to our surprise found it deserted. In one corner lay a great heap of bones, and on the far side we saw a broad bench, an open oven, pots and pans of enormous size, and many iron spits for roasting.

Exhausted and sick at heart, we lay down in the courtyard and were soon overcome by sleep. At sunset we were awakened by a noise like thunder. The earth shook beneath our feet and we saw a colossal black giant approaching from the doorway. He was a fearsome sight – tall as a palm-tree, with red eyes burning in his head like coals of fire; his mouth was a dark well, with lips that drooped like a camel's loosely over his chest, whilst his ears, like a pair of large round discs, hung back over his shoulders: his fangs were as long as the tusks of a boar and his nails were like the claws of a lion.

The sight of this monster struck terror to our hearts. We cowered motionless on the ground as we watched him stride across the yard and sit down on the bench. For a few moments he eyed us one by one in silence; then he rose and, reaching out towards me, lifted me up by the neck and began feeling my body as a butcher would a lamb. Finding me little more than skin and bone, however, he flung me to the ground and, picking up each of my companions in turn, pinched and prodded them and set them down until at last he came to the captain.

Now the captain was a corpulent fellow, tall and broad-shouldered. The giant seemed to like him well. He gripped him as a butcher grips a fatted ram and broke his neck under his foot. Then he thrust an iron spit through his body from mouth to backside and, lighting a great fire in the oven, carefully turned his victim round and round before it. When the flesh was finely roasted, the ogre tore the body to pieces with his finger-nails as though it were a pullet, and devoured it limb by limb, gnawing the bones and flinging them against the wall. The monster then stretched himself out on the bench and soon fell fast asleep. His snores were as loud as the grunts and gurgles that issue from the throat of a slaughtered beast.

Thus he slept all night, and when morning came he rose and went out of the palace, leaving us half-crazed with terror.

As soon as we were certain that the monster had gone, we began lamenting our evil fortune. 'Would that we had been drowned in the sea or killed by the apes!' we cried. 'That would surely have been better than the foul death which now awaits us! But that which Allah has ordained must surely come to pass.'

We left the palace to search for some hiding-place, but could find no shelter in any part of the island, and had no choice but to return to the palace in the evening. Night came, and with it the black giant, announcing his approach by a noise like thunder. No sooner had he entered than he snatched up one of the merchants and prepared his supper in the same way as the night before. Then, stretching himself out to sleep, he snored the night away.

Next morning, when the giant had gone, we discussed our desperate plight.

'By Allah,' cried one of the merchants, 'let us rather throw ourselves into the sea than remain alive to be roasted and eaten!'

'Listen, my friends,' said another. 'We must kill this monster. For only by destroying him can we end his wickedness and save good Moslems from his barbarous cruelty.'

This proposal was received with general approbation; so I rose in my turn and addressed the company. 'If we are all agreed to kill this monster,' I said, 'let us first build a raft on which we can escape from this island as soon as we have sent his soul to damnation. Perchance our raft will take us to some other island, where we can board a ship bound for our country. If we are drowned, we shall at least escape roasting and die a martyr's death.'

'By Allah,' cried the others, 'that is a wise plan.'

Setting to work at once, we hauled several logs from the great pile of wood stacked beside the oven and carried them out of the palace. Then we fastened them together into a raft, which we left ready on the seashore.

In the evening the earth shook beneath our feet as the black giant burst in upon us, barking and snarling like a mad dog. Once more he seized upon the stoutest of my companions and prepared his meal. When he had eaten his fill, he stretched himself upon the bench as was his custom and soon fell fast asleep.

Noiselessly we now rose, took two of the great iron spits from the oven, and thrust them into the fire. As soon as they were red hot we carried them over to the snoring monster and plunged their sharpened ends deep into his eyes, exerting our united weight from above to push them home. The giant gave a deafening shriek which filled our hearts with terror and cast us back on the ground many yards away. Totally blinded, he leapt up from the bench groping for us with outstretched hands, while we nimbly dodged his frantic clutches. In despair he felt his way to the ebony door and staggered out of the yard, groaning in agonies of pain.

Without losing a moment we made off towards the beach. As soon as we reached the water we launched our raft and jumped aboard; but scarcely had we rowed a few yards when we saw the blind savage running towards us, guided by a foul hag of his own kind. On reaching the shore they stood howling threats and curses at us for a while, and then caught up massive boulders and hurled them at our raft with stupendous force. Missile followed missile until all my companions, save two, were drowned; but we three who escaped soon contrived to paddle beyond the range of their fury.

Lashed by the waves, we drifted on in the open sea for a whole day and a whole night until we were cast upon the shore of another island. Half-dead with hunger and exhaustion, we threw ourselves upon the sand and fell asleep.

Next morning, when we awoke, we found ourselves encircled by a serpent of prodigious size, which lay about us in a knotted coil. Before we could move a limb the beast suddenly reared its head and, opening wide its deadly jaws, seized one of my companions and swallowed him to the shoulders; then it gulped him down entirely, and we heard his ribs crack in its belly. Presently, however, the serpent unwound its loathsome body and, heedless of my companion and myself, glided away, leaving us stricken with grief at the horrible fate of our comrade and amazed at our own narrow escape.

'By Allah,' we cried, 'we have fled from one form of death only to meet with another as hideous. How shall we now escape this serpent? There is no strength nor help save in Allah!'

The warmth of the new-born day inspired us with fresh courage, and we struck inland to search for food and water. Before nightfall we climbed into a tall tree, and perched ourselves as best we could upon the topmost branches. But as soon as darkness fell we heard a fearful hissing and a noise of heavy movement on the ground; and in a twinkling the serpent had seized my friend and gulped him down, cracking all his bones in its belly. Then the vile creature slid down the tree and disappeared among the vegetation. That was the end of the last of my companions.

At daybreak I climbed down from my hiding-place. My first thought was to throw myself into the sea and thus end a life which had already endured more than its share of hardships and ordeals. But when I was on the point of putting my resolve into execution, my courage failed me; for life is very precious. I clung instinctively to the hope of a speedy rescue, and a plan to protect myself from the serpent began to form in my mind.

I collected some thick planks of wood and fastened them together into a coffin-shaped box, complete with lid. When evening came I shut myself in, shielded on all sides by the strong boards. By and by the snake approached and circled round me, writhing and squirming. All night long its dreadful hissing sounded in my ears, but with the approach of morning it turned away and vanished among the undergrowth.

When the sun rose I came out of my shelter and cautiously made my way across the island. As I reached the shore, what should I see but a ship sailing far off upon the vast expanse of water!

At once I tore off a great branch from a tree, and, yelling at the top of my voice, waved it frantically above my head. The crew must have instantly observed my signal, for, to my great joy, the ship suddenly turned off its course and headed for the island.

When I came aboard the captain gave me clothes to cover my nakedness and offered me food and drink. Little by little I regained my strength, and after a few days of rest became my old self again. I rendered thanks to Allah for rescuing me from my ordeal, and soon my past sufferings were no more than half-forgotten dreams.

Aided by a prosperous wind, we voyaged many days and nights and at length came to the Isle of Salahitah. Here the captain cast anchor, and the merchants landed with their goods to trade with the people of the island. Whilst I was standing idly by, watching the busy scene, the captain of our ship came up to me, saying: 'Listen, my friend. You say you are a penniless stranger who has suffered much at sea. I will make you an offer which, I trust, will be greatly to your advantage. A few years ago I carried in my ship a merchant who, alas, was left behind upon a desert island. No news has since been heard of him, and no one knows whether he is alive or dead. Take his goods and trade with them, and a share of the profit shall be yours. The remainder of the money I will take back to the merchant's family in Baghdad.'

I thanked the captain with all my heart. He ordered the crew to unload the merchandise and called the ship's clerk to enter up the bales in his register.

'Whose property are they?' inquired the clerk.

'The owner's name was Sindbad,' replied the captain. 'But henceforth they will be in charge of this passenger.'

A cry of astonishment escaped my lips and I at once recognized him as the captain of the ship in which I had sailed on my second voyage.

'Why!' I exclaimed. 'I am Sindbad, that very merchant who many years ago was left behind on the Island of the Roc. I fell asleep beside a spring and awoke to find that the ship had gone. The merchants who saw me on the Diamond Mountains and heard my adventure will bear witness that I am indeed Sindbad.'

On hearing mention of the Diamond Mountains, one of the merchants, who by this time had gathered round us, came forward and, peering closely into my face, suddenly turned to his friends, crying: 'By Allah, not one of you would believe the wonder which I once witnessed on the Diamond Mountains, when a man was carried up from the valley by a mighty vulture! This is he; Sindbad the Sailor, the very one who presented me with those rare diamonds!'

The captain questioned me about the contents of my bales, and I readily gave him a precise description. I also reminded him of a certain incident which had occurred in the course of our voyage. He now recognized me and, taking me in his arms, congratulated me,

saying: 'Praise be to Him who has brought us together again and granted the restitution of all your
goods!'

My merchandise was brought ashore, and I sold it
forthwith at a substantial profit. Then we set sail and
after a few days came to the land of Sind, where we also
traded profitably.

In those Indian waters I witnessed many prodigies.
I saw a sea-monster which resembled a cow and another
with a head like a donkey's. I also saw a bird which
hatches from a sea-shell and remains throughout its life
floating on the water.

From Sind we set sail again, and, voyaging many days
and nights, came at length with Allah's help to Basrah.
I stayed there but a few days, and then voyaged upstream to Baghdad, where I was jubilantly welcomed
by my friends and kinsmen. I bestowed alms upon the
poor and gave generously to widows and orphans, for
I had returned from this voyage richer than ever before.

To-morrow, my friends, if Allah wills, I shall recount
to you the tale of my fourth voyage, which you shall
find even more extraordinary than the tales I have already related.

When the evening feast was ended, Sindbad the Sailor
gave Sindbad the Porter a hundred pieces of gold, and
the company took leave of their host and departed, marvelling at the wonders they had heard.

Next morning the porter returned, and when the
other guests had assembled, Sindbad the Sailor began:

The Fourth Voyage of Sindbad the Sailor

THE gay and extravagant life which I led after my return did not cause me to forget the delights and benefits of travel in distant lands; and my thirst for seeing the world, despite the perils I had encountered, continued as violent as ever. My restless soul at length yielded to the call of the sea, and, making preparations for a long voyage, I set sail with merchandise from Basrah, together with some eminent merchants of that city.

Blessed with a favouring wind, we sped upon the foamy highways of the sea, trading from port to port and from island to island. One day, however, a howling gale suddenly sprang up in mid-ocean, rolling against our ship massive waves as high as mountains. The captain at once ordered the crew to cast anchor, and we all fell on our knees in prayer and lamentation. A furious squall tore the sails to ribbons and snapped the mast in two; then a giant wave came hurtling down upon us from above, shattering our vessel and tossing us all into the raging sea.

With Allah's help, I clung fast to a floating beam, and bestriding it firmly fought the downrush of the waves with those of my companions who had managed to reach it also. Now paddling with our hands and feet, now swept by wind and current, we were at length thrown, half-dead with cold and exhaustion, on the shore of an island.

We lay down upon the sand and fell asleep. Next morning we rose, and striking inland came after a few hours in sight of a lofty building among the trees. As we drew nearer, a number of naked and wild-looking men emerged from the door, and without a word took

hold of my companions and myself and led us into the
building, where we saw their King seated upon a throne.

The King bade us sit down, and presently his servants set before us dishes of such meats as we had never
seen before in all our lives. My famished companions
ate ravenously; but my stomach revolted at the sight of
this food and, in spite of my hunger, I could not eat a
single mouthful. As things turned out, however, my
abstinence saved my life. For as soon as they had swallowed a few morsels my comrades began to lose their
intelligence and to act like gluttonous maniacs; so that
after a few hours of incessant guzzling they were little
better than savages.

Whilst my companions were thus feeding, the naked
men brought in a vessel filled with a strange ointment,
with which they anointed their victims' bodies. The
change my companions suffered was astonishing; their
eyes sank into their heads and their bellies grew hor-
ribly distended, so that the more they swelled the more
insatiable their appetites became.

My horror at this spectacle knew no bounds, especially when I soon discovered that our captors were
cannibals who fattened their victims in this way before
slaughtering them. The King feasted every day on a
roasted stranger; his men preferred their diet raw.

When my transformed companions had thus been
robbed entirely of all their human faculties, they were
committed to the charge of a herdsman, who led them
out every day to pasture in the meadows. I myself was
reduced to a shadow by hunger and fear and my skin
shrivelled upon my bones. Therefore the savages lost
all interest in me and no longer cared even to watch my
movements.

One day I slipped out of my captors' dwelling and

made off across the island. On reaching the distant grasslands I met the herdsman with his once-human charges. But instead of pursuing me or ordering me to return, he appeared to take pity on my helpless condition, and pointing to his right made signs to me which seemed to say: 'Go this way: have no fear.'

I ran on and on across the rolling plains in the direction he indicated. When evening came I ate a scanty meal of roots and herbs and lay down to rest upon the grass; but fear of the cannibals had robbed me of all desire to sleep, and at midnight I rose again and trudged painfully on.

Thus I journeyed for seven days and nights, and on the morning of the eighth day came at last to the opposite side of the island, where I could faintly discern human figures in the distance. Drawing nearer, I rejoiced to find that they were a party of peasants gathering pepper in a field.

They crowded round me, and speaking in my own language inquired who I was and whence I had come. In reply I recounted the story of my misfortunes, and they were all amazed at my adventure. They congratulated me on my escape and, after offering me food and water, allowed me to rest till evening. When their day's work was done, they took me with them in a boat to their capital, which was in a neighbouring island.

There I was presented to their King, who received me kindly and listened in astonishment to my story. I found their city prosperous and densely populated, abounding in markets and well-stocked shops, and filled with the bustle of commercial activity. The people, both rich and poor, possessed the rarest thoroughbred horses; but I was bewildered to see them ride their steeds bare-backed.

In my next audience with the King I ventured to express my surprise at his subjects' ignorance of the use of saddles and stirrups. 'My noble master,' I remarked, 'why is it that no one in this island uses a saddle? It makes both for the comfort of the rider and his mastery over his horse.'

'What may that be?' he asked, somewhat puzzled. 'I have never seen a saddle in all my life.'

'Pray allow me to make one for you,' I replied, 'that you may try it and find how comfortable and useful it can be.'

The King was pleased at my offer. At once I sought out a skilful carpenter and instructed him to make a wooden frame for a saddle of my own design; then I taught a blacksmith to forge a bit and a pair of stirrups. I fitted out the frame with a padding of wool and leather and furnished it with a girth and tassels. When all was ready, I chose the finest of the royal horses, saddled and bridled it, and led it before the King.

The King was highly delighted with the splendour and usefulness of his horse's novel equipment, and in reward bestowed on me precious gifts and a large sum of money.

When his Vizier saw the saddle he begged me to make one for him. I did so; and it was not long before every courtier and noble in the kingdom became the owner of a handsome saddle.

My skill soon made me the richest man in the island. The King conferred upon me many honours and I became a trusted courtier. One day, as we sat conversing together in his palace, he said: 'You must know, Sindbad, that we have grown to love you like a brother. Indeed, our regard for you is such that we cannot bear the thought that you might some day leave our kingdom. Therefore we will ask you a favour, which we hope you will not refuse.'

'Allah forbid,' I replied, 'that I should refuse you anything, your majesty.'

'We wish you to marry a beautiful girl who has been brought up in our court,' he said. 'She is intelligent and wealthy, and will make you an excellent wife. I trust that you will settle down happily with her in this city for the rest of your days. Do not refuse me this, I pray you.'

I was deeply embarrassed and did not know what to answer.

'Why do you not speak, my son?' he asked.

'Your majesty,' I faltered, 'I am in duty bound to obey you.'

The King sent at once for a cadi and witnesses and I was married that day to a rich woman of noble lineage. The King gave us a magnificent palace and assigned to us a retinue of slaves and servants.

We lived happily and contentedly together, although in my heart-of-hearts I never ceased to cherish a longing to return home with my wife; for I loved her dearly. But, alas, no mortal can control his destiny or trifle with the decrees of Fate.

One day death claimed to eternal rest my neighbour's wife, and, as he was one of my closest friends, I visited him at his house to offer my condolence. Finding him overcome with grief, I tried to comfort him, saying: 'Have patience, my friend. Allah in His great bounty may soon give you another wife as loving and as worthy as the one He has taken from you. May He lighten your sorrow and prolong your years!'

But he never raised his eyes from the ground.

'Alas!' he sighed. 'How can you wish me a long life when I have but a few hours to live?'

'Take heart, my friend,' I said, 'why do you speak of death when, thank Allah, you are in perfect health, sound in mind and body?'

'In a few hours,' he replied, 'I shall be consigned to the earth with the body of my wife. It is an ancient custom in this country that when a wife dies her husband is buried with her, and if he should die first his wife is buried with him: both must leave this world together.'

'By Allah,' I cried in horror, 'this is a most barbarous custom! No civilized people could ever tolerate such monstrous cruelty!'

Whilst we were talking, my neighbour's friends and kinsfolk, together with a large crowd, came into the house and began to condole with him upon his wife's and his own impending death. Presently the funeral preparations were completed; the woman's body was laid in a coffin, and a long procession of mourners, headed by the husband, formed outside the house. And we all set out towards the burial ground.

The procession halted at the foot of a steep mound overlooking the sea, where a stone was rolled away from the mouth of a deep pit, and into this pit the corpse was thrown. Next the mourners laid hold of my friend and lowered him by a long rope, together with seven loaves of bread and a pitcher of water. Then the stone was rolled back and we all returned to the city.

I hastened with a heavy heart to the King's palace, and when I was admitted to his presence I fell on my knees before him, crying: 'My noble master, I have visited many far countries and lived amongst all manner of men, but in all my life I have never seen or heard of anything so barbarous as your custom of burying the living with the dead. Are strangers, too, subject to this law, your majesty?'

'Certainly they are,' he replied. 'They must be interred with their dead wives. It is a time-hallowed custom to which all must submit.'

At this reply I felt as though my gall-bladder would burst open. I ran in haste to my own house, dreading lest my wife should have died since I last saw her. Finding her in perfect health, I comforted myself as best I could with the thought that I might one day find means of returning to my own country, or even die before my wife.

But Allah ordained otherwise. Soon afterwards my wife was stricken with an illness and in a few days surrendered her soul to the Merciful.

The King and all his courtiers came to my house to comfort me. The body of my wife was perfumed and arrayed in fine robes and rich ornaments. And when all was ready for the burial I was led behind the bier, at the head of a long procession.

When we came to the mound, the stone was lifted from the mouth of the pit and the body of my wife thrown in; then the mourners gathered round to bid me farewell, paying no heed to my protests and entreaties. They bound me with a long rope and lowered me into the pit, together with the customary loaves and pitcher of water. Then they rolled back the stone and went their way.

When I touched the bottom of the pit I found myself in a vast cavern filled with skeletons and reeking with the foul stench of decaying corpses. I threw myself upon the earth, crying: 'You deserve this fate, Sindbad! Here you have come to pay the last penalty for your avarice, your insatiable greed! What need had you to marry in this island? Would that you had died on the bare mountains or perished in the merciless sea!'

Tormented by the vision of a protracted death, I lay in an agony of despair for many hours. At length, feeling the effects of thirst and hunger, I unfastened the loaves and the pitcher of water, and ate and drank sparingly. Then I lay in a corner which I had carefully cleared of bones.

For several days I languished in that charnel cave, and at length the time came when my provisions were exhausted. As I lay down, commending myself to Allah and waiting for my approaching end, the covering of the pit was suddenly lifted and there appeared at its mouth a crowd of mourners, who presently lowered into the cavern a dead man accompanied by his screaming wife, together with seven loaves and a pitcher of water.

As soon as the stone was rolled back I rose and, snatching up a leg-bone from one of the skeletons, sprang upon the woman and dealt her a violent blow upon the head, so that she fell down lifeless upon the instant. Then I stole her provisions, which kept me alive for several days longer. When these in turn were finished, the stone was once again rolled away from the pit and a man lowered in with his dead wife. He, too, met the same end as the unfortunate woman before him.

In this way I lived on for many weeks, killing every new-comer and eating his food. One day, as I was sleeping in my accustomed place, I was awakened by a sound of movement near by. At once I sprang to my feet, and picking up my weapon followed the noise closely along until I could faintly discern the form of some animal scurrying before me. As I pressed forward in pursuit of the strange intruder, stumbling in the dark over the bones and corpses, I suddenly made out at the far side of the cavern a tremulous speck of light which grew

larger and brighter as I advanced towards it. When I
had reached the end of the cave the fleeing animal leapt
through the light and disappeared. To my inexpressible
joy, I realized that I had come upon a tunnel which the
wild beasts, attracted by the carrion in the cave, had
burrowed from the other side of the mound. I scrambled
into this tunnel, crawling on all fours, and soon found
myself at the foot of a high cliff, beneath the open
sky.

I fell upon my knees in prayer and thanked the Al-
mighty for my salvation. The warm and wholesome air
breathed new life into my veins, and I rejoiced to gaze
upon the loveliness of earth and sky.

Fortified with hope and courage, I made my way back
into the cave and brought out the store of food which
I had laid aside during my sojourn there. I also gathered
up all the jewels, pearls, and precious ornaments that I
could find upon the corpses, and, tying them in the
shrouds and garments of the dead, carried the bundles
to the seashore.

I remained there several days, surveying the horizon
from morning till night. One day, however, as I was sitting beneath a rock praying for a speedy rescue, I saw a
sail far off upon the ocean. I hoisted a winding-sheet
on my staff and waved it frantically as I ran up and down
the beach. The crew observed my signal, and a boat was
promptly sent off to fetch me.

'How did you find your way to this wild region?'
asked the captain in astonishment. 'I have never seen a
living man on this desolate spot in all the days of my
life.'

'Sir,' I replied, 'I was shipwrecked off this shore
many days ago. These bales are the remnants of my
goods which I managed to save.' And I kept the truth

from him, lest there should be some on board who were citizens of that island.

Then I took out a rare pearl from one of my packages and offered it to him. 'Pray accept this,' I said, 'as a token of my gratitude to you for saving my life.'

But the captain politely refused the gift. 'It is not our custom,' he said, 'to accept payment for a good deed. We have rescued many a shipwrecked voyager, fed him and clothed him and finally set him ashore with a little present of our own besides. Allah alone is the giver of rewards.'

I thanked him with all my heart and called down blessings upon him.

Then the ship resumed its voyage. And as we sailed from island to island and from sea to sea, I rejoiced at the prospect of seeing my native land again. At times, however, a memory of my sojourn with the dead would come back to me and I would be beside myself with terror.

At length, by the grace of Allah, we arrived safely in Basrah. I stayed a few days in that town, and then proceeded up the river to Baghdad. Loaded with treasure, I hastened to my own house, where I was rapturously welcomed by my friends and kinsfolk. I sold for a fabulous sum the precious stones I had brought back from that barbarous city, and gave lavish alms to widows and orphans.

That is the story of my fourth voyage. To-morrow, if Allah wills, I shall recount to you the adventures of my fifth voyage.

When the evening feast was over, Sindbad the Sailor gave Sindbad the Porter a hundred pieces of gold, and the company took leave of their host and departed, marvelling at all they had heard. Next morning the porter returned, and when the other guests had assembled, Sindbad the Sailor began:

The Fifth Voyage of Sindbad the Sailor

KNOW, my friends, that the gay and voluptuous life which I led after my return soon made me forget the suffering I had endured in the Land of the Cannibals and in the Cavern of the Dead. I remembered only the pleasures of adventure and the considerable gains which my travels had earned me, and once again longed to sail new seas and explore new lands. I equipped myself with commodities suitable for ready sale in foreign countries and, packing them in bales, took them to Basrah.

One day, as I was walking along the wharf, I saw a newly built ship with tall masts and fine new sails which at once caught my fancy. I bought her outright, and embarked in her my slaves and merchandise. Then I hired an experienced captain and a well-trained crew, and accepted as passengers several other merchants who offered to pay their fares beforehand.

Blessed with a favourable wind, we voyaged many days and nights, trading from sea to sea and from shore to shore, and at length came to a desert island where we caught sight of a solitary white dome, half-buried in the sand. This I recognized at once as a roc's egg; and the passengers begged leave to land, so that they might go near and gaze upon this prodigy.

As ill luck would have it, however, the light-hearted merchants found no better sport than to throw great stones at the egg. When the shell was broken, the passengers, who were determined to have a feast, dragged

F

out the young bird and cut it up in pieces. Then they returned on board to tell me of their adventure.

I was filled with horror and cried: 'We are lost! The parent birds will now pursue our ship with implacable rage and destroy us all!'

Scarcely had I finished speaking when the sun was suddenly hidden from our view as by a great cloud and the world grew dark around us as the rocs came flying home. On finding their egg broken and their offspring destroyed, the birds uttered deafening cries; they took to the air again, and in a twinkling vanished from sight.

'All aboard, quickly!' I exclaimed. 'We must at once fly from this island!'

The captain weighed anchor and with all speed we sailed off towards the open sea. But before long the world grew dark again, and in the ominous twilight we could see the gigantic birds hovering high overhead, each carrying in its talons an enormous rock. When they were directly above us, one of them let fall its missile, which narrowly missed the ship and made such a chasm in the ocean that for a moment we could see the sandy bottom. The waves rose mountain-high, tossing us up and down. Presently the other bird dropped its rock, which hit the stern and sent the rudder flying into twenty pieces. Those of us who were not crushed to death were hurled into the sea and swallowed up by the giant waves.

Through the grace of Allah I managed to cling to a floating piece of wreckage. Sitting astride this, I paddled with my feet, and, aided by wind and current, at length reached the shore of an island.

I threw myself upon the sand and lay down awhile to recover my breath. Then I rose and wandered about the island, which was as beautiful as one of the gardens of

Eden. The air was filled with the singing of birds, and wherever I turned my eyes I saw trees loaded with luscious fruit and crystal brooks meandering among banks of flowers. I refreshed myself with the fruit and water, and when evening came lay down upon the grass.

Early next morning I rose and set off to explore this solitary garden. After a long stroll among the trees I came to a rivulet where, to my astonishment, I saw, seated upon the bank, a decrepit old man cloaked in a mantle of leaves.

Taking him for a shipwrecked mariner like myself, I went up to him and wished him peace; but he replied only by a mournful nod. I asked him what luckless accident had cast him in that place, but instead of answering he entreated me with signs to take him upon my shoulders and carry him across the brook. I readily bent down and, lifting him upon my back, waded through the stream. When I reached the opposite bank I stooped again for him to get off; but instead of alighting the old wretch powerfully threw his legs, which I now saw were covered with a rough black skin like a buffalo's, round my neck and crossed them tightly over my chest. Seized with fear, I desperately tried to shake him off, but the monster pressed his thighs tighter and tighter round my throat until I could no longer breathe. The world darkened before my eyes and with a choking cry I fell senseless to the ground.

When I came to myself I found the old monster still crouching upon my shoulders, although he had now sufficiently relaxed his hold to allow me to breathe. As soon as he saw that I had recovered my senses he pushed one foot against my belly and, violently kicking my side with the other, forced me to rise and walk under some trees. He leisurely plucked the fruits and ate them, and every time I stopped against his will or failed to do his bidding he kicked me hard, so that I had no choice but to obey him. All day long he remained seated upon my shoulders, and I was no better than a captive slave; at night he made me lie down with him, never for one moment loosening his hold round my neck. Next morning he roused me with a kick and ordered me to carry him among the trees.

Thus he stayed rooted upon my back, discharging his natural filth upon me, and driving me relentlessly on from glade to glade. I cursed the charitable impulse which prompted me to help him, and longed for death to deliver me from my evil plight.

After many weeks of abject servitude I chanced one day to come upon a field where gourds were growing in abundance. Under one of the trees I found a large gourd which was sun-dried and empty. I picked it up and, after cleaning it thoroughly, squeezed into it the juice of several bunches of grapes; then, carefully stopping the hole which I had cut into its shell, left it in the sun to ferment.

When I returned with the old man a few days afterwards, I found the gourd filled with the purest wine. The drink gave me fresh vigour, and I presently began to feel so light and gay that I went tripping merrily among the trees, scarcely aware of my loathsome burden.

Perceiving the effect of the wine, my captor asked me to let him taste it. I did not dare to refuse. He took the gourd from my hand, and raising it to his lips gulped down the liquor to the dregs. When he was overcome with the wine, he began to sway from side to side and his legs gradually relaxed their clasp round my neck. With one violent jerk of my shoulders I hurled him to the ground, where he lay motionless. Then I quickly picked up a great stone from among the trees and, falling upon the old fiend with all my strength, crushed his skull to pieces and mingled his flesh with his blood. That was the end of my tormentor: may Allah have no mercy upon him!

Overjoyed at my new freedom, I roamed the island for many weeks, eating of its fruit and drinking from its springs. One day, however, as I sat on the shore musing on the vicissitudes of my life and recalling memories of my native land, I saw, to my great joy, a sail heading towards the island. On reaching the beach the vessel anchored, and the passengers went ashore to fill their pitchers with water.

I ran in haste to meet them. They were greatly astonished to see me and gathered round, inquiring who I was and whence I had come. I recounted to them all that had befallen me since my arrival, and they replied: 'It is a marvel that you had escaped from that fiend; for you must know that the monster who had crouched upon your shoulders was none other than the Old Man of the Sea. You are the first ever to escape alive from his clutches. Praise be to Allah for your deliverance!'

They took me to their ship, where the captain received me kindly and listened with astonishment to my adventure. Then we set sail, and after voyaging many days and nights cast anchor in the harbour of a city perched on a high cliff, which is known among travellers as the City of Apes on account of the hosts of monkeys that infest it by night.

I went ashore with one of the merchants from the ship and wandered about the town in search of some employment. We soon fell in with a crowd of men proceeding to the gates of the city with sacks of pebbles on their shoulders. At the sight of these men my friend the merchant gave me a large cotton bag, saying: 'Fill this with pebbles and follow these people into the forest. Do exactly as they do, and thus you will earn your livelihood.'

Following his instructions, I filled the sack with pebbles and joined the crowd. The merchant recommended me to them, saying: 'Here is a shipwrecked stranger; teach him to earn his bread and Allah will reward you.'

When we had marched a great distance from the city we came to a vast valley, covered with coconut-trees so straight and tall that no man could ever climb them. Drawing nearer, I saw among the trees innumerable monkeys, which fled at our approach and swiftly climbed up to the fruit-laden branches.

Here my companions set down their bags and began to pelt the apes with pebbles; and I did the same. The furious beasts retaliated by pelting us with coconuts, and these we gathered up and put into our sacks. When they were full we returned to the city and sold the nuts in the market-place.

Thenceforth I went out every day to the forest with the coconut hunters and traded profitably with the fruit. When I had saved enough money for my homeward voyage I took leave of my friend the merchant and embarked in a vessel bound for Basrah, taking with me a large cargo of coconuts and other produce of that city.

In the course of our voyage we stopped at many heathen islands, where I sold some of my coconuts at a substantial profit and exchanged others for cinnamon, pepper, and Chinese and Comarin aloes. On reaching the Sea of Pearls I engaged several divers into my service; and in a short time brought up a large quantity of priceless pearls.

After that we again set sail and, voyaging many days and nights, at length safely arrived in Basrah. I spent but a few days in that town, and then, loaded with treasure, set out for Baghdad. I rejoiced to be back in my native city, and hastening to my old street, entered my own house, where all my friends and kinsmen foregathered to greet me. I gave them gold and countless presents, and bestowed a large sum in charity among the widows and orphans.

That is the story of my fifth voyage. To-morrow, my friends, if Allah wills, I shall recount to you the tale of my sixth voyage.

When the evening feast was ended, Sindbad the Sailor gave Sindbad the Porter a hundred pieces of gold, and the company departed, marvelling at all they had heard.

Next morning the porter returned, and when the other guests had arrived, Sindbad the Sailor began:

The Sixth Voyage of Sindbad the Sailor

I was one day reclining at my ease in the comfort and felicity of a serene life, when a band of merchants who had just returned from abroad called at my house to give me news of foreign lands. The sight of these travellers recalled to my mind how great was the joy of returning from a far journey to be united with friends and kinsmen after a prolonged absence; and soon afterwards I made preparations for another voyage and set sail with a rich cargo from Basrah.

We voyaged leisurely many days and nights, buying and selling wherever the ship anchored and exploring the unfamiliar places at which we called. One day, however, as we were sailing in mid-ocean, we suddenly heard the captain of our ship burst out in a loud lament. He beat himself about the face, tore at his beard, and hurled his turban on the deck. We gathered round him, inquiring the cause of his violent grief.

'Alas, we are lost!' he cried. 'The ship has been driven off its course into an unknown ocean, where nothing can save us from final wreck but Allah's mercy. Let us pray to Him!'

Then, quickly rising, the captain climbed the mast to trim the sails, while the passengers fell on their knees weeping and bidding each other farewell. Scarcely had he reached the top when a violent gale arose, sweeping us swiftly along and dashing the ship against a craggy shore at the foot of a high mountain. At once the vessel split to pieces and we were all flung into the raging sea. Some were drowned outright, while others, like myself, managed to escape by clinging to the jutting rocks.

We found scattered all along the shore the remains of other wrecks, and the sands were strewn with countless bales from which rare merchandise and costly ornaments had broken loose. I wandered among these treasures for many hours, and then, winding my way through the rocks, suddenly came upon a river which flowed from a gorge in the mountain. I followed its course with my eyes and was surprised to find that instead of running into the sea, the river plunged into a vast rocky cavern and disappeared. The banks were covered with glittering jewels, and the bed was studded with myriads of rubies, emeralds, and other precious stones; so that the entire river blazed with a dazzling light. The rarest Chinese and Comarin aloe grew on the adjacent steeps, and liquid amber trickled down the rocks onto the beach below. Great whales would come out of the sea and drink of this amber; but, their bellies being gradually heated, they would at length disgorge it upon the surface of the water. There it would crystallize, and after changing its colour and other properties would finally be washed ashore, its rich perfume scenting the entire region.

Those of us who had escaped drowning lay in a sorrowful plight upon the shore, counting the days as they dragged by and waiting for the approach of death. One by one my companions died as they came to the end of their provisions, and we who were left washed the dead, and wrapped them in winding sheets made from the fabrics scattered on the shore, and buried them. Then my friends were stricken with a sickness of the belly, caused by the humid air, to which they all succumbed; and I had the melancholy task of burying with my own hands the last of my companions.

Realizing that death was at hand, I threw myself upon the earth, wailing: 'Would that I had died before my friends! There would at least have remained good comrades who would have washed my body and given it a decent burial! There is no strength nor help save in Allah!'

At length I rose and dug a deep grave by the sea, thinking to myself: 'When I sense the approach of death I will lie here and die in my grave. In time the wind will bury me with sand.' And as I thus prepared to meet my end, I cursed myself for venturing yet again upon the perils of the sea after having suffered so many misfortunes in my past voyages. 'Why,' I cried in my despair, 'O why were you not content to remain safe and happy in Baghdad? Had you not enough riches to last you twice a lifetime?'

Lost in these reflections, I wandered to the banks of

the river, and as I watched it disappear into the cavern
I struck upon a plan. 'By Allah,' I thought, 'this river
must have both a beginning and an end. If it enters the
mountain on this side it must surely emerge into day-
light again; and if I can but follow its course in some
vessel, the current may at last bring me to some in-
habited land. If I am destined to survive this peril,
Allah will guide me to safety; if I perish, it will not be
worse than the dismal fate which awaits me here.'

Emboldened by these thoughts, I collected some large
branches of Chinese and Comarin aloes and, laying these
on some planks from the wrecked vessels, bound them
with strong cables into a raft. This I loaded with sacks
of rubies, pearls, and other stones, as well as several
bales of the choicest ambergris; then, commending myself to Allah, I launched the raft upon the water and
jumped aboard.

The current carried me swiftly along, and I soon
found myself enveloped in the brooding darkness of the
cavern. My raft began to bump violently against the ragged sides, while the passage grew smaller and narrower
until I was compelled to lie flat upon my belly for fear
of striking my head. Very soon I wished I could return
to the open shore, but the current became faster and
faster as the river swept headlong down its precipitous
bed, and I resigned myself to certain death. At length,
overcome by terror and exertion, I sank into a death-
like sleep.

I cannot tell how long I slept, but when I awoke
I found myself lying on my raft close to the river bank,
beneath the open sky. The river was flowing gently
through a stretch of pleasant meadowland, and on the
bank stood many Indians and Abyssinians.

As soon as these men saw that I was awake, they

gathered about me, asking questions in a language I did not understand. Presently one of their number came forward and greeted me in Arabic.

'Who may you be?' he asked, 'and whence have you come? We were working in our fields when we saw you drifting down the river. We fastened your raft to this bank and, not wishing to disturb your slumbers, left you here in safety. But tell us, what accident has cast you upon this river, which takes its perilous course from beneath that mountain?'

I begged him first to give me some food, and promised to answer all their questions after I had eaten. They instantly brought me a variety of meats, and when I had regained my strength a little, I recounted to them all that had befallen me since my shipwreck. They marvelled at my miraculous escape, and said: 'We must take you to our King, so that you may yourself tell him of your adventure.'

Thereupon they led me to their city, carrying my raft with all its contents upon their shoulders. The King received me courteously and, after listening in profound astonishment to my story, congratulated me heartily on my escape. Then, opening my treasures in his presence, I laid out at his feet a priceless choice of emeralds, pearls, and rubies. In return he conferred upon me the highest honours of the kingdom, and invited me to stay as his guest at the palace.

Thus I rose rapidly in the King's favour, and soon became a trusted courtier. One day he questioned me about my country and its far-famed Caliph. I praised the wisdom, piety, and benevolence of Haroun Al-Rashid, and spoke at length of his glorious deeds. The King was profoundly impressed by my account. 'This monarch,' he said, 'must indeed be illustrious. We desire to send him a present worthy of his greatness, and appoint you the bearer of it.'

'I hear and obey,' I replied. 'I will gladly deliver your gift to the Prince of the Faithful, and will inform him that in your majesty he has a worthy ally and a trusted friend.'

The King gave orders that a magnificent present be prepared and commissioned a new vessel for the voyage. When all was ready for departure I presented myself at the royal palace and, thanking the King for the many favours he had shown me, took leave of him and of the officers of his court.

Then I set sail, and voyaging many days and nights at length safely arrived in Basrah. I hastened to Baghdad with the royal gift, and when I had been admitted to the Caliph's presence, I kissed the ground before him and told him of my mission. Al-Rashid marvelled greatly at my adventure and gave orders that the story be inscribed on parchment in letters of gold, so that it might be preserved among the treasures of the kingdom.

Leaving his court, I hastened to my old street and, entering my own house, rejoiced to meet my friends and kinsfolk. I gave them gold and costly presents, and distributed lavish alms among the poor of the city.

Such is the story of my sixth voyage. To-morrow, my friends, I shall recount to you the tale of my seventh and last voyage.

When the evening feast was ended, Sindbad the Sailor gave Sindbad the Porter a hundred pieces of gold, and the guests departed, marvelling at all they had heard.

Next morning the porter returned, and when the other guests had assembled, Sindbad the Sailor began:

The Last Voyage of Sindbad the Sailor

FOR many years after my return I lived joyfully in Baghdad, feasting and carousing with my boon companions and revelling away the riches which my far-flung travels had earned me. But though I was now past the prime of life, my untamed spirit rebelled against my declining years, and I once again longed to see the world and travel in the lands of men. I made preparations for a long voyage and, boarding a good ship in company with some eminent merchants, set sail from Basrah with a fair wind and a rich cargo.

We voyaged peacefully for many weeks, but one day, whilst we were sailing in the China Sea, a violent tempest struck our ship, drenching us with torrents of rain. We hastily covered our bales with canvas to protect them from the wet, and fervently prayed to Allah to save us from the fury of the sea; while the captain, rolling up his sleeves and tucking the skirts of his robes into his belt, climbed the mast and from the top scanned the horizon in all directions. Presently he climbed down again, all in a tremble with terror, and, staring at us with an expression of blank despair, beat his face and plucked the hairs of his beard.

'Pray to Allah,' he cried, 'that He may save us from the peril into which we have fallen! Weep and say your farewells, for the treacherous wind has got the better of us and driven our ship into the world's farthermost ocean!'

Thereupon the captain opened one of his cabin chests and took from it a small cotton bag filled with an ash-like powder. He sprinkled some water over the powder and, after waiting a little, inhaled it into his nostrils;

then, opening a little book, he intoned aloud some strange incantations and at length turned to us, crying: 'Know that we are now approaching the Realm of Kings, the very land where our master Solomon son of David (may peace be upon him) lies buried. Serpents of prodigious size swarm about that coast, and the sea is filled with giant whales which can swallow vessels whole. Farewell, my friends; and may Allah have mercy upon us all!'

Scarcely had the captain uttered these words when suddenly the ship was tossed high up in the air and then flung down into the sea, while an ear-splitting cry, more terrible than thunder, boomed through the swelling ocean. Terror seized our hearts as we saw a gigantic whale, as massive as a mountain, rushing swiftly towards us, followed by another no less huge, and a third greater than the two put together. This last monster bounded from the surging billows and, opening wide its enormous mouth, seized in its jaws the ship with all that was in it. I hastily ran to the edge of the tilting deck and, casting off my clothes, leapt into the sea just before the whale swallowed up the ship and disappeared beneath the foam with its two companions.

With Allah's help I clung to a piece of timber which had fallen from the lost vessel and, contending with the mighty waves for two days and nights, was at length cast on an island covered with fruit-trees and watered by many streams. After refreshing myself I wandered aimlessly about, and soon came to a fast-flowing river which rolled its waters towards the interior of the island. As I stood upon the bank I hit upon the idea of building a raft and allowing myself to be carried down by the current, as I had done in my last voyage. 'If I succeed in saving myself this time,' I said, 'all will be well with me and I solemnly vow never in all my life to let the mere thought of voyaging cross my mind again. If I fail, I shall at last find rest from all the toils and tribulations which my incorrigible folly has earned me.'

I cut down several branches from an exotic tree which I had never seen before and bound them together into a raft with the stems of some creeping plants. I loaded the raft with a large quantity of fruit, and, commending myself to Allah, pushed off down the river.

For three days and nights I was hurried swiftly along by the current, until, overcome by dizziness, I sank into a dead faint. When I recovered consciousness I found myself heading towards a fearful precipice, down which the waters of the river were tumbling in a mighty cataract. I clung with all my strength to the branches of the raft and, resigning myself to my fate, prayed silently for a merciful end. When I had reached the very edge of the precipice, however, I suddenly felt the raft halted upon the water and found myself caught in a net which a crowd of men had thrown from the bank. My raft was quickly hauled to land, and I was released from the net half-dead with terror and exhaustion.

As I lay upon the mud, I gradually became aware of a venerable old man who was bending over me. He wrapped me in warm garments and greeted me kindly; and when my strength had returned a little he helped me to rise and led me slowly to the baths of the city, where I was washed with perfumed water. Then the old man took me to his own house. He regaled me sumptuously with excellent meats and wines, and when the feast was ended, his slaves washed my hands and wiped them with napkins of the rarest silk. After this my host conducted me to a noble chamber and left me alone after assigning several of his slaves to my service.

The kind old man entertained me in this fashion for three days. When I had completly recovered, he visited me in my chamber and sat conversing with me for an hour. Just before leaving my room, however, he turned to me and said: 'If you wish to sell your merchandise, my friend, I will gladly come down with you to the market-place.'

I was greatly puzzled at these words and did not know what to answer, as I had been cast utterly naked in that city.

'Do not be troubled over your goods, my son,' went on the old man. 'If we receive a good offer, we will sell them outright; if not, I will keep them for you in my own storehouse until they fetch a better price.'

Concealing my perplexity, I replied: 'I am willing to do whatever you advise.' With this I rose and went out with him to the market-place.

There I saw an excited crowd admiring an object on the ground with exclamations of enthusiastic praise. Pushing my way among the gesticulating merchants, I was astonished to find the centre of attention to be no other than the raft aboard which I had sailed down the river. And presently the old man ordered a broker to begin the auction.

'Who will make the first bid for this rare sandal-wood?' began the broker.

'A hundred dinars!' cried one of the merchants.

'A thousand!' shouted another.

'Eleven hundred!' exclaimed my host.

'Agreed!' I cried.

Upon this the old man ordered his slaves to carry the wood to his store and walked back with me to his house, where he paid me eleven hundred pieces of gold locked in an iron coffer.

One day, as we sat conversing together, the old man said: 'My son, pray grant me a favour.'

'With all my heart,' I replied.

'I am a very old man, and have not been blessed with a son,' went on my benefactor. 'Yet I have a young and beautiful daughter, who on my death will be sole mistress of my fortune. If you will have her for your wife, you will inherit my wealth and become chief of the merchants of this city.'

I readily consented to the sheikh's proposal. A sumptuous feast was held, a cadi and witnesses were called in, and I was married to the old man's daughter amidst great rejoicings. When the wedding guests had departed I was conducted to the bridal chamber, where I was allowed to see my wife for the first time. I found her incomparably beautiful, and rejoiced to see her decked with the rarest pearls and jewels.

My wife and I grew to love each other dearly, and we lived together in happiness and contentment. Not long afterwards my wife's father died, and I inherited all his possessions. His slaves became my slaves and his goods my goods, and the merchants of the city appointed me their chief in his place.

One day, however, I discovered that every year the people of that land experienced a wondrous change in their bodies. All the men grew wings upon their shoulders and for a whole day flew high up in the air, leaving their wives and children behind. Amazed at this prodigy, I importuned one of my friends to allow me to cling to him when he next took his flight, and at length prevailed on him to let me try this novel adventure. When the long-awaited day arrived, I took tight hold of my friend's waist and was at once carried up swiftly in the air. We climbed higher and higher into the void until I could hear the angels in their choirs singing hymns to Allah under the vault of heaven. Moved with awe, I cried: 'Glory and praise eternal be to Allah, King of the Universe!'

Scarcely had I uttered these words when my winged carrier dropped headlong through the air and finally alighted on the top of a high mountain. There he threw me off his back and took to the air again, calling down curses on my head. Abandoned upon this desolate mountain, I lifted my hands in despair and cried: 'There is no strength nor help save in Allah! Every time I escape from one ordeal I find myself in another as grievous. Surely I deserve all that befalls me!'

Whilst I was thus reflecting upon my plight, I saw two youths coming up towards me. Their faces shone with an unearthly beauty, and each held a staff of red gold in his hand. I at once rose to my feet, and, walking towards them, wished them peace. They returned my greeting courteously, and I inquired: 'Who are you, pray, and what object has brought you to this barren mountain?'

'We are worshippers of the True God,' they replied. With this, one of the youths pointed to a certain path upon the mountain and, handing me his staff, walked away with his companion.

Bewildered at these words, I set off in the direction he had indicated, leaning upon my gold staff as I walked. I had not gone far when I saw coming towards me the flyer who had so unceremoniously set me down upon the mountain. Determined to learn the reason of his displeasure, I went up to him and said gently: 'Is this how friends behave to friends?'

The winged man, who was now no longer angry, replied: 'Know that my fall was caused by your unfortunate mention of your god. The word has this effect upon us all, and this is why we never utter it.'

I assured my friend that I had meant no harm and promised to commit no such transgression in future. Then I begged him to carry me back to the city. He took me upon his shoulders and in a few moments set me down before my own house.

My wife was overjoyed at my return, and when I told her of my adventure, she said: 'We must no longer stay among these people. Know that they are the brothers of Satan and have no knowledge of the True God.'

'How then did your father dwell amongst them?' I asked.

'My father was of an alien race,' she replied. 'He shared none of their creeds, and he did not lead their life. As he is now dead, let us sell our possessions and leave this blasphemous city.'

Thereupon I resolved to return home. We sold our houses and other property, and hiring a vessel set sail with a rich cargo.

Aided by a favouring wind, we voyaged many days and nights and at length came to Basrah and thence to Baghdad, the City of Peace. I conveyed to my stores the valuables I had brought with me, and, taking my wife to my own house in my old street, rejoiced to meet my kinsfolk and my old companions. They told me that this voyage had kept me abroad for nearly twenty-seven years, and marvelled exceedingly at all that had befallen me.

I rendered deep thanks to Allah for bringing me safely back to my friends and kinsfolk, and solemnly vowed never to travel again by sea or land. Such, dear guests, was the last and longest of my voyages.

When the evening feast was ended, Sindbad the Sailor gave Sindbad the Porter a hundred pieces of gold, which he took with thanks and blessings and departed, marvelling at all he had heard.

The porter remained a constant visitor at the house of his illustrious friend, and the two lived in amity and peace until there came to them the Spoiler of worldly mansions, the Dark Steward of the graveyard; the Shadow which dissolves the bonds of friendship and ends alike all joys and all sorrows.

THE TALE OF
KAFUR THE BLACK EUNUCH

❦

Know, my friends, that when no more than eight years of age I had already cultivated a remarkable habit of telling one big lie a year.

Unable to bear with me any longer, my old master, who was a slave merchant, decided to sell me. He took me to his broker and ordered him to cry through the market-place: 'Who will buy a little slave with one fault?'

While the broker was thus declaiming the terms of the bargain, a certain merchant came forward and inquired what my fault might be. He was told that I lied once a year, and he finally agreed to buy me, fault and all, for the moderate sum of six hundred dirhams. Thereupon the broker took me to the merchant's house, and departed after receiving his commission.

My new master clad me in a fine suit of clothes, and I remained in his service for the rest of that year. With the new year the merchants hailed a season of fruitfulness and abundance, regaling each other at convivial feasts. When his turn came, my master made elaborate preparations for a pleasure-trip to a garden not far from the city. On the appointed day he and his guests went there and sat eating and carousing till noon, when my master, having forgotten something at his house, ordered me to ride back and return with it post-haste.

At once I mounted my mule and set out on my errand. But as soon as I drew near the house, I began to cry out and to shed a flood of tears. The neighbours, old and young, flocked around me; and, hearing my cries, my master's wife and daughters rushed to the door and asked me what had happened. With tears running down my face, I sobbed: 'My master and his guests were sitting in the garden beneath an old wall, and the wall fell down on them and crushed them to death. I mounted my mule and came with all speed to tell you.'

When they heard this, my master's wife and daughters shrieked and rent their clothes and beat their faces, while the neighbours thronged around to comfort them. My mistress proceeded to mourn her husband's death in a noble fashion. She set the entire house in chaos, smashing up the furniture, tearing down the doors and the windows, and smearing the walls with mud and soot. When half the business of destruction had been accomplished, she cried out to me to help her in the mourning rites. I gladly offered my services, setting myself the task of making havoc of all that remained. I knocked out the cupboards, pulled down the shelves with all that stood upon them, shattered to fragments the vessels and the china, and went around battering at the walls and the ceilings until the whole house lay in ruin. And all the while I cried: 'My master, oh, my master!'

Then my mistress rushed out into the street, with face unveiled and tresses flowing, followed by all her sons and daughters. 'Come, Kafur,' they cried, 'lead us to the place where your master lies buried, so that we may take him from beneath the ruins, and lay him in a coffin, and give him a fitting funeral!'

So I marched ahead of them, crying out: 'My master, oh, my master!'

A great multitude of men, women, and children followed at our heels, all beating their faces and joining in a chorus of shrill lament. I led them at an easy pace from one end of the city to the other; and as we advanced from street to street, more and more people joined the procession, crying, when they learnt of the tragedy: 'There is no strength nor help save in Allah!'

Just before we reached the gates of the city, some neighbours counselled my mistress to report the disaster to the Governor. When he heard the news, the Governor rose at once and, ordering some labourers to follow him with spades and baskets, joined the vast crowd; and they all resumed the march towards the garden.

Wailing aloud, beating my face, and scattering dust upon my head, I ran on as fast as I could go until I left the mourners far behind me. As soon as I approached the gates of the garden, I began to howl: 'My mistress, oh, my mistress! Who will ever be as kind to me as my poor, dead mistress!'

Alarmed at my lament, my master rushed out to meet me. He cried: 'In Allah's name, Kafur, what has happened?'

'Sir,' I replied, 'when I reached home, I found that the walls of the house had fallen down upon my mistress and her children.'

My master stood aghast.

'But my wife!' he exclaimed. 'Was she not saved?'

'Alas, she was not,' I answered. 'They were all crushed beneath the ruins; your eldest daughter was the first to die.'

'But my youngest girl!' he cried. 'Did she not escape?'

'Alas, she did not,' I replied.

'And what became of my mule?' he then cried. 'Is she safe?'

'No, by Allah,' I answered. 'The walls of both the house and the stable collapsed and buried beneath them every living thing, even the sheep, the geese, and the hens. Nothing is now left but a heap of decaying flesh.'

'But my eldest son?' he exclaimed.

'Dead, dead!' I moaned. 'Not a trace is left of house or family. As for the sheep, the geese, and the hens, the cats and dogs of the entire neighbourhood are even now devouring their dead flesh.'

The world darkened before my master's eyes. Stunned by the terrible news and trembling all over, he could scarcely stand upright and was like one suddenly stricken with the palsy. He rent his clothes, tore his beard, hurled his turban to the ground, and beat his face until his cheeks were covered with blood. 'My wife!' he cried out. 'My children! Oh, my great sorrow!'

His friends the merchants gathered around him, wailing and tearing their clothes.

Still beating himself about the head with great violence, my master staggered forward towards the road, followed by his guests. Scarcely had he reached the gates of the garden, when he saw in the distance a great cloud of dust, from which proceeded cries of wild lamentation. And soon the Governor appeared with my master's family, together with the rest of the mourners.

My master was confounded at the sight of his own wife and children hurrying towards him. For a moment he stood speechless, and then broke out into a fit of laughter.

'Thank Allah you are alive!' shouted his wife and children, throwing themselves upon him.

'Thank Allah you are safe!' exclaimed my master.

'But how were you rescued from beneath the ruins of the wall, you and your friends the merchants?' cried his wife.

'What happened to you in the house?' asked my master.

'We are all safe and well,' answered his wife. 'Nothing has happened save that your servant Kafur came to us unturbaned and with his clothes all torn, telling us that the garden wall had fallen upon you and killed you.'

'But, by Allah,' burst out my master, 'Kafur came to me just now and told me that you were all crushed beneath the ruins of the house!'

Here my master turned round and saw me still wailing and throwing dust upon my bare head. He beckoned me to draw near, crying: 'Ill-omened slave, son of a pitch-faced whore, damned offspring of a monstrous race, what is the reason of this fiendish act? By Allah, I will flay your skin from your flesh and tear your flesh from your bones!'

'Upon my life,' I retorted, 'you can do no such thing. You have bought me with my fault; and there are honest men who will bear witness that you did so knowing that my fault was the telling of one lie a year. Now this, let me hasten to add, is only half a lie. The other half shall be told before the year is out.'

'Dog, and son of a dog!' exclaimed my master. 'Do you call that half a lie? Why, it is an entire calamity! By Allah, let the world note, I free you here and now: you are no more slave of mine!'

'By Allah,' I rejoined, 'if you are willing to free me, I will not free you until my year is ended and I have treated you to the other half of my lie. Then, and only then, you can take me to the market-place and sell me. But you must sell me with my fault. Free me you cannot, for I know no trade with which to earn a living. Such is the law of the land.'

While we were thus arguing, the great crowd, headed by the Governor and his men, gathered around us. My master and the other merchants explained what had happened, adding: 'This, mark you, is only half a lie.'

The crowd marvelled greatly, but everyone said that it was a whole lie, and a big one. So they reviled me and showered curses on my head, while I stood grinning at them.

'How can my master punish me,' I laughed triumphantly, 'when he bought me with my fault?'

When at last we returned to the town and entered the quarter where my master lived, he found a heap of ruins where his house once stood. But my mistress chose to forget her own exploits and told him that I had done all the damage.

'Son of a whore!' he cried, foaming with rage. 'If this was only half a lie, what would have happened if you had told a whole one? A couple of cities, I suppose, would have been levelled to the ground!'

With that he dragged me to the Governor's house, where I was treated to such a trouncing that I at length dropped down unconscious. Whilst I was lying senseless they called in a barber, who cut off my testicles and cauterized the wound: so that when I recovered my senses I found myself a eunuch with nothing left. My master wagged his finger at me with evident satisfaction, saying: 'You have taken away from me things that I valued dearly: I have taken away from you things which you held most precious.'

Soon afterwards, he took me to the market-place and sold me at an enormous profit, for I was now a eunuch.

Thus I continued to bring trouble and misfortune to

every household that employed me until at length I entered the service of the Prince of the Faithful. But now, alas, my old spirit is broken; for I have lost much of my youthful vigour since I became a eunuch.

That, my friends, is the story of my castration; and peace be with you.

THE TALE OF
KHALIFAH THE FISHERMAN

ONCE upon a time, in the reign of the Caliph Haroun Al-Rashid, there lived in the city of Baghdad a fisherman who was so poor that he could not afford to take even one woman in marriage. He was called Khalifah.

It so happened one morning that he took his net upon his back and went down to the river, before the other fishermen arrived. When he reached the bank he rolled up his sleeves and tucked his skirt into his belt; then he spread his net and cast it into the water. He cast his net ten times, but did not catch a single fish. In despair he threw himself upon the river bank, crying: 'There is no strength nor help save in Allah! He gives bread to whom He will, and denies it to whom He pleases.' Then thought Khalifah: 'Trusting in Allah, I will cast my net once more.'

So saying, he rose and, wading knee-deep into the water, threw his net as far as his arms could send it. He waited a long time, and then pulled hard on the cords. But when at last he managed, with much skill and effort, to haul the heavy net ashore, he was astonished to find in it a lame, one-eyed ape. His astonishment, however, soon gave way to anger. He tied the ape to a tree upon the river bank, and would have fallen upon the beast with his whip had not Allah made the ape speak with an eloquent tongue.

'Stay your hand, Khalifah,' said the ape, 'and do not whip me. Leave me tied here to this tree and cast your net again. Allah will give you all that you desire.'

On hearing the ape's words, the fisherman once more spread his net and cast it into the water. Shortly afterwards he felt the net grow heavy; but when he had succeeded in bringing it to land, he found in it another ape of even more grotesque appearance. His eyelids were darkened with kohl, his hands dyed with henna, and he wore a tattered vest about his middle. His front teeth, set wide apart, gleamed as he stared at the fisherman with an awkward grin.

'Praise be to Allah who has changed the fishes of the river into apes!' exclaimed the amazed Khalifah. Then, running towards the first beast, he cried: 'Look upon the fruit of your counsel, monster of ill omen! I began the day with the sight of your deformity and I shall doubtless end it in starvation and ruin.'

He lifted his whip high above his head and was again about to fall upon the one-eyed ape, when the beast begged him for mercy, crying: 'Spare me, Khalifah, in the name of Allah! Go to my brother: he will give you good advice.'

The bewildered fisherman flung away his whip and turned to the second ape, who said: 'If you mark my counsel and do my bidding, Khalifah, you shall prosper.'

'What would you have me do?' asked the fisherman.

'Leave me on this bank,' said the second ape, 'and once more cast your net.'

Khalifah spread his net again and cast it into the water. He waited patiently, and when he felt the net grow heavy, he gently hauled it in, only to find in it yet another ape. His hair was red, his eyelids lengthened with kohl, his hands and feet dyed with henna, and he wore a blue vest about his middle.

'Glory to Allah, King of the Universe!' exclaimed Khalifah when he saw the third ape. 'Surely this is a blessed day from first to last! It began with a sinister-looking monkey; and if the purport of a scroll can be divined from its title, this must indeed be a day of monkeys! There is not a single fish left in the river and we shall catch nothing to-day but apes!' Then, turning to the red-haired beast, he cried: 'In heaven's name what are you?'

'Do you not know me, Khalifah?' replied the ape.

'I do not, indeed,' protested the fisherman.

'Know, then,' said the beast, 'that I am the ape of Abu Sa'adah the Jew, chief of the money-changers. To me he owes his good fortune and all his riches. On greeting me in the morning he gains five pieces of gold, and on bidding me good-night he gains five more.'

'Mark that,' said Khalifah, turning to the first ape. '*You* cannot boast of such liberality: seeing your face this morning has brought me nothing but ill luck!'

'Leave my brother in peace, Khalifah,' said the red-haired ape, 'and cast your net once more into the river. Then come back and show me your catch. I shall instruct you how to use it to your best advantage.'

'I hear and obey, King of all monkeys!' answered the fisherman.

Khalifah did as the ape told him, and when he drew in his net he rejoiced to find a splendid fish with a large head, broad fins, and eyes that glittered like gold coins. Marvelling at the quaintness of his prize, he carried it to the red-haired ape and showed it to him.

'Now gather some fresh grass,' said the beast, 'and spread it at the bottom of your basket: lay the fish upon it and cover it with more grass. Then carry the basket to the city of Baghdad. Should anyone speak to you on your way, you must make no answer, but proceed directly to the market of the money-changers. In the midst of it stands the shop of Abu Sa'adah the Jew, chief of the money-changers. You will find him seated on a mattress with an embroidered cushion at his back, surrounded by his slaves and servants. In front of him you will see two coffers, one for gold and one for silver. Go up to him, and set your basket before him, and say: "Sir, I went down to the Tigris this morning and in your name cast my net. Allah sent me this fish." He will ask: "Have you shown it to any other man?" "No, by Allah," you must answer. Then he will take the fish and offer you one dinar. You must refuse to sell it for that price. He will offer you two dinars, but you must still refuse. Whatever he offers, you must not accept, though it be the fish's weight in gold. He will ask: "What, then, would you have?" And you will reply: "I will sell this fish only for a few plain words." "What are they?" he will ask, and you will answer: "Stand up and say: 'Bear witness, all who are present in this market, that I give Khalifah the fisherman my ape in exchange for his ape, and that I barter my fortune for his fortune.' That is the price of my fish: I demand no gold." If the Jew consents to this,' continued the red-haired ape, 'you will become my master; I will bless you every morning and every evening, and you will every day gain ten pieces of gold. As for Abu Sa'adah, he will be cursed with the sight of my lame, one-eyed brother, and daily afflicted with extortionate tolls and taxes until he is reduced to beggary. Bear in mind what I have told you, Khalifah, and you shall prosper.'

'I will obey you in every particular, royal ape!' said

the fisherman. He unbound the three beasts, who leapt into the water and disappeared.

Khalifah washed the fish, placed it in his basket upon some fresh grass, and covered it over. Then he set out for the city, singing merrily.

As he made his way through the streets of Baghdad, many people greeted him and asked him if he had any fish to sell. But he walked on, heeding no one, until he entered the market of the money-changers and stopped before the shop of Abu Sa'adah the Jew. The fisherman found him surrounded by numerous servants, who were attending him with such ceremony as can be found only in the royal courts of Khorasan. He went up to him and stood before him.

'What can we do for you, Khalifah?' asked Abu Sa'adah. 'If any man has wronged or slandered you, we will gladly take up your cause with the Governor, and you shall have justice.'

'Chief of the Jews,' replied Khalifah, 'I come to you with no such grievance. This morning I went down to the Tigris, and in your name cast my net. I caught this fish.'

Khalifah opened the basket and proudly held out the fish to the money-changer.

'By the Five Books of Moses, the Psalms, and the Ten Commandments,' cried the delighted Jew, 'a holy man appeared to me in a dream last night, saying: "You shall receive a present from me to-morrow." This must be the present; only tell me, on your life, have you shown this fish to any other man?'

'I swear by Allah, chief of the Jews,' replied the fisherman, 'and by the honoured memory of Abu Bakr, that no one else has seen it.'

When he heard this the Jew turned to one of his

slaves and said: 'Take this fish to my house and ask my
daughter to have it dressed for dinner: tell her to fry
one half and to grill the other.'

'Do you hear, my lad?' echoed Khalifah. 'Tell your
mistress to fry one half and to grill the other. Tell her
it is a most excellent fish.'

'I hear and obey,' answered the slave, and departed
with it to his master's house.

The Jew took a dinar from one of his coffers and
offered it to Khalifah, saying: 'Spend this on your family.' Now Khalifah, who had never before earned such
a sum for a single day's labour, impulsively held out his
hand and took the coin. But as he was about to leave the
money-changer, he remembered the ape's instructions.

'Take your dinar and give me back my fish,' he cried,
throwing down the coin before the Jew. 'Would you
make a laughing-stock of me?'

Thinking that the fisherman was jesting with him,
the Jew smiled and handed him three dinars; but Khalifah refused the gold, saying: 'Since when have you
known me to sell my fish for such a trifle?'

The Jew then gave him five dinars and said: 'Take
these and do not be greedy.'

The fisherman took the five dinars and left the shop,
scarcely believing his eyes. 'Glory be to Allah!' he
thought. 'The Caliph himself has not as much gold in
his coffers as I have in my purse to-day!' It was not until
he had reached the end of the market-place, however,
that he remembered the ape's advice. He hurried back
to the Jew and again threw down the coins before him.

'What has come over you, Khalifah?' asked Abu
Sa'adah. 'Would you rather have the money in silver?'

'I want neither your gold nor your silver,' returned
the fisherman. 'Give me back my fish.'

G

'I have given you five dinars for a fish that is not worth one dirham,' cried the money-changer impatiently, 'and yet you are not satisfied. In heaven's name what is your price?'

'A few plain words,' replied Khalifah.

When he heard this the Jew grew so angry that his eyes sank into their sockets. 'You nail-paring of the Moslems!' he exclaimed, grinding his teeth with rage. 'Would you have me give up my faith, renounce my religion, and disavow the laws of my holy ancestors for a mere fish?' Then, turning to his slaves, he cried: 'Take hold of this rascal and beat him soundly!'

The slaves immediately set upon the fisherman and beat him until their master cried: 'Enough!' But as soon as they let go of him, Khalifah rose to his feet as though he felt no pain at all.

'Sir,' said the fisherman, 'you should have known that Khalifah can take more blows than ten donkeys put together.'

At this the Jew laughed heartily, and said: 'Enough of this fooling. How much do you wish me to pay you?'

'I ask only for a few brief words,' repeated Khalifah, 'and these have nothing to do with your religion; for if you were to become a Moslem, your conversion would neither benefit the Moslems nor harm the Jews; and if you persist in your error, your heresy will neither benefit the Jews nor harm the Moslems. I wish you only to rise up and say: "Bear witness, all who are present in this market, that I give Khalifah the fisherman my ape in exchange for his ape, and that I barter my fortune for his fortune."'

'Nothing can be easier than that,' said the Jew. And he instantly rose to his feet and proclaimed the words in

the market-place. Then, turning to Khalifah, he asked:
'Is there any other thing that I am required to do?'

'No,' answered the fisherman.

'Then peace be with you,' said the money-changer.

Khalifah placed the empty basket upon his shoulder
and hurried back to the river. As soon as he reached
the bank he spread his net and cast it into the water.
When he drew it in he found it filled with fish of every
kind. Presently a woman came up to him with a basket
on her shoulder, and bought a dinar's worth of fish.
Then there passed by a slave who also bought a dinar's
worth. When the day was done Khalifah had earned ten
dinars. And he continued to earn ten dinars a day until
he piled up a hundred pieces of gold.

Now Khalifah the fisherman dwelt in a hovel of a
house at the end of the Lane of the Merchants. One
night, as he lay in his lodging befuddled with hashish,
he thought to himself: 'All your neighbours, Khalifah,
think that you are a penniless, unfortunate fisherman.
They have not seen your hundred pieces of gold. But
they will soon hear of your wealth; and before long the
Caliph himself will get to know of it. One day, when
his treasury is empty, he will send for you and say:
"I need some money. I hear that you have a hundred
dinars. You must lend them to me." "Prince of the
Faithful," I will answer, "your slave is a poor, humble
fisherman. The man who told you that is a wicked liar."
The Caliph, of course, will not believe me. He will hand
me over to the Governor, who will strip me naked and
whip me mercilessly. The best course for me now is
to inure my body to whipping. I will rise and prepare
myself.'

Khalifah rose and put off all his clothes. He placed
beside him an old leather cushion, and, taking up his

whip, began lashing himself, aiming every other stroke at the cushion and yelling out: 'A wicked lie! Oh! Oh! I have no money!'

His cries, and the sound of the whipping, echoed in the stillness of the night and startled the neighbours out of their slumbers. They all rushed out into the street inquiring the cause of the disturbance. Thinking that thieves had broken in upon the fisherman, the neighbours hurried to his rescue; but they were surprised to find the door of his lodging locked and bolted.

'The thieves must have got in from the neighbouring terrace,' they said to each other. So they climbed up to the adjoining terrace and from there descended into the fisherman's house, only to find him thrashing his naked body.

'What demon has possessed you to-night, Khalifah?' they cried in amazement. And when he had told the neighbours the very secret he had been so anxious to keep from them, they laughed at him and said: 'Enough of this jest! May Allah give you no joy in your treasure!'

When the fisherman woke up next morning his mind was still obsessed with the fear of losing his gold. 'If I leave my hundred dinars at home,' he thought, 'it is certain they will be stolen; if I carry them in my belt, thieves will lie in wait for me in some deserted place, and cut my throat, and rob me of them. I must think of a better device.' At length Khalifah decided to sew a pocket in the breast of his robe, and to carry in it the hundred dinars tied in a bundle. This done, he took up his net, his basket, and his staff, and went down to the Tigris.

When he reached the river he stepped down the bank and cast his net into the water. But the net brought up nothing at all. Farther and farther away he moved along the bank until he had travelled half a day's journey from the city; but all to no purpose. At last he summoned up all his strength and hurled the net with such desperate force that the bundle of coins flew from his pocket and plunged into the river.

At once Khalifah threw off his clothes and dived after his gold; but it was swept away by the swift current, and he soon had to abandon the search. Bedraggled and utterly exhausted, he walked back to the spot where he had left his clothes. But his clothes, too, had disappeared and were nowhere to be found. In despair he wrapped himself in his net, and, like a raging camel or a rebel jinnee just let loose from King Solomon's prison-house, he began jumping blindly in all directions. So much for Khalifah the fisherman.

Now it so chanced that the Caliph Haroun Al-Rashid (who is the other hero of our tale) had at that time a friend among the jewellers of Baghdad called Ibn-al-Kirnas. He was known to all the merchants of the city as the Caliph's own broker; and his influence was such that nothing choice or rare, from jewels to eunuchs and slave-girls, was put up for sale that was not first shown to him.

One day, as Ibn-al-Kirnas was attending to his customers, the chief of the brokers ushered into his shop a slave-girl of incomparable beauty. Not only was she peerless in her physical perfection, but she was also graced with rare accomplishments; she could recite pretty verses, sing, and make music upon all manner of instruments. Her name was Kut-al-Kulub. Ibn-al-Kirnas bought her upon the instant for five thousand dinars; and after he had arrayed her in rich robes and adorned her with jewels worth a thousand more, he took her to the Prince of the Faithful.

Al-Rashid spent that night with Kut-al-Kulub, and was so delighted with her talents that next morning he sent for Ibn-al-Kirnas and gave him, in payment for the girl, ten thousand dinars. The Caliph loved his new favourite with such violent passion that he forsook for her his wife, the Lady Zubaidah, and all his concubines. He stayed a whole month by her side, leaving her chamber only for the Friday prayers.

It was not long, however, before resentment grew among the Caliph's lieutenants and the officers of his court. They could keep silence no longer, and voiced their complaints before Ja'afar the Vizier.

The following Friday, whilst he was attending upon the Caliph at the mosque, Ja'afar discreetly broached the subject of his infatuation with Kut-al-Kulub.

'By Allah, Ja'afar,' replied the Caliph, 'my will is powerless in this matter; for my heart is caught in the snares of love, and, try as I may, I cannot release it.'

'Prince of the Faithful,' said Ja'afar, 'this girl Kut-al-Kulub is now a member of your household, a servant among your servants; and it is a common saying that what the hand possesses the soul never pines for. Think of the pleasures of riding and hunting and other sports; for these may help you to forget her.'

'You have spoken wisely, Ja'afar,' replied the Caliph. 'Come, we will go hunting this very day.'

As soon as the service was over they mounted their steeds and rode out into the open country, followed by the troops.

It was a hot day. When they had travelled a long way from the city, Al-Rashid felt very thirsty, and, looking round to see if there was any sign of an encampment near by, he faintly descried an object far off upon a mound.

'Can you see what that is?' he asked Ja'afar.

'It seems to be the figure of a man,' replied the Vizier. 'He is perhaps the keeper of an orchard or a cucumber garden. He can no doubt give us some water. I will ride and fetch some.'

But Al-Rashid ordered Ja'afar to stay and wait for the troops, who had lingered behind, and he himself galloped off, more swiftly than the wind that blows in the wilderness or the cataract that thunders down the rocks. On reaching the mound he saw a man swathed in a fishing-net, with hair dishevelled and dusty, and bloodshot eyes blazing like lurid torches.

Al-Rashid greeted the strange-looking figure, and Khalifah muttered a few angry words in reply.

'Have you a drink of water to give me?' asked the Caliph.

'Are you blind or mad?' broke out the fisherman. 'Can you not see that the Tigris flows behind this mound?'

Al-Rashid walked round the hillock, and finding that the river did indeed run behind it, drank and watered his horse. Returning to Khalifah, he said: 'What are you doing here, and what is your trade?'

'That question is even sillier than the last!' cried Khalifah. 'Do you not see the implement of my trade about my shoulders?'

'So you are a fisherman,' said the Caliph. 'But where have you left your cloak, your gown, and your belt?'

It so chanced that those were the very things of which the fisherman had been robbed. Therefore, when he heard the Caliph name them, he did not doubt that the thief stood before him. At once he darted, like a flash of lightning, from the top of the mound and caught the Caliph's horse by the bridle, crying: 'Give me back my clothes and stop this foolish joke!'

'By Allah, my friend,' replied the Caliph, 'I have never seen your clothes; nor do I understand what you are shouting about.'

Now Al-Rashid had a small mouth and round, plump cheeks; so that Khalifah took him for a professional piper. 'Give me back my clothes, you scraper of beggarly tunes,' threatened the fisherman, 'or I will cudgel your bones with this staff till you wet your drawers!'

When he saw the fisherman brandishing his heavy staff, the Caliph thought to himself: 'By Allah, even a light stroke from this cudgel would be too much for me.' He at once took off his splendid satin cloak and handed it to Khalifah, saying: 'Take this in place of the things you lost.'

'My clothes were worth ten times as much as this frivolous garment,' muttered Khalifah, as he turned the cloak about with evident contempt. At length, however, he was prevailed upon by Al-Rashid to try it on. But finding it too long, he took the knife which was tied to the handle of his basket and cut off the lower third of its skirt, so that it hung just above his knees.

'Tell me, good piper,' said the fisherman, 'how much a month does your playing bring you?'

'Ten dinars,' replied the Caliph.

'By Allah,' said Khalifah, 'you make me feel sorry for you. Why, I make ten dinars every day. If you are willing to enter my service, I will teach you my trade and share with you my gain. You will thus become my partner and earn a good round sum every day. And should your old master have any objections, this staff of mine will protect you.'

'I accept your offer,' replied the Caliph.

'Then get off your ass,' said the fisherman, 'and follow me. We will begin work at once.'

Al-Rashid dismounted, and having fastened his horse to a near-by tree he rolled up his sleeves and tucked his robe into his belt.

'Hold the net thus,' said the fisherman, 'spread it over your arm thus, and cast it into the water – thus. ...'

Al-Rashid summoned up all his strength and did as the fisherman told him. When, after a few moments, he tried to draw in the net, it was so heavy that the fisherman had to come to his aid.

'Piper of ill omen!' burst out Khalifah, as the two tugged together at the cords. 'A moment ago I was willing to accept your cloak in compensation for my clothes: but now, if you cause my net to be torn or damaged, I will take from you your ass and beat you black and blue. Do you hear?'

When they at length succeeded in hauling the net ashore, they rejoiced to find it filled with fish of every kind and colour.

'Although you are but an ill-favoured piper,' said Khalifah, 'you may yet become an excellent fisherman. Ride now to the market-place and fetch me two large baskets. I will stay here and watch over the fish till you return. We will then load the catch on your ass's back and take it to the fish market. All that you have to do there is to hold the scales and receive the money. Be off, and waste no time!'

'I hear and obey,' replied the Caliph, and, mounting his horse, galloped away, scarcely able to repress his laughter.

When Al-Rashid had re-joined Ja'afar and the troops, the Vizier, who had become anxious about his master's delay, said: 'You no doubt came upon some pleasant garden on the way and rested there all this while.'

At this the Caliph burst out laughing, and proceeded

to tell the company of his adventure with the fisherman. 'My master is now waiting for me,' he continued gleefully. 'He and I are to go to the market-place and sell the fish and share the profit.'

'Then let me provide you with some customers,' laughed the Vizier.

But a mischievous fancy suddenly took possession of the Caliph's mind. 'By the honour of my holy ancestors,' he cried, 'whoever brings me a fish from my master Khalifah shall receive one gold dinar.'

Thereupon the crier proclaimed the Caliph's wish among the guards, and they all made at once for the river, in the direction of the mound.

While the fisherman was waiting for Al-Rashid, the guards swooped down upon him like vultures, each grabbing as many fish as his hands could hold.

'There must surely be something miraculous about these fishes!' cried Khalifah in terror and amazement. Then, holding one fish in each hand, he jumped into the water, crying: 'O Allah, send your servant the piper quickly to my aid!'

The guards wrapped up the spoil in their large, gold-embroidered handkerchiefs and rode back to their master at full gallop. As soon as they were gone, however, the chief of the Caliph's eunuchs (who had been delayed through his horse stopping on the road to make water) appeared on the bank of the river.

'Come here, fisherman,' said the Negro, when he saw Khalifah holding up the fish.

'Be off, impudent scoundrel,' answered Khalifah.

But the eunuch drew nearer. 'Give me your fish,' he said persuasively. 'I will pay you well.'

The fisherman still refused, and the slave lifted his lance and aimed it at him.

'Dog, do not throw!' cried Khalifah. 'I would rather give you all than lose my life.'

So saying, he contemptuously flung the fish at the Negro, who picked them up and wrapped them in his handkerchief. Then the chief of the eunuchs put his hand in his pocket in order to pay the fisherman. But, as chance would have it, he found not a single coin.

'I fear you have no luck to-day,' he said, 'for, by Allah, I have not one piece of silver about me. But if you will come to the Caliph's palace to-morrow and ask for Sandal the black eunuch, you shall receive a hearty welcome and a generous reward.' With this the slave leapt upon his horse and galloped away.

'This is indeed a blessed day!' groaned Khalifah. In despair, he threw his net upon his shoulder and set out for the city.

As he walked through the streets of Baghdad, the passers-by were puzzled to see the fisherman wrapped in a cloak worth a thousand dinars. Presently he entered the market-place and passed by the shop of the Caliph's tailor, who recognized the garment which he himself had made for the Prince of the Faithful.

The tailor stopped Khalifah, saying: 'How did you come by that cloak?'

'What is that to you?' returned the fisherman angrily. 'Yet, if you must know, it was given me by an apprentice of mine. The rascal had stolen all my clothes; but I took pity on him, and, rather than have his hand cut off for theft, I contented myself with this cloak, which he offered me in their place.'

The tailor was greatly amused to hear this, and understood at once that the fisherman was the victim of one of the Caliph's latest pranks.

Meanwhile, a plot against Kut-al-Kulub was being hatched at the Caliph's palace. For when the Lady Zubaidah, the Caliph's queen and cousin, learnt of her husband's new attachment, she was stung with such consuming jealousy that she thenceforth refused meat and drink, and eagerly awaited an opportunity to avenge herself on Kut-al-Kulub. Now when she heard that Al-Rashid had gone out hunting, she held a sumptuous feast and sent for her husband's favourite to entertain the guests with her music.

Not knowing what Destiny held in store for her, the girl took up her instruments and allowed herself to be conducted to the Queen's chambers.

When her eyes fell upon Kut-al-Kulub, the Lady Zubaidah marvelled in her heart at the girl's exquisite beauty, and concealing her bitter thoughts with a welcoming smile requested her to be seated. Kut-al-Kulub sang to the accompaniment of the lute and the tambourine. So sweetly did she sing that her audience were charmed into a magic trance, the birds paused in their flight, and the whole palace echoed with a thousand mellifluous voices.

'Al-Rashid is hardly to blame for loving her,' thought the Lady Zubaidah, as the girl ended her performance and gracefully bowed to the ground before her.

Presently the servants set before Kut-al-Kulub a dish of sweetmeats in which the Queen had cunningly mixed a potent drug. Scarcely had the girl swallowed one morsel when her head fell backward and she sank to the ground unconscious. The Lady Zubaidah ordered her women to carry the girl to her private chambers. She then had it announced that Kut-al-Kulub had choked while eating and died, threatening her attendants with a cruel death if they betrayed her secret. Lastly she ordered a mock burial to take place and a marble tomb to be erected in the grounds of the palace.

When the Caliph returned from the hunt and the news of the supposed death of his favourite was broken to him, the world darkened before his eyes and he was overwhelmed with grief. He bitterly wept for Kut-al-Kulub and stayed by the tomb a full hour.

Her plot having succeeded, the Lady Zubaidah gave orders that the senseless Kut-al-Kulub be locked into a chest and carried to the market-place. She instructed one of her trusted slaves to sell the chest without delay, making it a condition that the contents should not be declared beforehand. And she ordered the slave to give away the money in alms.

Now to return to the fisherman. Early next morning, Khalifah thought to himself: 'I can do nothing better to-day than go to the Caliph's palace and demand of the black slave the debt he owes me.'

So he rose and betook himself to Al-Rashid's court. As soon as he entered the great portals of the palace, he saw Sandal, the chief eunuch, in the doorway, with a crowd of slaves waiting upon him. As the fisherman drew closer, one of the slaves rose to bar his way and would have turned him back had not Khalifah called out to the black eunuch: 'I have not failed you, my golden tulip!'

Recognizing the fisherman, Sandal greeted him with a laugh and put his hand into his pocket to produce his purse. It so chanced, however, that at that moment a great shout announced the approach of Ja'afar. At once Sandal sprang to his feet and, heedless of his creditor, hurried off to the Vizier and fell into a long conversation with him.

Khalifah repeatedly tried to draw the slave's attention

to his presence, but all to no purpose. At length, observing the fisherman's impatient gesticulations, Ja'afar asked: 'Who is that stranger?'

'That,' replied Sandal, 'is the self-same fisherman whose fish we seized yesterday at the Caliph's orders.' And he proceeded to explain to Ja'afar the occasion of Khalifah's visit.

When he had heard Sandal's account, the Vizier smiled and said: 'This fisherman is the Caliph's instructor and business partner. He has come at a time when we need him most. To-day our master's heart is heavy with grief for the death of his beloved, and perhaps nothing can cheer him better than this fisherman's antics. Let him stay here while I ask the Prince of the Faithful if he wishes to see him.'

Ja'afar left the eunuch and hurried back to the Caliph's chamber. He found him bowed down with sorrow, still brooding over the loss of Kut-al-Kulub. The Vizier wished him peace, and bowing low before him, said: 'On my way to you just now, Prince of the Faithful, I met at the door your teacher and partner, Khalifah the fisherman. He is loud in his complaint against you. "Glory to Allah!" I heard him say. "Is this how masters should be treated? I sent him to fetch me a couple of baskets and he never came back. What kind of partnership is this, I ask?" Now, I pray you, Prince of the Faithful,' went on Ja'afar, 'if you still have a mind to be his partner, let him know of it; but if you wish to end your joint labours, tell him that he must seek another man.'

The Caliph smiled at Ja'afar's words, and his sorrow seemed to be lightened. 'Is this true, Ja'afar?' he asked. 'Upon my life, this fisherman shall have his reward!' Then added Al-Rashid with a mischievous twinkle in his eye: 'If it is Allah's wish that he should prosper through me, it shall be done; and if it is His wish to scourge him through me, it shall be done also.'

So saying, Al-Rashid took a large sheet of paper and, cutting it into numerous pieces, said to the Vizier: 'Write down on twenty of these papers sums of money from one dinar to a thousand, and all the dignities of the State from the smallest office to the Caliphate itself; also twenty kinds of punishment from the lightest beating to a hideous death.'

'I hear and obey,' replied Ja'afar, and did as the Prince of the Faithful bade him.

Then said the Caliph: 'I swear by my holy ancestors and by my kinship with Hamzah and Akil that Khalifah the fisherman shall have the choice of one of these papers, and that I will reward him accordingly. Go and bring him before me!'

'There is no strength nor help save in Allah,' thought Ja'afar, as he left the Caliph's chamber. 'Who knows what lies in store for this poor wretch! But the Caliph has sworn; and that which Allah has ordained must surely come to pass.'

When he found Khalifah, Ja'afar took him by the hand and, followed by a crowd of slaves, proceeded with him through seven vast vestibules until they stood at the door of the Caliph's chamber.

'Be careful,' said the Vizier to the terrified fisherman. 'You are about to be admitted to the presence of the Prince of the Faithful, Defender of the Faith.' With this, he led him in; and Khalifah, who was so perplexed at the commotion that he could not understand the Vizier's words, suddenly saw the Caliph seated on a couch with all the officers of his court standing around him. The fisherman recognized his former apprentice with a shout of surprise.

'It is good to see you again, my piper!' he cried. 'But was it right to go away and leave me by the river all alone with the fish, and never to return? Know, then, that thanks to your truancy I was attacked by a band of mounted slaves, who carried off the entire catch. Had you returned promptly with the baskets, we would have made a hundred dinars. And what is worse, the treacherous rogues have now arrested me. But, tell me, who has imprisoned *you* in this place?'

Al-Rashid smiled and held out the cuttings to the fisherman, saying: 'Come closer, Khalifah, and draw one of these papers.'

'Only yesterday you were a fisherman,' replied Khalifah. 'Now I see that you have turned astrologer. But you have doubtless heard the common adage: "A rolling stone gathers no moss."'

'Enough of this chatter,' interrupted Ja'afar. 'Draw one of these papers at once, and do as the Prince of the Faithful bids you.'

The fisherman took one paper and handed it to the Caliph, saying: 'Read me my fortune, good piper, and keep nothing back.'

Al-Rashid passed the paper to Ja'afar and asked him to read out the contents. Such was Khalifah's luck, however, that his choice decreed a hundred blows of the stick. Accordingly, he was at once thrown down and given a hundred strokes.

'This unfortunate man has come to the river of your bounty, Prince of the Faithful,' said Ja'afar. 'Pray do not turn him back with his thirst unquenched.' And the Vizier persuaded the Caliph to let the fisherman draw again.

The second paper decreed that Khalifah be given nothing at all. Ja'afar, however, prevailed upon the

Caliph to let the fisherman draw a third. Khalifah drew again, and the Vizier unfolded the paper and announced: 'One dinar.'

'What!' cried the angry fisherman. 'One dinar for a hundred strokes? Then may Allah justly requite you.'

The Caliph laughed, and Ja'afar took the fisherman by the hand and led him from his master's presence.

As Khalifah was about to leave the palace, Sandal called out to him, saying: 'Come, my friend, give me my share of the Caliph's reward.'

'You want your share, do you, thick-lips?' broke out Khalifah. 'All I have earned was a hundred strokes and one dinar. You would indeed be welcome to half of my beating; as for the miserable coin, why, you can have that too!' So saying, he flung the dinar at him and rushed out, bursting with indignation.

Moved with pity, the eunuch ordered some slaves to run after him and bring him back. They did so, and Sandal took out a red purse and emptied from it a hundred dinars into the fisherman's hands, saying: 'Take this in payment of my debt, and go hence in peace.'

Khalifah rejoiced. He put the gold into his pocket, together with the dinar which Al-Rashid had given him, and went out of the palace, his troubles all forgotten.

Now it so chanced that as the fisherman was walking along the streets, lost in happy fancies, Destiny conducted his steps to the market-place, where he saw a great concourse of people. Pushing his way among the wealthy merchants, he found the centre of attention to be a large chest with a young slave seated upon it. Beside the chest stood an old man calling out: 'Gentlemen, merchants, worthy citizens! Who will be the first bidder for this chest of unknown treasure from the harem of the Lady Zubaidah, daughter of Al-Kasim, wife of the Prince of the Faithful?'

'By Allah,' said one of the merchants, 'there is much risk in this; but I will say twenty dinars.'

'Fifty!' cried another.

'A hundred!' shouted a third.

'Who will give more?' cried the auctioneer.

Breathless with excitement, Khalifah the fisherman lifted his voice, crying: 'Be it mine for a hundred and one dinars!'

At this the merchants laughed incredulously; but the auctioneer, who was impressed by the fisherman's earnestness, replied: 'The chest is yours: hand in your gold, and may Allah bless the bargain!'

Having paid the slave, Khalifah placed the chest upon his shoulder, and carried it to his house. As he staggered along under its weight, he wondered what the precious contents might be. Presently he reached his dwelling, and after he had managed to get the chest through the door, he applied himself to open it. But the chest was securely locked.

'What devil possessed me to buy a box that cannot even be opened!' he cried. Then he decided to break the chest to pieces: but it stoutly defied all his kicks and blows. Utterly exhausted, he at length stretched himself out on the lid and sank into a heavy sleep.

Scarcely an hour had passed, however, when the fisherman was awakened by a sound of movement beneath him. Half-demented with terror, he leapt to his feet, crying: 'This chest must be haunted by jinn! Praise be to Allah who prevented me from opening it! For had I freed them in the dark they would have put me to a miserable death!'

His terror increased as the noise gradually became

more distinct. He searched in vain for a lamp and finally rushed out into the street yelling at the top of his voice: 'Help! Help, good neighbours!'

Roused from their sleep, the neighbours appeared at every door and window. 'What has happened?' they shouted.

'Jinn! Jinn!' cried the fisherman. 'My house is haunted! Give me a lamp and a hammer, in the name of Allah!'

The neighbours laughed. One gave him a lamp, and another lent him a hammer. His confidence restored, the fisherman went back to his house determined to break open the chest. He battered its locks with the hammer and pulled back the lid.

Inside, he was astonished to see a girl as beautiful as a houri. Her eyes were half-opened, as if she had just waked from a heavy sleep. Khalifah marvelled at her loveliness. 'In Allah's name, who are you?' he whispered, kneeling down before her.

Kut-al-Kulub opened her eyes and murmured: 'Bring me Jasmine and Narcissus.' *

'Alas, my mistress,' he replied, 'I have nothing here but a few henna flowers.'

On hearing the stranger's words the girl completely regained her senses. 'Who are you? Where am I?' she asked, gazing intently into his face.

'I am Khalifah the fisherman, and you are in my house,' he answered.

'Am I not in the palace of the Caliph Haroun Al-Rashid?' asked the girl.

'Are you mad?' exclaimed the fisherman. 'Let me tell you at once that you belong to no one but me; it was only this morning that I bought you for a hundred and

* The names of two slave-girls.

one dinars. Allah be praised; my luckless star has turned auspicious!'

Khalifah would have long continued in this strain had not Kut-al-Kulub, who was beginning to feel the pangs of hunger, interrupted him, saying: 'Give me something to eat.'

'By Allah,' replied the fisherman, 'there is nothing to eat or drink in this house. I myself have scarcely tasted anything for two days past.'

'Have you any money, then?' she asked.

'Allah preserve this chest!' he answered bitterly. 'This bargain has swallowed up every dirham that I had.'

'Then go to your neighbours,' she said, 'and bring me something to eat, for I am very hungry.'

The fisherman rushed out into the street, crying: 'Good neighbours, who will give a hungry man something to eat?' This he repeated several times at the top of his voice, until the unfortunate neighbours, once more awakened by his cries, opened their windows and threw down some food to him: one gave him half a loaf of bread, another a piece of cheese, a third a cucumber.

Returning home, he set the food before Kut-al-Kulub and invited her to eat. But the girl said: 'Bring me a drink of water; I am very thirsty.'

So Khalifah took up his empty pitcher and again ran out into the street, begging the neighbours for some water. The neighbours replied with angry curses; but, unable to stand his persistent cries any longer, they carried water to him in jugs, pails, and ewers. Khalifah filled his pitcher and took it to the slave-girl.

When she had eaten and drunk her fill, the fisherman asked her how she had come to be locked into the chest. She recounted to him all that had happened at the

Caliph's palace, adding: 'All this is no doubt destined to make your fortune. For when Al-Rashid hears the news of my rescue you shall not lose your reward.'

'But is not this Al-Rashid the dull-witted piper whom I but recently taught fishing?' cried Khalifah. 'Never in all my life have I met such a niggardly rascal.'

'My friend,' said the girl, 'you must cease this churlish talk and make yourself worthy of the new station that awaits you. Above all, you must bear yourself respectfully and courteously in the presence of the Prince of the Faithful.'

Such was the influence of Kut-al-Kulub's words on Khalifah that a new world seemed to unfold before him. The dark veil of ignorance was lifted from his eyes and he became a wiser man.

The fisherman and the girl slept (the two lying far apart) till morning, when Kut-al-Kulub asked Khalifah to bring her pen, ink, and paper. She wrote to Ibn-al-Kirnas, the Caliph's jeweller, informing him of her whereabouts and of the events of the previous day. Then she directed Khalifah to the shop of Ibn-al-Kirnas and asked him to deliver the letter without delay.

When he entered the jeweller's shop the fisherman bowed to the ground before him and wished him peace. But, taking Khalifah for a common beggar, the merchant ordered one of his slaves to give him half a dirham and show him out. Khalifah refused the coin, saying: 'I beg no alms. Read this, I pray you.'

As soon as he finished reading the girl's letter, the jeweller lifted it to his lips and, rising, bade the fisherman a courteous welcome. 'Where is your house, my friend?' he asked.

Khalifah directed him to his dwelling. The merchant then called two of his servants and said to them: 'Take my friend to the shop of Muhsin the money-changer and ask him to pay him a thousand dinars in gold. Then return with him forthwith.'

The servants took the fisherman to the money-changer, and he was paid a thousand dinars. When they returned with him to their master's shop, Khalifah found the jeweller mounted on a magnificent dappled mule with all his servants gathered around him. Near by stood another splendid mule, richly saddled and bridled, which Ibn-al-Kirnas invited Khalifah to mount. The fisherman, who had never been on a mule's back in all his life, at first refused, but having been finally prevailed upon by the merchant, he decided to risk a trial and resolutely leapt upon the animal's back – facing the wrong way and grasping its tail instead of the bridle. The mule reared at once, and Khalifah was violently thrown to the ground to the cheers and shouts of the onlookers.

Ibn-al-Kirnas left the fisherman behind and rode off to the Caliph's palace. Al-Rashid was overjoyed to hear the news of his favourite's deliverance, and he ordered the merchant to bring her immediately to his court.

When the girl was admitted to the Caliph's presence, she kissed the ground before him, and he rose and welcomed her rapturously. Kut-al-Kulub related to him the story of her adventure and told him that her rescuer was a fisherman called Khalifah. 'He is now waiting at the door of the palace,' she added.

Al-Rashid sent at once for the fisherman, and when he entered upon him he kissed the ground before him and humbly wished him joy and everlasting glory.

The Caliph marvelled at the fisherman's transformation, his humility and politeness. He bestowed upon him a generous reward, giving him fifty thousand dinars, a magnificent robe of honour, a noble mare, and slaves from the Sudan.

When his audience with the Caliph ended, the fisherman again kissed the ground before him and left his chamber a proud, rich man. As he passed through the gates of the palace, Sandal approached him and wished him joy of his new fortune. Khalifah produced from his pocket a purse containing a thousand dinars and offered it to him. But the slave refused the gold and marvelled at his liberality and the goodness of his heart.

Then Khalifah mounted the mare which Al-Rashid had given him and, with the help of two slaves who held her by the bridle, rode majestically through the streets of the city until he reached his house. As he dismounted, his neighbours flocked around him inquiring about his sudden prosperity. The fisherman related to them all that had happened and they marvelled at his story.

Khalifah became a constant visitor at the court of Al-Rashid, who continued to lavish on him high dignities and favours. He bought a magnificent house and had it furnished with rare and costly objects. Then he married a well-born, beautiful maiden, and lived happily with her until he was visited by the Spoiler of worldly mansions, the Dark Minister of the graveyard.

THE TALE OF
MA'ARUF THE COBBLER

ONCE upon a time there lived in the city of Cairo a
poor and honest cobbler who earned his living by
patching old shoes. His name was Ma'aruf.

He was married to a spiteful termagant called Fatimah, nicknamed by her neighbours 'The Shrew' on account of her sour disposition and scolding tongue. She
used her husband with heartless cruelty, cursing him a
thousand times a day and making his life a burden and
a torment. Ma'aruf was a sensitive man, jealous of his
good name, and in time he grew to fear her malice and
dread her fiery temper. All his daily earnings he gladly
spent on her, but if, by ill fortune, he returned home
with an empty purse, she abused and scolded him, giving
him no rest and making his night hideous as her scowl.

It happened one day that his wife came to Ma'aruf
and said: 'See that you bring me a kinafah cake to-
night, and let it be dripping with sweet honey.'

'May Allah send me good custom to-day,' replied the
cobbler, 'and you shall gladly have one. At present I
have not a single copper, but the bounty of Allah is
great.'

'A fig for the bounty of Allah!' rejoined the shrew.
'If you do not bring me back a kinafah, dripping with
sweet honey, I will make the night blacker for you than
the fate which cast you into my hands!'

'Allah is merciful,' sighed Ma'aruf. Perplexed and downcast, he left his house and went to open his shop, saying: 'O Allah, grant me this day the means to buy a honey-cake for my wife, that I may save myself from the spleen of that wicked woman!'

But, as ill luck would have it, no customer entered his shop that day and he did not earn enough even to buy a loaf of bread. Weary and sick at heart, he locked his shop and walked along the street. Presently he came to a pastry-cook's, and as he gazed upon the delicacies displayed in the window, his eyes filled with tears. Noticing his dejected countenance, the pastry-cook called out to him, saying: 'Why so sad, Ma'aruf? Come in, and tell me your trouble.'

When the cook had heard the cause of the cobbler's unhappiness, he laughed and said: 'No harm shall come to you, my friend. What quantity of kinafah do you require?'

'Five ounces,' muttered Ma'aruf.

'I will gladly let you have it,' said the cook, 'and you can pay me some other time.'

He cut a large slice of kinafah and added: 'I fear that I have no honey, but only sugar-cane syrup. I assure you it is just as good.'

The cook put the kinafah in a dish and poured over it syrup and melted butter until it was worthy of a king's table. Then he handed the dish to the cobbler, together with a cheese and a loaf of bread for his supper. Ma'aruf could scarcely find words to express his gratitude, and, calling down fervent blessings on the good man, went off to his house.

As soon as his wife saw him she cried: 'Have you brought me the kinafah?'

Ma'aruf placed the dish before her, but no sooner

had the vixen set eyes on the cake than she burst out in a menacing voice: 'Did I not tell you it must be made with honey? You have brought me a syrup cake to spite me! Did you think I would not know the difference?'

Abjectly, Ma'aruf stammered out his explanation, saying: 'Good wife, I did not buy this cake; it was given me on credit by the kind-hearted pastry-cook.'

'This babble will not help you!' shrieked the furious woman. 'There, take your miserable syrup dish!' And she flung the cake in her husband's face and ordered him to go and fetch her another made with honey. Then she dealt him a savage blow on the jaw, knocking out one of his teeth, so that the blood trickled down his beard and chest.

Losing all patience, the long-suffering Ma'aruf impulsively lifted his hand and gave the woman a mild slap on the head. At this the termagant flew into a desperate rage; she gripped his beard with both her hands, and, raising her voice to its loudest pitch, shrieked out: 'Help, good Moslems! Help, my husband is murdering me!'

Hearing her cries, the neighbours came rushing into the house. After a long struggle they succeeded in freeing the cobbler's beard from his wife's clutches, but when they saw the injury she had inflicted on him and heard the cause of the dispute, they rebuked her and said: 'We are all content to eat syrup kinafah, and find it as good as the other kind. What has your poor husband done that you should torment him so?'

At length, thinking that peace had been restored between husband and wife, the neighbours went their way. Left alone with Fatimah, Ma'aruf attempted to pacify her. He gathered up the scattered remnants of the kinafah and offered it to her with a trembling hand, say-

ing: 'Eat a little of this, my love, and to-morrow, if
Allah wills, I shall bring you a kinafah dripping with
honey.'

But the shrew gave no heed to his entreaties, and
swore that nothing would persuade her to touch it. At
last, beginning to feel the pangs of hunger, Ma'aruf sat
down to eat the kinafah himself. This he did to the accompaniment of an uninterrupted flow of abuse from
his wife; and she continued to call down curses on him
throughout the night.

Early next morning Ma'aruf went to the mosque and
prayed to Allah to grant him the means wherewith to
gratify his wife's demand. Then he opened his shop, but
had scarcely sat down to his work when two guards
burst in upon him, saying: 'We hold a warrant from
the Cadi So-and-so for your arrest.' With this they manacled the cobbler and dragged him to their master's
court.

When he was led into the Cadi's presence, Ma'aruf
saw his wife standing all in tears, with a bandaged arm
and her head wrapped in a blood-stained veil.

'Wretch!' cried the Cadi, as soon as he set eyes on
Ma'aruf. 'Have you no fear of Allah that you beat this
poor woman and break her arm and knock out her
tooth?'

The cobbler was utterly confounded, and proceeded
to tell the Cadi what had passed between him and his
wife. Convinced that the unhappy man was telling the
truth, the Cadi took pity on Ma'aruf and gave him a
quarter of a dinar, saying: 'Take this and buy her a
honey kinafah.' Then he exhorted the pair to use each
other kindly and, having made peace between them,
dismissed them from his presence.

Ma'aruf gave his wife the quarter of a dinar and returned to his shop. Presently, however, the guards who had marched him to the court came back to demand payment. When Ma'aruf told them that he had not a copper in his purse, they dragged him out into the market-place and would have given him a sound beating had he not instantly sold his cobbler's tools and paid them half a dinar.

As he sat in his empty shop brooding over his ill fortune, two ruffianly guards from the court of another cadi burst in, saying: 'We have a warrant for your arrest.' Without more ado they led him to the court, where Ma'aruf was astounded to see his wife standing as before, with bandaged arm and a blood-stained veil about her head, heaping up monstrous charges against him.

Again the cobbler related his story to the judge, adding: 'The Cadi So-and-so had but an hour ago made peace between us.'

'Woman,' cried the Cadi, addressing the shrew, 'if you are already reconciled, why have you come to me?'

'He has beaten me again!' protested Fatimah.

The Cadi rebuked them both and, after ordering Ma'aruf to pay the guards, dismissed them from his presence.

The harassed cobbler parted with his last copper and trudged dolefully back to his shop. Scarcely an hour had passed, when one of his friends came running to the door and cried: 'Rise, Ma'aruf, and fly for your life, for the shrew has brought an action against you at the Governor's court! His guards are even now on their way to arrest you!'

The terrified cobbler closed his shop and made off towards the Victory Gate. It was a grey winter afternoon, and as soon as he came to the outskirts of the city and found himself amongst the garbage heaps, the rain began to fall in torrents, drenching him to the skin. On and on he ran, and at nightfall came to a ruined hovel where he took shelter from the storm. He sat down on the ground and wept bitterly, crying: 'Oh, how shall I save myself from this fiend? O Allah, help me fly to some far-off land, where I shall never see her more!'

Whilst he was thus lamenting, the wall of the hovel suddenly opened and there appeared before him a colossal jinnee whose fearsome aspect struck terror to his soul.

'Son of Adam,' roared the jinnee, 'what calamity can have befallen you that you disturb my midnight slumbers with your wailing? I am the jinnee of this ruin and have dwelt here these hundred years; yet have I never seen the like of this behaviour.' Then, moved with pity, the jinnee added: 'Tell me what you desire, and I will do your bidding.'

Ma'aruf told him the story of his misfortunes, and the jinnee said: 'Mount on my back, and I will take you to a land where your wife shall never find you.'

The cobbler climbed onto the back of the jinnee, who flew with him between earth and sky all night and at daybreak set him down on the top of a mountain.

'Son of Adam,' said the jinnee, 'go down this mountain and you will come to the gates of Ikhtiyan-al-Khatan. In that city you will find refuge from your wife.' And so saying, the jinnee vanished.

Amazed and bewildered, Ma'aruf remained where the jinnee had left him until the sun rose. Then he climbed down the mountain and at length came to a well-built city surrounded by high walls. He entered the gates, and, as he walked through the streets, the townsfolk stared at him with wondering eyes and gathered about him, marvelling at his strange costume. Presently a man stepped forward and asked him whence he had come.

'From Cairo,' replied Ma'aruf.

'When did you leave Cairo?' inquired the man.

'Last night,' he answered, 'just after the hour of evening prayers.'

At these words his questioner laughed incredulously, and, turning to the by-standers, cried: 'Listen to this madman! He tells us that he left Cairo only last night!'

The crowd greeted this remark with loud laughter, and, pressing round Ma'aruf, shouted: 'Have you taken leave of your senses? How was it that you left Cairo only last night? Do you not know that Cairo is a year's journey from this city?'

Ma'aruf swore that he was speaking the truth, and to prove his story took from his pocket a loaf of Cairo bread and showed it to them. They were all astonished to see the loaf, which was of a kind unknown in their country, and still soft and fresh. A few believed him, whilst others ridiculed him. As this was going forward, a wealthy merchant, followed by two slaves, came riding by and, stopping near the crowd, admonished them sternly, saying: 'Are you not ashamed to make game of this stranger?'

Then, turning to Ma'aruf, the merchant spoke to him kindly and invited him to his house.

There his host clad Ma'aruf in a merchant's robe worth a thousand dinars, seated him in a splendid hall, and entertained him at a sumptuous meal. When they had finished eating, the merchant said to the cobbler: 'Pray tell me, my brother, what land you have come from, for, by your dress, you would seem to be an Egyptian.'

'You are right, my master,' replied Ma'aruf. 'I am an Egyptian, and Cairo is the city of my birth.'

'What is your trade?' inquired the merchant.

'I am a cobbler; I patch old shoes.'

'In what part of Cairo did you live?'

'In Red Lane,' replied Ma'aruf.

'What folk do you know there?'

Ma'aruf named several of his neighbours in that street.

'Do you know Sheikh Ahmed the perfume-seller?' asked the merchant eagerly.

'Do I know him?' laughed Ma'aruf. 'Why, he is my next-door neighbour!'

'How is he faring?'

'Thanks be to Allah, he is in the best of health,' replied the cobbler.

'How many sons has he now?'

'He has three sons: Mustapha, Mohammed, and Ali.'

'What do they do for their living?' inquired the host.

'The eldest, Mustapha,' replied Ma'aruf, 'is a schoolmaster. Mohammed, the second, is a perfume-seller and has set up a shop of his own next to his father's. His wife has but recently borne him a son, whom they called Hassan. As for Ali, he was the playmate of my childhood. Together we would enter the churches of the Christians and steal their prayer-books; then we would sell them in the market-place and buy sweetmeats with the money. One day the Christians caught us red-handed and complained to our parents. They threatened Ali's father, saying: "If you do not restrain your son, we will inform the King of this sacrilege." Sheikh Ahmed gave his son a thrashing and poor little Ali ran away from home. No news has been heard of him these twenty years.'

Here the merchant threw his arms round the cobbler's neck and wept for joy, crying: 'Praise be to Allah! O Ma'aruf, I am that very Ali, the son of Sheikh Ahmed the perfume-seller!'

Then Ali asked his friend what had brought him to Ikhtiyan-al-Khatan, and the cobbler recounted to him the tale of his misfortunes and all that had befallen him since his disastrous marriage. He explained how he had chosen to fly the city rather than remain at the mercy of his heartless wife, how he met the jinnee in the ruined hovel, and how he was carried overnight to Ikhtiyan-al-Khatan. Then Ma'aruf asked his friend to tell him how he rose to such prosperity.

'After I left Cairo,' said Ali, 'I wandered for many years from place to place and at length arrived, forlorn and penniless, in this city. I found its people honest and kind-hearted, hospitable to strangers and always ready to help the poor. I told them that I was a rich merchant, the owner of a great caravan which would shortly arrive in their city. They believed my story and gave me a splendid mansion for my use. Then I borrowed a thousand dinars, telling my creditor that I needed a few necessities before my merchandise arrived. With this money I bought a quantity of goods and sold them the following day at a profit of fifty pieces of gold. I bought more goods, and, to enhance my reputation, I sought the acquaintance of the richest merchants in the town and entertained them liberally in my house. I continued to buy and sell until I had amassed a large fortune.

'The old proverb says: "Where candour fails, cunning thrives." Now, my friend, if you tell the people of this city that you are a poor cobbler, that you have run away from a nagging wife and left Cairo only yesterday, no one will believe you and you will become the laughing-stock of the whole town. If you tell them that you were carried here by a jinnee, you will frighten everyone away and they will think: "This man is possessed with an evil spirit." No, my friend, this will not do.'

'Then what am I to do?' asked the perplexed Ma'aruf.

'To-morrow morning,' said Ali, 'you shall mount my finest mule and ride to the market-place, with one of my slaves walking behind you all the way. There you will find me sitting among the richest merchants of the city. When I see you I will rise and greet you, I will kiss your hand and receive you with the utmost deference. When you have taken your seat among the other merchants, I shall question you about many kinds of merchandise, saying: "Have you such-and-such a cloth?" And you must answer: "Plenty! Plenty!" When they ask me who you are, I shall say you are a merchant of great wealth, and praise your munificence. If a beggar holds out his hand to you, give him gold. These proceedings will earn you great consideration in the merchants' eyes. They will seek your acquaintance and wish to trade with you, and before long you will become indeed a merchant of great wealth.'

Next morning Ali dressed Ma'aruf in a magnificent robe, gave him a thousand dinars, and mounted him upon his best mule. At the appointed time the cobbler rode to the market-place, where he found his friend sitting among the merchants. As soon as Ali saw him approaching he rose, threw himself at his feet, kissed his hand, and helped him from his mule, saying: 'May your day be blessed, great Ma'aruf!'

When the new-comer had gravely taken his seat, the wondering merchants came to Ali one after another and asked him in a low voice: 'Who may this sheikh be?' Ali replied: 'He is one of the chief merchants of Egypt.

H

His wealth and the wealth of his father and forefathers is of proverbial fame, and his munificence is boundless as the sea. He possesses shops and storehouses in all the corners of the earth, and his agents and partners are the pillars of commerce in every city from Egypt and Yemen to India and the far-flung hills of Sind. Indeed the wealthiest merchant in this city is but a poor pedlar when compared with him.'

Hearing this encomium, the merchants thronged around Ma'aruf, vying with each other to welcome him and offering him sherbets. The chief of the merchants himself came to greet him, and questioned him eagerly about the goods he had brought.

'Doubtless, my master,' he said, 'you have many bales of yellow silk?'

'Plenty! Plenty!' answered Ma'aruf, without a moment's hesitation.

'And gazelle blood-red?' asked another.

'Plenty! Plenty!' replied the cobbler gravely.

To all their questions he made the same answer, and when one of the merchants begged him to show them a few samples, Ma'aruf replied: 'Certainly, as soon as my caravan arrives.' Then he explained to the company that he was expecting a caravan of a thousand mules within the next few days.

Now whilst the merchants were chatting together and marvelling at the extraordinary richness of the caravan, a beggar came round and held out his hand to each in turn. A few gave him half a dirham, some a copper, but most of them gave him nothing. Ma'aruf, however, calmly drew out a handful of gold and gave it to the beggar.

The merchants marvelled at this, and thought to themselves: 'By Allah, this man must be richer than a king!'

Then a poor woman approached him, and to her also he gave a handful of gold. Scarcely believing her eyes, the woman hurried away to tell the other beggars, and they all came flocking round Ma'aruf with outstretched hands. The cobbler gave each a handful of gold, until the thousand dinars were finished. Then he clapped his hands together, saying: 'By Allah, to think there are so many beggars in this city! Had I known of this I would have come prepared, for it is not my way to refuse alms. What shall I do now if a beggar solicits me before my caravan arrives? If only I had, say, a thousand dinars!'

'Do not let that trouble you,' said the chief of the merchants. And he at once sent for a thousand dinars and handed the money to Ma'aruf.

The cobbler continued to give gold to every beggar who passed by. When the muezzin's call summoned the Faithful to afternoon prayers, he went with the merchants to the mosque, and what remained of the thousand dinars he scattered over the heads of the worshippers.

As soon as the prayers were over he borrowed another thousand, and these also he gave away. By night-fall Ma'aruf had obtained five thousand dinars from the merchants and given them all away, while the dismayed Ali watched the proceedings helplessly. And to all his creditors he said: 'When my caravan arrives, if you want gold, you shall have gold; and if you want goods, you shall have goods: for I have vast quantities of them.'

That night Ali entertained the merchants at his house. Ma'aruf was given the seat of honour, and all night spoke of nothing but jewels and rich silks. And whenever they asked him if he had this or that merchandise in his caravan, the cobbler replied: 'Plenty! Plenty!'

Next morning he again went to the market-place, where he talked to the merchants about his caravan and borrowed more money and gave it to the beggars. This he repeated each day for twenty days, and by the end of this time he had taken sixty thousand pieces of gold on credit. And still no caravan arrived; no, not as much as a half-cooked pie.

At length the merchants, who were becoming impatient at the caravan's delay, began to clamour for their money. They voiced their anxiety to their friend Ali, who, himself alarmed at the cobbler's munificence, took him aside and remonstrated with him, saying: 'Have you taken leave of your senses? I told you to toast the bread, not to burn it! The merchants are demanding their money and say that you owe them sixty thousand dinars. You have squandered all this gold among the beggars; how will you ever pay it back, idle as you are, with no work to do or goods to trade with?'

'No matter,' replied Ma'aruf. 'What is sixty thousand dinars? When my caravan arrives, if they want gold, they shall have gold; and if they want goods, they shall have goods: for I have vast quantities of them.'

'Now glory be to Allah!' exclaimed Ali. 'What goods are you talking about?'

'Why, the goods in my caravan,' replied Ma'aruf. 'I have countless bales of merchandise.'

'Impudent dog!' cried Ali. 'Are you telling me that story? Why, I will denounce you to the whole world!'

'Be off!' said Ma'aruf. 'Did you suppose I was a poor man? Know, then, I have priceless riches on the way. As soon as my caravan arrives, the merchants shall be repaid twofold!'

At this Ali grew very angry and cried: 'Scoundrel! I will teach you to lie to me!'

'Do your worst!' replied the cobbler. 'They must wait until my caravan arrives, and then they shall have their money back and more.'

In despair Ali left Ma'aruf and went away thinking: 'If I now abuse him after so highly commending him, I shall, as the saying goes, be a twofold liar.'

When the merchants returned, inquiring the outcome of his audience with Ma'aruf, the harassed Ali replied: 'My friends, I had not the heart to speak to him about his debts, for I myself have lent him a thousand dinars. When you advanced him so much money, you did not seek my advice; therefore you cannot hold me responsible. Speak to him yourselves. If he fails to pay his debts, denounce him to the King as an impostor and a thief.'

The merchants went in a body to the King and told him all that had passed between them and Ma'aruf. 'Your majesty,' they said, 'we are in great perplexity about this merchant, whose generosity knows no bounds. He has borrowed of us sixty thousand dinars and scattered them in handfuls among the poor. Were he a poor man, he would never be so foolish as to squander such a fortune; and if he is indeed a man of wealth, why has his vaunted caravan not yet arrived?'

Now the King was an avaricious old miser. When he heard the merchants' account of Ma'aruf's prodigality, greed took possession of his soul and he said to his Vizier: 'This merchant must surely be a man of extraordinary wealth, or he would never have been capable of such munificence. His caravan is certain to arrive. Now I will not suffer these wolves of the market-place to grab all the treasures for themselves, for they are already too rich. I must seek his friendship, so that when his caravan arrives I, too, will have a share. Why, I

might even give him my daughter in marriage and join
his wealth to mine.'

But the Vizier replied: 'This man is an impostor, your
majesty. Beware of avarice, for avarice brings ruin and
repentance.'

'I will put him to the test,' said the King, 'and we will
soon discover if he is a trickster. I will show him a
costly pearl and ask him his opinion. If he can tell its
worth, we shall know that he is a man of affluence accustomed to such rarities. If he cannot, then we shall
know that he is a liar and a fraud, and I will put him to
a cruel death.'

The Vizier sent at once for Ma'aruf, and when he had
been admitted to the King's presence and exchanged
greetings with him, the King asked: 'Is it true that you
owe the merchants sixty thousand pieces of gold?'

When Ma'aruf replied that it was true, he asked:
'Why do you not pay them their money?'

'The day my caravan arrives,' replied Ma'aruf, 'they
shall be paid twofold. If they want gold, they shall have
gold; if they want silver, they shall have silver; and if
they prefer goods, they shall have goods: for I have
vast quantities of them.'

Then, to test Ma'aruf, the King handed him a rare
pearl worth a thousand dinars. 'Have you such pearls
in your caravan?' he asked.

Ma'aruf examined the pearl for a moment, and,
throwing it disdainfully to the ground, crushed it beneath his heel.

'What is the meaning of this?' cried the King indignantly.

'This pearl,' replied the cobbler with a laugh, 'is
scarcely worth a thousand dinars. I have vast quantities
of infinitely larger pearls in my caravan.'

At this the King's avarice knew no bounds. He at once sent for the merchants, told them that their fears were groundless, and assured them that the caravan would soon arrive. Then he summoned the Vizier and said: 'See that the merchant Ma'aruf is received with all magnificence at the palace. Speak to him about my daughter the Princess. Perhaps he will consent to marry her, and so we shall gain possession of all his wealth.'

'Your majesty,' replied the Vizier, 'I do not like the manner of this foreigner. His presence bodes evil to the court. I pray you to wait until we have visible proof of his caravan.'

Now the Vizier himself had once sought the Princess's hand in marriage and his suit had been rejected. So when the King heard this warning, he flew into a passion and cried: 'Treacherous dog, you slander this merchant only because you wish to marry the Princess yourself. You would have her left on my hands until she is old and unacceptable. Could she ever find a more suitable husband than this accomplished, generous, and opulent young man? Not only will he make her a perfect husband, but he will make us all rich into the bargain!'

Afraid of the King's anger, the Vizier kept his own counsel and said no more. He betook himself to Ma'aruf and said to him: 'His majesty the King desires you to marry his daughter the Princess. What answer shall I give him?'

'I am honoured by the King's proposal,' replied Ma'aruf with an air of dignified reserve. 'But do you not think it would be better to wait until my caravan arrives? The dowry of such a bride as the Princess would be a greater expense than I can at present afford. I must give my wife a marriage-portion of at least five

thousand purses of gold. Among the poor of the city
I shall have to distribute a thousand purses on the bridal
night; to those who walk in the wedding procession I
must give a thousand more; and I shall need another
thousand to entertain the troops. On the next morning
I must present a hundred rich diamonds to the Princess, and as many jewels to the slave-girls and the eunuchs of the palace. All this is an expense which cannot
be met before my caravan arrives.'

When the Vizier went back to the King and repeated
to him Ma'aruf's reply, the King was overwhelmed at
the prodigious recital and sent the Vizier to bring him
to his presence. As soon as the cobbler entered the
King said: 'Honoured and most distinguished merchant, let us celebrate this happy union forthwith! I myself will meet the expenses of the marriage. My treasury
is full; I give you leave to take from it all that you require. You can settle the Princess's dowry when your
caravan comes in. By Allah, I will take no refusal!'

Without a moment's delay the King sent for the
Imam of the royal mosque, who drew up a marriage
contract for Ma'aruf and the Princess.

The city was gaily decorated at the King's orders,
drums and trumpets sounded in the streets, and Ma'aruf
the cobbler sat enthroned in the great parlour of the
palace. A troop of singers, dancers, wrestlers, clowns,
and acrobats capered round the court to entertain the
guests, whilst the royal treasurer brought Ma'aruf bag
after bag of gold to scatter among the merry throng.
He had no rest that day, for no sooner had he come to
Ma'aruf staggering under the weight of a hundred thousand dinars, than he was sent back for another load.
The Vizier watched the spectacle with rage in his heart,
whilst Ali the merchant, aghast at the proceedings, ap-

proached Ma'aruf and whispered in his ear: 'May Allah have no mercy upon you! Is it not enough that you have frittered away the wealth of all the merchants? Must you also drain the royal treasury?'

'What is that to you?' replied Ma'aruf. 'Be sure that when my great caravan arrives, I will repay the King a thousandfold.'

The extravagant rejoicings lasted forty days, and then came the wedding-day. The King, accompanied by his viziers and the officers of his troops, walked in the bridal procession, and as he passed by, Ma'aruf threw handfuls of gold to the crowds that lined the way.

When the couple were at length left alone in the bridal chamber, and the Princess lay down beneath the velvet curtains of the bed, Ma'aruf sat on the floor and wrung his hands in despair. Perceiving his grief, the Princess tenderly asked him: 'Why so sad, my lord?'

'There is no strength nor help save in Allah!' replied Ma'aruf with a sigh. 'It is all your father's fault!'

'How so?' she asked.

'He has exposed me to ridicule in the eyes of the whole world!' sighed Ma'aruf. 'Surely everyone must have noticed my meanness, my miserly treatment of you and the royal guests! If only he had waited till my great caravan arrived! At least I should have been able to give you a few rich presents befitting your degree, and bestow upon your women jewels and ornaments in honour of this happy occasion. But your father would hurry on the wedding and put me to this shame! It was like burning green grass!'

'Instead of worrying about such trifles,' replied the Princess, 'undress and come to bed. Put away all thoughts of presents and caravans, my dear, and gird your loins for the merry sport!'

Ma'aruf cast off his clothes, and climbing into bed threw himself upon the Princess as she lay on her back. He clasped her tight, and she pressed close to him, so that tongue met tongue in that hour when men forget their mothers. He slipped his hands under her armpits and strained her to his breast, squeezing all the honey and setting the dainties face to face. Then, threading the needle, he kindled the match, put it to the priming, and fired the shot. Thus the citadel was breached and the victory won.

After a night of such dalliance, Ma'aruf rose and went to the bath. Then he dressed himself in a princely robe and entered the King's council-chamber, where he sat down by the side of his father-in-law to receive the felicitations of the viziers and the chief officers of the kingdom. He sent for the treasurer and ordered him to give robes of honour to all who were present; then he called for sacks of gold and gave handfuls to every member of the royal palace from the highest courtier to the humblest kitchen boy. And for twenty days he thus continued to dissipate the King's treasure.

At the end of this time there was still no news of Ma'aruf's caravan, and at length the day came when the treasurer found his coffers empty. He went to the King with a heavy heart and said: 'Your majesty, the treasure chests are empty and the great caravan of your son-in-law has not yet come to fill them.'

Alarmed at these words, the King turned to his Vizier and said: 'By Allah, it is true there is still no sign of the caravan. What shall we do?'

'Allah prolong your days, my master,' replied the Vizier with an evil smile. 'Did I not warn you against the wiles of this impostor? I swear he has no caravan: no, not as much as a half-cooked pie! He has married your daughter without a dowry and defrauded you of all your treasure. How long will your majesty tolerate this vagabond?'

'If only we could find the truth about him!' sighed the King in great perplexity.

'Your majesty,' said the Vizier, 'no one is better able to find out a man's secrets than his wife. I beg you to call your daughter here and permit me to question her from behind the curtain.'

'It shall be done!' replied the King. 'On my life, if it be proved that he has deceived us, he shall die the cruellest of deaths!'

At once the King had a curtain drawn across the hall, and, summoning the Princess, bade her sit behind it and speak with the Vizier.

'What do you wish to know?' she asked.

'Honoured lady,' began the Vizier, 'the chests of the treasury are empty, thanks to the extravagance of Prince Ma'aruf, and the wondrous caravan, about which we have heard so much, has not yet come. Therefore the King has given me leave to ask what you know of this stranger and whether you have reason to suspect him.'

'Night after night,' replied the Princess, 'he has promised me pearls and jewels, and treasures without number. But of these I have yet seen nothing.'

'Your highness,' said the Vizier, 'I counsel you to question him to-night, that we may know the answer to this riddle. Beg him to tell you the truth, and promise to keep his secret.'

'I hear and obey,' replied the Princess. 'I will speak to Ma'aruf to-night and tell you what he says.'

In the evening, when the pair lay side by side, the Princess threw her arms around Ma'aruf and, assuming that sweet and endearing air with which subtle women coax their husbands, said to him: 'Light of my eyes and flower of my heart, may Time and Destiny never part us! Your love has kindled in my breast such fires that I will gladly die for you. Tell me the truth about your caravan and conceal nothing from me. How long will you delude my father with such lies? For I fear that he will find you out at last and make you pay dearly for this deception. Tell me everything, my love, and I will contrive a means to help you.'

'Sweet Princess,' replied Ma'aruf, 'I will tell you all. I am no wealthy merchant, no master of caravans. In my own land I was a poor cobbler, cursed with a vixen of a wife called ...' And he recounted to the Princess the tale of his connubial misfortunes from the adventure of the honey-cake to his flight to Ikhtiyan-al-Khatan.

When she heard the cobbler's story, the Princess burst into a fit of laughter and said: 'Truly, Ma'aruf, you are a subtle rogue! But what are we to do? What will my father say when he learns the truth? The Vizier has already sown suspicions in his mind. He will surely kill you, and I shall die of grief. Take this fifty thousand dinars and leave the palace this very hour. Ride away to some far country, and then send a courier to acquaint me with your news.'

'I am at your mercy, mistress,' replied the cobbler.

After he had dallied with the Princess for a while, he rose, disguised himself in the livery of a slave, and, mounting the fastest horse in the King's stables, rode out into the night.

Next morning, the King sat in the council-chamber with the Vizier by his side and summoned the Princess to his presence. When she had taken her seat behind the curtain as before, the King asked: 'Tell us, my daughter, what you have learned about Prince Ma'aruf.'

'May Allah confound all slanderous tongues,' exclaimed the Princess, 'and blacken the face of your Vizier, as he would have blackened mine in my husband's eyes!'

'How so?' asked the King.

'Last night,' continued the Princess, 'soon after my husband came to my chamber, the chief of the eunuchs brought in a letter from ten richly dressed slaves who begged an audience with their master Ma'aruf. I took the letter and read aloud: "From the five hundred slaves of the caravan to their master the merchant Ma'aruf. We would have you know that soon after you left us we were attacked by a host of two thousand mounted bedouin. A bloody battle ensued, and lasted thirty days and thirty nights. The caravan lost fifty of its slaves, a hundred mules, and two hundred loads of merchandise. This is the cause of our delay."

'Yet at this bad news the Prince was undismayed; he did not even ask further details from the waiting messengers. "What are two hundred bales and a hundred wretched mules?" he said. "At worst the loss cannot be more than seventy thousand pieces of gold. Think no more about it, my dear. One thing alone distresses me, that I shall have to leave you for a few days in order to go myself and hasten the arrival of the caravan." He rose with a carefree laugh, embraced me tenderly, and bade me farewell. When he had gone I looked through the window of my chamber and saw him chatting with ten handsome slaves dressed in uniforms of rare magnificence. Presently he mounted his horse and rode away with them to bring the caravan home. Allah be praised that I did not question my husband in the manner you requested,' added the Princess bitterly. 'I would have lost his love and he would have ceased to trust me. It was all the fault of your hateful Vizier, whose only thought is to revile my husband and discredit him in your eyes.'

The King rejoiced at these words and exclaimed: 'May Allah increase your husband's wealth and prolong his years, my daughter!' Then, turning to the Vizier, he rebuked him angrily and bade him henceforth hold his tongue. So much for the King, the Vizier, and the Princess.

As for Ma'aruf, he journeyed disconsolately far into the desert, his heart yearning for his beloved princess, until he came at midday to the outskirts of a little village. By this time he was tired and very hungry. Seeing a ploughman driving two oxen in a field, he went up to him and greeted him, saying: 'Peace be with you!'

The peasant returned his greeting, and, noticing the stranger's garb, inquired: 'Doubtless, my master, you are one of the King's servants?'

When Ma'aruf replied that he was, the ploughman welcomed him, saying: 'Pray dismount and be my guest this day!'

The cobbler thanked the poor peasant for his generosity and politely declined. But the kind old man would take no refusal. 'Pray dismount,' he insisted, 'and grant me the honour of entertaining you. I will go instantly to the village, which is close at hand, and bring you food and hay for your horse.'

'Since the village is so near, my friend,' protested Ma'aruf, 'I can easily ride there myself and buy food in the market-place.'

But the peasant smiled and shook his head. 'I fear you will find no market-place in a poor hamlet such as ours,' he replied. 'I beg you, in Allah's name, to rest here with your horse while I quickly run to the village.'

Not wishing to offend the old man, Ma'aruf dismounted and sat down on the grass, while his host hurried away.

As he waited for the peasant's return, Ma'aruf thought: 'I am keeping this poor man from his work. I will make up for his lost time by working at the plough myself.'

He rose, and, going up to the oxen, drove the plough along the furrow. The beasts had not gone far, however, when the share struck against an object in the ground and came to a sudden halt. Ma'aruf goaded the oxen on, but though they strained powerfully against the yoke, the plough remained rooted in the ground. Clearing away the soil about the share, Ma'aruf found that it had caught in a great ring of gold set in a marble slab the size of a large mill-stone. He exerted all his strength, and when he had moved the slab aside, he saw below it a flight of stairs. Going down the stairs he found himself in a square vault as large as the city baths containing four separate halls. The first was filled with gold from floor to ceiling; the second with pearls, emeralds, and coral; the third with jacinths, rubies, and turquoises; and the fourth with diamonds and other precious stones. At the far side of the vault stood a coffer of clearest crystal, and upon it a golden casket no larger than a lemon.

The cobbler marvelled and rejoiced at this discovery. He went up to the little casket, and, lifting its lid, found in it a gold signet-ring finely engraved with strange talismanic inscriptions that resembled the legs of creeping insects. He slipped the ring upon his finger, and, as he did so, rubbed the seal.

At once a mighty jinnee appeared before him, saying: 'I am here, master, I am here! Speak and I will obey! What is your wish? Would you have me build a capital, or lay a town in ruin? Would you have me slay a king, or dig a river-bed? I am your slave, by order of the Sovereign of the Jinn, Creator of the day and night! What is your wish?'

Amazed at the apparition, Ma'aruf cried: 'Creature of Allah, who are you?'

'I am Abul-Sa'adah, the slave of the ring,' replied the jinnee. 'Faithfully I serve my master, and my master is he who rubs the ring. Nothing is beyond my power; for I am lord over seventy-two tribes of jinn, each two-and-seventy thousand strong: each jinnee rules over a thousand giants, each giant over a thousand goblins, each goblin over a thousand demons, and each demon over a thousand imps. All these owe me absolute allegiance; and yet for all my power, I cannot choose but to obey my master. Ask what you will, and it shall be done. Be it on land or sea, by day or night: should you need me you have but to rub the ring, and I will be at hand to do your bidding. Of one thing only I must warn you; if you twice rub the ring I shall be consumed in the fire of the powerful words engraved on the seal, and you will lose me for ever.'

'Abul-Sa'adah,' said Ma'aruf, 'can you tell me what this place is, and who imprisoned you in this ring?'

'This vault in which you stand, my master,' replied the jinnee, 'is the ancient treasure-house of Shaddad Ibn Aad, King of the many-columned city of Iram. While he lived I was his servant and dwelt in this ring. Just before his death he locked it away in this treasure-house, and it was your good fortune to find it.'

'Slave of the ring,' said the cobbler, 'can you carry all this treasure to the open?'

'That is very easy,' replied the jinnee.

'Then do so without delay,' said Ma'aruf, 'and leave nothing in this vault.'

Scarcely had he uttered these words when the earth opened and there appeared before him several handsome youths with baskets upon their heads. These they quickly filled with gold and jewels and carried them above ground; and in a few moments the four halls were emptied of their treasure.

'Who are these boys?' asked Ma'aruf.

'They are my own sons,' replied the jinnee. 'A light task such as this does not require the mustering of a mighty band of jinn. What else do you wish, my master?'

'I require a train of mules loaded with chests,' replied Ma'aruf, 'to carry these marvels to Ikhtiyan-al-Khatan.'

The jinnee uttered a great cry, and there appeared seven hundred richly saddled mules laden with chests and baskets, and a hundred slaves magnificently clad. In a twinkling the chests and baskets were filled with treasure and placed upon the mules, and the caravan stood in splendid array, guarded by mounted slaves.

'And now, slave of the ring,' said Ma'aruf, 'I require a few hundred loads of precious stuffs.'

'Would you have Syrian damask or Persian velvet, Indian brocade or Roman silk or Egyptian gaberdine?'

'A hundred loads of each!' cried Ma'aruf.

'I hear and obey,' replied the slave. 'I will at once dispatch my jinn to those distant lands, and they shall return to-morrow morning with all that you require.'

Then Ma'aruf ordered the slave of the ring to set up

a pavilion and serve him food and wine. The jinnee promptly provided his master with a silk pavilion and a sumptuous meal, and departed on his mission.

As Ma'aruf was about to sit down to his feast, the old peasant returned from the village, carrying a large bowl of lentils for his guest and a sack of hay for the horse. When he saw the great caravan drawn up in the field, and Ma'aruf reclining in the tent, attended by innumerable slaves, he thought that his guest must be no other than the King. 'I will hurry back,' he reflected, 'and kill my two fowls and roast them in butter for him.'

The peasant was on the point of turning back when Ma'aruf saw him and ordered his slaves to bring him into the pavilion.

The slaves led the peasant to the tent, with his bowl of lentils and his sack of hay. Ma'aruf rose to receive him and welcomed him, saying: 'What is it you are carrying, my brother?'

'My master,' replied the peasant, all abashed, 'I was bringing you your dinner and some hay for your horse. Forgive my scant courtesy, I pray you. Had I known you were the King, I would have killed my two fowls and roasted them in butter for you.'

'Do not be dismayed, my friend,' replied Ma'aruf, 'I am not the King, but only his son-in-law. A certain misunderstanding arose between us and I left the palace. He has sent these messengers to fetch me and these presents as a token of his forgiveness. To-morrow morning I shall return to the city.' Then Ma'aruf thanked the peasant for his generosity and seated him by his side, saying: 'By Allah, I will eat nothing but the food of your hospitality.'

He ordered the slaves to serve the peasant with the

choice meats and ate the lentils himself. When the meal was finished he filled the empty bowl with gold and gave it to the peasant. 'Take this to your family,' he said, 'and if you come to see me at the palace, you shall receive a hearty welcome and a generous reward.'

The peasant took the gold and returned to the village, scarcely believing his good fortune.

When darkness fell, the slaves of the caravan brought into the tent beautiful young girls, who danced and made music. At daybreak Ma'aruf perceived a great cloud of dust in the distance, and presently saw a long procession of mules approaching. They were laden with innumerable bales of merchandise, and at their head rode the jinnee in the semblance of a caravan-leader, alongside a four-pillared litter of pure gold inlaid with diamonds. When the caravan came to the tent, the jinnee dismounted and, kissing the ground before Ma'aruf, said: 'The task is accomplished, my master. Pray mount into this litter and put on the garment which I have brought especially for you. You will find it worthy of a king.'

'One thing more remains to be done,' said Ma'aruf. 'Before I set forth with the caravan, I wish you to hasten to Ikhtiyan-al-Khatan and announce my coming to the King.'

'I hear and obey,' replied the jinnee, and instantly transforming himself into the semblance of a courier made off towards the city.

He arrived at the palace just as the Vizier was saying to the King: 'Be no longer deceived, your majesty, by the lies of this impostor. Give no credence to your daughter's story; for I swear by your precious life that it was not to hurry on the arrival of his caravan that Prince Ma'aruf fled the city, but to save his skin.'

The Vizier had not finished speaking, when the courier entered the royal presence and kissed the ground before the King, saying: 'Your majesty, I bring you greetings from the illustrious Prince your son-in-law, who is now approaching the city with his noble caravan.'

With this the courier again kissed the ground before the King and hurried out of the palace. The King rejoiced, and, turning to the Vizier, exclaimed: 'May Allah blacken your face, traitor of ill omen! How long will you revile my son-in-law to my face and call him thief and liar?'

The dumbfounded Vizier hung his head, whilst the King hastened to give orders for the decoration of the city and to send out a procession to meet the caravan. Then he went to his daughter's chamber and told her the joyful news. The Princess was astounded to hear her father speak of the caravan, and thought: 'Can this be another of Ma'aruf's tricks? Or was he testing my love with an invented tale of poverty?'

But even more astonished than the Princess was her husband's friend, Ali the merchant. When he beheld the great commotion in the city and learnt the news of Ma'aruf's imminent arrival at the head of a splendid caravan, he thought: 'What new roguery is this? Can it be possible that this patcher of old slippers is really coming with a caravan? Or is it some fresh trick which he has contrived with the aid of the Princess? May Allah preserve my old friend from dishonour!'

Before long the procession, which had gone out to meet the caravan, returned to the city. Arrayed in a magnificent robe, Ma'aruf rode triumphantly by the King's side in the golden litter, and as the interminable caravan wound its way through the streets, the merchants flocked around their prodigal debtor and kissed the ground before him as he passed. Ali the merchant pushed his way through the throng, and whispered to Ma'aruf: 'How has this come about, sheikh of mad swindlers? And yet, by Allah, you deserve your good fortune!'

The procession halted at the royal palace, and Ma'aruf sat with the King in the great council-chamber. He ordered his slaves to fill the royal coffers with gold and jewels, and to unpack the bales of precious merchandise. He chose out the finest stuffs and said to the attendants: 'Carry these silks to the Princess that she may distribute them among her women; and take to her this chest of jewels that she may share its contents among the slaves and eunuchs.'

Then he proceeded to deal out the treasures to the officers of the King's troops, to the courtiers and their wives, to his creditors the merchants and to the poor of the city, while the King writhed upon his throne in an agony of greed. As Ma'aruf threw handfuls of pearls and emeralds to right and left, the King would whisper to him: 'Enough, my son! There will be nothing left for us!' But Ma'aruf would answer: 'My caravan is inexhaustible.'

Soon the Vizier came and told the King that the treasury was full and could hold no more. And the King cried: 'Fill another hall!'

Then Ma'aruf hastened to his wife, who received him in a transport of joy and kissed his hand, saying: 'Was it to mock me or to test my love that you pretended to be a poor cobbler fleeing from a nagging wife? Whichever it was, I thank Allah I did not fail you.'

Ma'aruf embraced her and gave her a gown splendidly embroidered in gold, a necklace threaded with forty orphan pearls, and a pair of anklets fashioned by the art of mighty sorcerers. His wife cried out for joy as she saw these marvels, and said: 'I will keep them for festivals and state occasions only.'

'Not so, my love,' replied Ma'aruf, 'I will give you ornaments like these each day.'

Then he summoned the slave-girls of the harem and bestowed upon each of them an embroidered robe adorned with ornaments of gold. Arrayed in this splendour, they were like the black-eyed houris of Paradise, whilst the Princess shone in their midst like the moon amongst the stars.

At nightfall the King said to the Vizier: 'What have you to say now? Does not the wealth of my son-in-law surpass all wonders?'

'Indeed, your majesty,' replied the Vizier, 'the Prince's prodigality is that of no ordinary merchant; for where can a merchant find such pearls and jewels as your son-in-law has thrown away? Kings and princes have not treasures like these. There must surely be some strange reason for his conduct. I suggest, my master, that you make Prince Ma'aruf drunk if you wish to discover the source of his riches. When he is overcome with wine, we will ply him with questions until he tells us all. Indeed, I already fear the consequences of this extraordinary munificence; for it is more than likely that he will in time win the troops with his favours and drive you from your kingdom.'

'You have spoken wisely, my Vizier,' said the King. 'To-morrow we must find out the whole truth.'

Next morning, whilst the King was sitting in his council-chamber, the grooms of the royal stables rushed in, begging leave to speak with him. 'Your majesty,' they cried, 'the entire caravan of Prince Ma'aruf is gone!

MA'ARUF THE COBBLER   233

All the slaves, the horses, and the mules disappeared during the night, and nowhere can we find a trace of them.'

Greatly troubled at this news, the King hastened to Ma'aruf's chamber and told him what had happened. But Ma'aruf laughed aloud.

'Pray calm yourself, your majesty,' he said. 'The loss of these trifles is nothing to me. For what is a caravan of mules?'

'By Allah,' thought the King in amazement, 'what manner of man is this, to whom wealth counts for nothing? There must surely be a reason for all this!'

When evening came, the King sat with Ma'aruf and the Vizier in a pavilion in the garden of the palace. Wine flowed freely; and when Ma'aruf was flushed with drink so that he could not tell his left hand from his right, the Vizier said to him: 'Your highness, you have never told us the adventures of your life. Pray let us hear how you achieved your prodigious wealth, and the marvellous vicissitudes of fortune which have befallen you.'

Thereupon the drunken cobbler related the story of his life, from his marriage in Cairo to the finding of the magic ring in the peasant's field.

Then said the Vizier: 'Will you not permit us to see the ring, your highness?'

Without a moment's thought the foolish cobbler slipped the ring from his finger and handed it to the Vizier, saying: 'Look at the seal! My servant the jinnee dwells within it!'

The Vizier instantly passed the ring upon his own finger and rubbed the seal; and the jinnee appeared before him, saying: 'I am here! Ask and receive! Would you have me build a capital, or lay a town in ruin?

Would you have me slay a king, or dig a river-bed?'

'Slave of the ring,' replied the Vizier, pointing to Ma'aruf, 'take up this rascal and cast him down upon some barren desert where he shall perish from hunger and thirst!'

At once the jinnee snatched up Ma'aruf and flew with him between earth and sky until he set him down in the middle of a waterless desert.

Then said the Vizier to the King: 'Did I not tell you that this dog was a liar and a cheat? But you gave no heed to my counsel.'

'You were right, my Vizier,' replied the King. 'Give me the ring that I may examine it.'

But the Vizier spat in his face and cried: 'Miserable old fool, do you expect me to remain your servant when I can be your master?'

So saying, the Vizier rubbed the ring and said to the jinnee: 'Take up this wretch and cast him down by the side of his cobbler son-in-law!'

The jinnee at once carried the old man upon his shoulder and, flying with him through the void, set him down in the middle of the desert, where King and son-in-law sat wailing together. So much for them.

The Vizier summoned the nobles and the captains of the troops and proclaimed himself Sultan of the city. He explained that he had banished the King and Ma'aruf by the power of a magic ring, and threatened the assembly, saying: 'If anyone dares resist my rule, he shall join them in the desert of hunger and thirst!'

Perforce the courtiers swore fealty, and the Vizier, after exalting some and dismissing others, sent to the Princess, saying: 'Prepare to receive me this night, for my heart yearns for you!'

The Princess, who was stricken with grief at the

downfall of her father and Ma'aruf, sent back to say:
'I cannot receive you until you have drawn up a marriage-contract and become my lawful husband.' But the
Vizier replied: 'I know nothing of marriage-contracts,
and accept no such excuses. I desire to visit you at once.'

'Come, then, you will be welcome,' answered the
Princess through her eunuch.

When evening came she arrayed herself in silks and
jewels, perfumed herself, and received the Vizier with
a seductive smile. 'What an honour, my master,' she
said. 'What a night we shall pass together!'

She seated him on her couch and dallied with him
until he was roused to a frenzy of desire. But as he was
about to throw himself upon her, she uttered a cry of
terror and started back, covering her face.

'What is the matter, my mistress?' asked the Vizier.

'Would you show me naked to that stranger?' she
cried.

'Where? Where?' exclaimed the Vizier angrily.

'There, in your ring!' she answered.

The Vizier laughed and said: 'Dear lady, that is no
man, but only my faithful jinnee.'

But the Princess screamed still louder and cried: 'I
am terrified of jinn! Put him away, for my sake!'

Impatient to do that for which he had come, the
Vizier took off the ring from his finger and hid it under
the cushions. The Princess let him approach and, when
he had come near, kicked him so violently in the belly
that he rolled over senseless on the floor. Thereupon she
gave a loud cry, and at once forty slave-girls burst into
the room and laid hold of the Vizier, whilst she hastily
snatched up the ring and rubbed the seal, saying to the
jinnee: 'Cast this traitor into a dark dungeon and bring
me back my father and my husband!'

'I hear and obey!' replied the jinnee, and, carrying the Vizier on his shoulder, threw him in the darkest dungeon of the palace. Then he flew towards the desert and presently returned with the King and Ma'aruf, both half-dead with fright and hunger.

The Princess rejoiced to see them. She offered them food and wine and told them how she had outwitted the Vizier.

'We will tie him to the stake and burn him alive!' cried the King. 'But first give me back the ring, my daughter.'

But the Princess replied: 'The ring shall stay on my finger. I myself will look after it in future.'

Early next morning the King and Ma'aruf entered the council-chamber, and the courtiers, who were astonished to see them, kissed the ground before them and gave them a jubilant welcome. The stake was set up in the grounds of the palace and the Vizier was burnt alive in sight of all the people.

Ma'aruf was appointed Vizier and heir to the throne. He governed jointly with the King, and lived happily with his wife, who after a few months gave birth to a son.

Five years later the King died, and soon the Princess followed him to eternal rest. Before she died she commended the young Prince to the care of Ma'aruf, and gave him the ring and counselled him to guard it well.

King Ma'aruf reigned wisely and justly for many years, so that all his subjects loved him. One night, however, when he had retired to his sleeping chamber, a hideous old woman jumped out of his bed and flung her arms around him.

'Allah preserve us from the wiles of the Evil One!' exclaimed Ma'aruf in terror. 'Who are you?'

'Have no fear!' replied the hag. 'I am your wife, Fatimah!'

Ma'aruf recognized her by her long teeth and her black ugliness. 'But how came you here?' he asked in amazement. 'Who brought you to this city?'

'Last night,' answered Fatimah, 'as I sat in a street by the wall of a ruined house, begging alms from the passers-by and bewailing my woeful plight, a jinnee appeared, saying: "Why are you weeping, old woman?" When I recounted to him my misfortunes since you left me and told him that my name was Fatimah, wife of Ma'aruf, one time cobbler in Red Lane, the jinnee said: "I know your husband. He is now King of Ikhtiyan-al-Khatan, and if you wish I will take you to him." The jinnee carried me upon his back and flew with me between earth and sky until he alighted on the roof of this palace and set me down upon your bed.'

The old shrew wept and, kneeling down before her husband, begged forgiveness of him. Ma'aruf took pity on his wife. He bade her rise, and, seating her by his side, related to her all that had befallen him since his flight from Cairo. He set apart a magnificent palace for her use and assigned twenty slave-girls to her service.

When Fatimah saw, however, that her husband held aloof from her bed and sought his pleasure with other women, she became jealous and her evil soul prompted her to seek his ruin. One night, whilst Ma'aruf was fast asleep with the magic ring under his pillow, she entered the palace and stealthily made her way to his room. She softly approached her husband's bed and took the ring from under the pillow.

Now it so chanced that as she was stealing out, with the ring in her hand, Ma'aruf's son, the young Prince, was passing by the door of his father's room. He followed her unnoticed until she came to the vestibule of the palace. Here she slipped the ring on her finger and was about to rub the seal, when he drew his sword and struck her through the neck. With a piercing scream she dropped dead to the ground.

The young Prince hurried to his father's chamber and roused him from his sleep. Ma'aruf praised his son for his bravery, and recovered the ring from his wife's finger. Then he called out to his attendants and ordered them to take the body and bury it in the grounds of the palace. Such was the end of Fatimah.

King Ma'aruf reigned through many joyful years, until he was visited by the Destroyer of all earthly pleasures, the Leveller of mighty kings and humble peasants.

EPILOGUE

Now during this time Shahrazad had borne King Shahriyar three sons. On the thousand and first night, when she had ended the tale of Ma'aruf, she rose and kissed the ground before him, saying: 'Great King, for a thousand and one nights I have been recounting to you the fables of past ages and the legends of ancient kings. May I make so bold as to crave a favour of your majesty?'

The King replied: 'Ask, and it shall be granted.'

Shahrazad called out to the nurses, saying: 'Bring me my children.'

Three little boys were instantly brought in; one walking, one crawling on all fours, and the third sucking at the breast of his nurse. Shahrazad ranged the little ones before the King and, again kissing the ground before him, said: 'Behold these three whom Allah has granted to us. For their sake I implore you to spare my life. For if you destroy the mother of these infants, they will find none among women to love them as I would.'

The King embraced his three sons, and his eyes filled with tears as he answered: 'I swear by Allah, Shahrazad, that you were already pardoned before the coming of these children. I loved you because I found you chaste and tender, wise and eloquent. May Allah bless you, and bless your father and mother, your ancestors, and all your descendants. O, Shahrazad, this thousand and first night is brighter for us than the day!'

Shahrazad rejoiced; she kissed the King's hand and called down blessings upon him.

The people were overjoyed at the news of Shahrazad's salvation. Next morning King Shahriyar summoned to his presence the great ones of the city, the chamberlains, the nabobs, and the officers of his army. When they had all assembled in the great hall of the palace, Shahriyar proclaimed his decision to spare the life of his bride. Then he called his Vizier, Shahrazad's father, and invested him with a magnificent robe of honour, saying: 'Allah has raised up your daughter to be the salvation of my people. I have found her chaste, wise, and eloquent, and repentance has come to me through her.'

Then the King bestowed robes of honour upon the courtiers and the captains of his troops, and gave orders for the decoration of his capital.

The city was decked and lighted; and in the streets and market-squares drums rattled, trumpets blared, and clarions sounded. The King lavished alms on the poor and the needy, and all the people feasted at the King's expense for thirty days and thirty nights.

Shahriyar reigned over his subjects in all justice, and lived happily with Shahrazad until they were visited by the Destroyer of all earthly pleasures, the Annihilator of men.

Now praise and glory be to Him who sits throned in eternity above the shifts of time; who, changing all things, remains Himself unchanged; who alone is the Paragon of all perfection. And blessing and peace be upon His chosen Messenger, the Prince of Apostles, our master Mohammed, to whom we pray for an auspicious

END